ERNESTO QUIÑONEZ

BODEGA DREAMS

Ernesto Quiñonez studied writing at The City College of New York. He currently teaches bilingual fourth grade in the New York public school system and is at work on his second novel. He lives in New York City.

BODEGA DREAMS

BODEGA DREAMS

Ernesto Quiñonez

VINTAGE CONTEMPORARIES

VINTAGE BOOKS

A DIVISION OF RANDOM HOUSE, INC.

NEW YORK

A VINTAGE CONTEMPORARIES ORIGINAL, MARCH 2000
FIRST EDITION

Grateful acknowledgment is made to Arte Publico Press for permission to reprint an excerpt from "La Bodega Sold Dreams" from *La Bodega Sold Dreams* by Miguel Pinero (Houston: Arte Publico Press—University of Houston, 1980).

A portion of this work was originally published, in somewhat different form, in *Bomb* magazine.

Library of Congress Cataloging-in-Publication Data
Quiñonez, Ernesto.
Bodega dreams / Ernesto Quiñonez.
p.   cm.
ISBN 0-375-70589-9
1. Puerto Ricans—New York (State)—New York—Fiction.   I. Title
PS3567.U3618L3   2000
813'.54—dc21   99-33380
CIP

Author photograph © Joyce Ravid
Book design by JoAnne Metsch

www.vintagebooks.com

Printed in the United States of America
10   9   8   7   6   5   4   3   2

CONTENTS

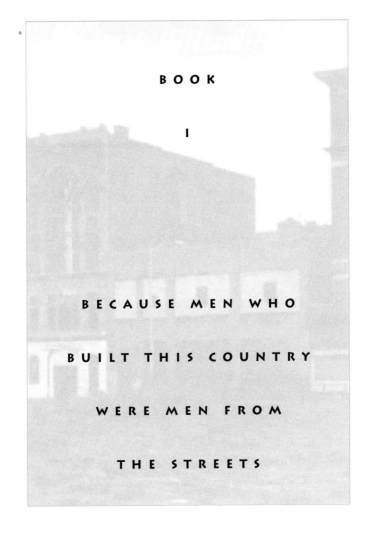

BOOK

I

BECAUSE MEN WHO

BUILT THIS COUNTRY

WERE MEN FROM

THE STREETS

All died

hating the grocery stores

that sold them make-believe steak and bullet-proof rice
   and beans

All died waiting dreaming and hating

PEDRO PIETRI
— "Puerto Rican Obituary"

Spanish for "Toad"

SAPO was different.

Sapo was always Sapo, and no one messed with him because he had a reputation for biting. "When I'm in a fight," Sapo would spit, "whass close to my mouth is mine by right and my teeth ain't no fucken pawn-shop."

I loved Sapo. I loved Sapo because he loved himself. And I wanted to be able to do that, to rely on myself for my own happiness.

Sapo, he relied on himself. He'd been this way since we met back in the fourth grade when he threw a book at Lisa Rivera's face because she had started to make fun of his looks by calling out, "ribbit, ribbit." But in truth, Sapo did look like a toad. He was strong, squatty, with a huge mouth framed by fat lips, freaking *bembas* that could almost swallow you. His eyes bulged in their sockets and when he laughed there was no denying the resemblance. It was like one huge, happy toad laughing right in front of you.

As far back as I could remember Sapo had always been called Sapo and no one called him by his real name, Enrique. Usually Enriques are nicknamed Kiko or Kique. But Sapo didn't look like an Enrique anyway, whatever an Enrique is supposed to look like. Sapo could only be Sapo. And that's what everyone called him. It was rumored around the neighborhood that when Sapo came out, the nurses cleaned him up and brought him over to his father. His father saw the baby and said, "*Coño*, he looks like a frog," and quickly handed the baby to the mother. "Here, you take him." I think this story is true. But Sapo never bitched, as if he had said, "Fuck that shit. I'll love myself." And that's how I wanted to be.

To have a name other than the one your parents had given you meant you had status in school, had status on your block. You were somebody. If anyone called you by your real name you were *un mamao*, a useless, meaningless thing. It meant that you hadn't proved yourself, it was open season for anybody who wanted to kick your ass. It was Sapo who taught me that it didn't matter if you lost the fight, only that you never backed down. The more guys that saw you lose fights without ever backing down, the better. This didn't mean you were home free, it simply meant bigger guys would think twice before starting something with you.

Getting a name meant I had to fight. There was no way out of it. I got beat up a few times, but I never backed down. "You back down once," Sapo had told me, "and you'll be backin' down f' the res' of your life. It's a Timex world, everyone takes a lickin' but you got to keep on tickin'. Know what I'm sayin', *papi*?" Sapo was one of those guys who went around beating other kids up, but Sapo was different. Sapo loved himself. He didn't need teachers or anyone else telling him this. The meanest and ugliest kid on the block loved himself and not only that, he was my *pana*, my friend. This gave me hope, and getting a name seemed possible. So I decided that I no longer wanted to be called by the name my parents had given me, Julio. I wanted a name like Sapo had and so I looked for fights.

It was always easy to get into fights if you hated yourself. So what if you fought a guy bigger than you who would kick your ass? So what if you got stabbed with a 007 in the back and never walked again? So what if someone broke your nose in a fight? You were ugly anyway. Your life meant shit from the start. It was as if you had given up on the war and decided to charge the tanks with your bare fists. Nothing brave in it, you just didn't give a shit anymore. It was easy to be big and bad when you hated your life and felt meaningless. You lived in projects with pissed-up elevators, junkies on the stairs, posters of the rapist of the month, and whores you never knew were whores until you saw men go in and out of their apartments like through revolving doors. You lived in a place where vacant lots grew like wild grass does in Kansas. Kansas? What does a kid from Spanish Harlem know about Kansas? All you knew was that one day a block would have people, the next day it would be erased by a fire. The burned-down buildings would then house junkies who made them into shooting galleries or become playgrounds for kids like me and Sapo to explore. After a few months, the City of New York would send a crane with a ball and chain to wreck the gutted tenements. A few weeks later a bulldozer would arrive and turn the block into a vacant lot. The vacant lot would now become a graveyard for stolen cars. Sapo and I played in those cars with no doors, tires, windows, or steering wheels, where mice had made their nests inside the slashed seats. Sapo loved killing the little mice in different ways. I liked to take a big piece of glass and tear open what was left of the seat. I always hoped to find something the car thieves had hidden inside but had forgotten to take when they ditched the car. But I never found anything except foam and sometimes more mice.

Fires, junkies dying, shootouts, holdups, babies falling out of windows were things you took as part of life. If you were a graffiti artist and people knew you were a good one, death meant an opportunity to make a few bucks. Someone close to the deceased, usually a woman, would knock on your door. "*Mira*, my cousin Freddy just passed away. Can you do him a R.I.P.?" You would bemoan Freddy's death whether you knew him or not, say you were sorry and ask what had happened, like you really cared. "Freddy? Freddy was shot by mistake. He wasn't stealin' not'en." You'd nod and then ask the person on what wall she wanted the R.I.P. and what to paint on it. "On the wall of P.S. 101's schoolyard. The back wall. The one that faces 111th Street. Freddy would hang there all night. I want it to say, 'Freddy the best of 109th Street, R.I.P.' And then I want the flag of Borinquen and a big conga with Freddy's face on it, can you paint that?" You would say, "Yeah, I can paint that" and never ask for the money up front, because then you wouldn't get tipped.

I painted dozens of R.I.P.s for guys in El Barrio who felt small and needed something violent to jump-start their lives and at the same time end them. It was guys like these who on any given day were looking to beat someone up, so it was up to me to either become like them or get the shit kicked out of me.

Junior High School 99 (aka Jailhouse 99), on 100th Street and First Avenue, became the outlet I needed. It was violently perfect and in constant turmoil within itself. It was a school that was divided by two powers, the white teachers and the Hispanic teachers. The white teachers had most of the power because they had seniority. They had been teaching before the chancellor of the Board of Education finally realized that the school was located in Spanish Harlem and practically all of the students were Latinos, and so changed the school's name from Margaret Knox to Julia de Burgos.

To the white teachers we were all going to end up delinquents. "I get paid whether you learn or not," they would tell us. So we figured, hey, I ain't stealing food from your kid's mouth, why should I do my work? The whole time I was at Julia de Burgos, I had no idea the school was named after Puerto Rico's greatest poet, had no idea Julia de Burgos had emigrated to New York City and lived in poverty while she wrote beautiful verses. She lived in El Barrio and had died on the street. But we weren't taught about her or any other Latin American poets, for that matter. As for history, we knew more about Italy than our own Latin American countries. To Mr. Varatollo, the social studies teacher, everything was Italy this, Italy that, Italy, Italy, Italy. Didn't he know the history of the neighborhood? Hadn't he ever seen *West Side Story*? We hated Italians. At least that part of *West Side Story* was correct. Some Italians from the old days of the fifties and sixties were still around. They lived on Pleasant Avenue off 116th Street, and if you were caught around there at night you'd better have been a light-skinned Latino so you could pass yourself off as Italian.

So, since we were almost convinced that our race had no culture, no smart people, we behaved even worse. It made us fight and throw books at one another, sell loose joints on the stairways, talk back to teachers, and leave classrooms whenever we wanted to. We hated the white teachers because we knew they hated their jobs. The only white teacher who actually taught us something, actually went through the hassle of making us respect her by never taking shit from us, was the math teacher, Ms. Boorstein. She once went toe-to-toe with Sapo. He was about to walk out of her classroom because he was bored, and she said to him, "Enrique, sit back down!" Sapo kept walking and she ran toward the door and blocked his path. She dared him to push her. She said to him, "I'll get your mother. I bet she hits harder." And Sapo had no choice but to go back to his seat. From that day on, no one messed with her. She might have been Jewish, but to us she was still white. Ms. Boorstein could yell like a Latin woman. To us she was always "that bitch." But we knew she cared, for the simple reason that she never called us names; she would yell but never call us names. She only wanted us to listen, and when we did well on her math tests she was all smiles.

The Hispanic teachers, on the other hand, saw themselves in our eyes and made us work hard. Most of them were young, the sons and daughters of the first wave of Puerto Ricans who immigrated to El Barrio in the late forties and the fifties. These teachers never took shit from us (especially Sapo), and they were not afraid to curse in class: "*Mira*, sit down or I'll kick your ass down." At times they spoke to us harshly, as if they were our parents. This somehow made us fear and listen to them. They were not Puerto Ricans who danced in empty streets, snapping their fingers and twirling their bodies. Nor were they violent, with switchblade tempers. None of them were named Maria, Bernardo, or Anita. These teachers simply taught us that our complexion was made up of many continents, Africa, Europe, and Asia. To them our self-respect was more important than passing some test, because you can't pass a test if you already feel defeated. But the Hispanic teachers had very little say in how things were run in that school. Most of them had just graduated from a city university and couldn't rock the boat. Any boat.

So we hated ourselves and fought every day. And finally, after a while, when I lost the fear of hitting someone else (not the fear of getting hit but of hitting someone else), I looked for fights. With Sapo watching my back, getting into fights was fun. During my three years at Julia de Burgos, I had more fights than Sapo. And since I was born with high, flat cheekbones, almond-shaped eyes, and straight black hair (courtesy of my father's Ecuadorian side of the family), and because kung fu movies were very popular at the time, when I was in the eighth grade, I was tagged Chino.

I was happy with the name. Chino was a cool name, *qué chévere*. There were many guys named Chino in East Harlem but it wasn't a name that was just given to you. First, you had to look a bit Chinese, and second, you had to fight. It was an honor to be called Chino. But there were other honorable names in the neighborhood: Indio, if you had straight black hair, tan skin, and looked like a Taino; Batuka, if you liked Santana music and played the congas real good; Biscocho, if you were fat but told good jokes; and so on. Then there were names that were added to your name because of who you were, what you were known for, or what was said about you. Like a guy I knew named Junior, of 109th and Madison. Junior not only carried a knife, a *jiga*, in his back pocket, he had used it to cut someone's face. It was no big deal to carry a knife in your back pocket. Everyone did and everyone knew that 80 percent of it was just for show, *puro aguaje*. The other 20 percent you hoped would never come your way. But Junior was notorious for going straight for his *jiga* when he got into a fight. He didn't waste any time. It was Junior who introduced the phrase "Kool-Aid smile" when he cut a guy's face so bad, from ear to ear, that he was left looking like the chubby, smiling cartoon logo from Kool-Aid packets. Soon this term caught on and it became a street phrase: "Shut the fuck up or I'll give you a Kool-Aid smile." Junior was no longer just Junior, but sometimes Junior Jiga of 109th Street.

Then there were the names your parents had called you since you were a kid, bullshit names like Papito, Tato, Chave, Junito, Googie, Butchy, Tito. Those names meant shit around school, around the block, around the neighborhood. They carried no weight and it was usually guys stuck with those names that were always getting their asses kicked.

·

SAPO WAS the same around everybody, it didn't matter if it was the president of the United States or some junkie, Sapo was himself. He was that way around any girl, too. See, there were girls in the neighborhood that you could curse around, act stupid, and all that, and then there were girls that you just didn't. Sapo couldn't care less.

Nancy Saldivia was the second type. First, she was a Pentecostal girl. More important, she was fine. All the guys from the neighborhood liked Nancy Saldivia. Her face could envelop you, almost convert you. She had light tan skin, hazel eyes, and a beautiful mane of semibrown, semiblond hair. Nancy exuded a purity rarely found among the church girls. She was as genuine as a statue of a saint you want to light candles to, steal flowers for, or pray in front of. When she'd say, *"Gloria a Dios!"* she meant it. She was intelligent, polite, and friendly, and since she never cursed everyone called her Blanca.

Blanca wasn't allowed to wear jeans but she made up for it by wearing tight, short skirts. She always carried a Bible with her and never talked bad about anybody and at school she only hung around with her Pentecostal friend, Lucy. Lucy was a hairy girl who never shaved her legs because it was against her religion. Blanca had hairy legs as well, but Lucy's legs were so hairy that everyone called her Chewbacca. As if that wasn't enough, Lucy also had huge breasts. Because of them she was at times tagged Chewbacca *la vaca*. When the cruelty toward Lucy became too much for Blanca, she'd punish the boys by being the coldest, most serious person in school. Only Blanca could get away with this because she had an angelic face that almost made you want to sing Alleluia. Made you want to pick up a tambourine and join her one night in her church. Make a joyful noise to the Lord so she would begin to jump up and down to all that religious salsa. And maybe you'd be lucky enough to cop a cheap feel as the Holy Ghost took over her body.

All the guys felt this need to be nice to Blanca, to protect her in any way they could, even though she was a church girl and all they'd ever get would be a peck on the cheek. All the guys, I mean, except Sapo.

"Shit, man, she ain't gold. She ain't the fucken Virgin Mary."

"Blanca's Pentecostal, bro. Not Catholic."

"Whatevah the fuck she is. All the guys really want is to fuck her, so why do they keep her in some fucken glass case?"

"Yo, respect that shit, Sapo."

"Wha' for? She ain't no angel. Yo, my aunt was Pentecostal and she, bro, she has fucked half the men in her congregation. *Esa ha cojido mas huevos que una sartén.*"

"Respect, Sapo. Blanca believes in that shit, so—" Sapo would cut me off.

"So you like her, thass all. Because it's really bullshit. But you like her so you riding that shit, bro. But you know it's all bullshit. Yo, check this out, my moms prays to her saint, Santa Clara, every day at Saint Cecilia's. She lights all these fucken candles so the Virgin will give her the numbers. When that bitch saint tells my moms the Lotto numbers, then I'll believe. Yo, I'll believe. Yo, I'll believe so bad I'll buy Santa Clara a fucken wax museum."

•

MY MOTHER hated Sapo. "I don't want to see you hanging around with that *demonio*," she'd say to me. But I never listened, because Sapo meant adventure. Sapo meant we could steal beer and drink it together. He meant flying kites on the roof of a tenement building, both high on his weed. We loved flying kites but it wasn't the pot that made the flying adventurous, it was the Gillette blades. We would buy one pack of those thin blades and glue razors onto the edges of our kites. Now we had flying weapons, kites able to cut the strings of other people's kites in midair. It was aerial warfare. We would look up at the sky and see a kite and then maneuver our kites toward it. Sapo was brilliant at this. He didn't really have to get that close or as high, all he had to do was get his kite with its blade edges to brush up against the string of the other kite. Then, without that person knowing it, his string would go limp and he'd think that it had just snapped, but no, Sapo had cut it. Then I would run downstairs and track the kite, which would soon come crashing to the ground or on some rooftop or some-where. I would collect our spoils of war, which we would sell to some kid and split the money.

My father understood where we were living. He knew, and when I would come home with bruises or a black eye he never lost his cool. I liked my father, and my father liked Sapo. He knew the importance of having someone there to watch your back. It was important to have a *pana*, a *broqui*. But my mother didn't get it. And like my mother, that's what Blanca could never understand. Sapo was important to me. Sapo had arrived at a time when I needed someone there, next to me, so I could feel valuable. My childhood and adolescent life had been made up of times with him, as I later wanted my adult life to be made up of times with Blanca. It was hard to split the two.

"You know, Sapo," I said to him one day as we were preparing to fly kites on the roof of a project, "if we could ride on top of these things, we could get out of here. You know?"

"Why would you wanna fucken leave this place?" he said with his Sapo smile, showing all his teeth as he glued some razors to his kite. "This neighborhood is beautiful, bro."

"Yeah, you're right, *pana*," I said to him, but knew I didn't mean it. I gave my kite to the wind, which took it with a hiss, and I thought of Blanca and let out more string.

Willie Bodega

I n the eighth grade I applied to the High School of Art and Design on Fifty-seventh Street and Second Avenue. When I was accepted a lot of things seemed possible. I now left East Harlem every day and without my quite knowing it, the world became new.

Little by little the neighborhood's petty street politics became less important. I started to hang out less with Sapo, who had already dropped out. When we did meet on the street it was like we were long-lost brothers who hadn't seen each other in years. Regardless of the distance created, I did know that he was still my *pana*, my main-mellow-man. I knew that if I went to Sapo and said some guys wanted to jump me, he'd round up a crew for me, a clique from 112th and Lex or from another block. Sapo knew a lot of blocks. He knew just about all the guys that lived in the neighborhood. Most of them owed Sapo one thing or another, or were just scared of him and would do as he said, no questions asked.

In my senior year at Art and Design, I learned about the Futurists. I wanted to do something like they had done. The Futurists had been a malcontent group of artists at the beginning of the century who loved speed and thought war was good, the "hygiene of humanity." To them it was important to begin again. Culture was dead and it was time for something new. Burn all the museums! Burn all the libraries! Let's begin from scratch! were some of their battle cries, and although most of them were, like their leader, Marinetti, from upper-middle-class backgrounds and not from the slums like myself, I liked them because I could relate to their anger. I realized that by reinventing culture, they were reinventing themselves. I wanted to reinvent myself too. I no longer wanted the world to be just my neighborhood anymore. Blanca thought the same, and when we started going out we would talk about this all the time.

"Julio, don't you hate it when people from the neighborhood who somehow manage to leave change their names? Instead of Juan, they want to be called John."

"I see your point. But what's in a name, anyway? A Rivera from Spanish Harlem by any other name would still be from Spanish Harlem."

Blanca laughed and called me stupid. Then she said, "I have an aunt named Veronica. When she married this rich guy from Miami, she changed her name to Vera."

"That's wack," I said.

"I'm not going to do that. I'm going to keep my name, Nancy Saldivia, and my friends can always call me Blanca. The only time I'll change my name is when I get married."

I could have married Blanca right then and there. Instead we enrolled at Hunter College, because we knew we needed school if we were ever going to change ourselves. We got married the following year. Those were the days when all conversations seemed as important as a cabinet crisis. We'd always talk about graduating and saving up to buy a house. About children who looked like me and slept like her. With Blanca next to me, El Barrio seemed less dirty, life less hard, God less unjust. Those were the good days, when Blanca and I worked hard to invent new people. It was important to have someone help you as you grew and changed.

•

THAT'S WHAT it was always about. Shedding your past. Creating yourself from nothing. Now I realize that that's what attracted me to Willie Bodega. Willie Bodega didn't just change me and Blanca's life, but the entire landscape of the neighborhood. Bodega would go down as a representation of all the ugliness in Spanish Harlem and also all the good it was capable of being. Bodega placed a mirror in front of the neighborhood and in front of himself. He was street nobility incarnated in someone who still believed in dreams. And for a small while, those dreams seemed as palpable as that dagger Macbeth tried to grab. From his younger days as a Young Lord to his later days as Bodega, his life had been triggered by a romantic ideal found only in those poor bastards who really wanted to be poets but got drafted and sent to the front lines. During that time Bodega would create a green light of hope. And when that short-lived light went supernova, it would leave a blueprint of achievement and desire for anyone in the neighborhood searching for new possibilities.

It was always about Bodega and nobody else but Bodega and the only reason I began with Sapo was because to get to Bodega, you first had to go through Sapo.

Anyway, it was Sapo who introduced me. Sapo would knock at my door at crazy hours of the night.

"Yo, Chino, man, whass up? You know yo'r my *pana*, right? And like, you know yo'r the only guy I can trust, right? I mean, we go way back." He'd rattle out credentials as if I might deny him the favor. Then after recapping our friendship from the fourth grade to the adult present he would say, "So, *mira*, I have this package here and bein' that yo'r the only guy I can trust, you know, can I leave it here wi'choo, Chino?" Of course I knew what was in the paper bag. Blanca did too, and she had fits.

"You know he's bad news. Always has been. I don't want you around Enrique."

"What are you, my mother?"

"He's a drug dealer, Julio."

"Man, you're brilliant, Blanca. What could have possibly given him away?" The honeymoon had been over for months.

"What is your problem? You know, Julio, I married you because I thought you had brains. I thought you had more brains than most of the f-f-fucks in this neighborhood." When Blanca cursed, I knew she was mad. Even when she was angry I could detect some hesitation, a stutter before the curse. Blanca measured her curses very carefully. She didn't waste too many.

"Just look at Enrique," she continued. "He has all these women who sleep with him hoping to rip him off when he falls asleep. So he brings his dope here so you, my idiot husband, can guard it while he has a great time!"

"So what's wrong with that? It's not like we have to change it and make a bottle for it."

"*Dios mío!* Enrique might have some money and drive a BMW but he still lives in the same roach-infested buildings that we do. He can't leave because his money is only good here. You don't see him living on Eighty-sixth Street with the *blanquitos,* do you?"

"Did you figure all this out by yourself, Blanca?" I acted more interested in looking for the remote, so I could switch on the television.

"Did it ever occur to you," I said after finding it under the sofa cushions, "that maybe Sapo likes it here? Maybe, like a pig, Sapo likes the mud. Not everybody wants to go to college, Blanca." I switched on the TV and began to surf. "Not everyone wants to save up. Buy a little house in the Bronx. Raise some brats. You think everyone wants what you want?"

"What *we* want, Julio, what *we* want." She pointed at the two of us.

"Blanca, I hate that supermarket job and I've no classes tonight so don't ask me right now what I want. Right now just let me watch *Jeopardy,* okay?" She went over to switch the television off. She stood in between the remote and the television so that I couldn't turn it back on from the sofa.

"I don't like that receptionist desk, either." Blanca stepped forward and snatched the remote from my hand. "But unlike you, I'm almost finished at Hunter. Maybe if you would stop hanging around with Sapo, you could finish up before the baby arrives. We're going to need real money, real jobs."

"Ahh, Blanca, this is all reruns. It's all been said before. Come on. You may know what to do when you get that degree; me, I don't care. I'm getting it because I like books and all that stuff. Give me the remote." Blanca sat down on the edge of the sofa next to me. She was calm, staring straight ahead, avoiding any possibility of eye contact. When she did this, I knew a little speech was coming.

"Julio, I know how you feel about your studies. I do. But I'm only thinking about the baby. I would have preferred to have waited a year or two after we graduated, but it didn't work out that way."

"Oh, so it's my fault, right?"

"It's no one's fault. Look, I don't intend to keep badgering you about finishing school. And who knows what you'll do when you finish. I wish you'd talk to me about it." Her tone changed, a bit more angry. "But if you're up to something, something stupid with Sapo that's going to get you in some trouble, I want to hear about it. I want to hear it from you." Blanca faced me. Her hazel eyes stared fiercely into mine. I blinked. She didn't. She poked a finger in my chest. "I want to hear it, understand? From you and not from someone else's mouth. From you. So I can decide if I'm going to stay with you or not. I want to know. At least give me that. One hundred percent of that. If you are up to something illegal, you tell me. Let me decide for myself if I want to stay with you, if I'm going to be one of those wives whose husbands are in jail. I'm willing to put up with a lot, but I want to be told. If you keep me in the dark it's like insulting me. And you know Enrique is trouble."

"Blanca, I'm here with you, right? Have I ever been in any trouble? I'm here, right?"

"But what if one day Enrique doesn't tell you where he is taking you and actually takes you somewhere bad? What if the police bust him and since you were with him you get in trouble too? That happens a lot, you know."

"Sapo would never do that to me."

"How do you know?"

"Because I know."

"Julio, when we were teenagers at Julia de Burgos, I knew guys had to play this macho game and I knew you didn't really want to play but you had to. Even though you were this kid who just wanted to paint. I liked you even back then."

"I liked you too—"

"No, let me say this, okay?"

"Okay."

"I remember when they would call you on the loudspeaker to go down to the office and paint this for Mrs. So-and-So, or paint a mural for an assembly. It happened a lot. Sometimes you would miss all eight periods because you were painting something for some teacher. I remember how cool you thought it was that you were singled out and had this special privilege. But I knew you were being ruined by those terrible teachers. You were just a kid. You should have been in a classroom and they didn't care about you, they only wanted you to make their assemblies look good."

"So what are you getting at, Blanca?"

"Listen, I know this neighborhood, Julio. Just because I go to church doesn't mean I don't know this neighborhood. Here it only matters what they can break, take, or steal from you. I know that Sapo is your friend. I know that. But his friends are not your friends. His friends don't have friends." I saw her point. It was a good one. But I just played it off as if she was wrong and told her to go to sleep. Without saying another word Blanca handed the remote back and slowly walked into the bedroom. I guess she'd had her say and was leaving it up to me.

·

BUT THE fights with Blanca over Sapo only got worse. Finally, during her second trimester, Blanca didn't even bother, more out of preoccupation with the baby than out of hopelessness. When she knew I was going to hang with Sapo, she would throw her hands up in disgust and ask the Lord for forgiveness. To forgive me, that is, never her. Always me. This also meant I couldn't touch her. I was impure and her body, round as the moon, was still the temple.

I can't say I blamed her. When I asked her to marry me, her pastor, Miguel Vasquez, had warned her that if she married me—a worldly person, a mundane—she'd lose the privilege of playing the tambourine in front of the congregation. That meant a lot to Blanca. At times she'd beg me to convert so she could be in good grace again. Besides, she hated going to church by herself. Now I know about wanting some sort of recognition, of wanting to have some sort of status, but when I think about yelling things like *Cristo salva!* I get the heebie-jeebies. You don't know what it's like inside a Pentecostal church full of Latinos. They really get down to some serious worshiping, with tambourines here, tambourines there, some guy beginning to wiggle on the floor because he has the Holy Ghost in him. The pastor gives his speech, yelling about Christ coming, every week Christ is coming. *Christo viene pronto! Arrepiéntete! Arrepiéntete!* Then an entire band goes to the platform and begins to jam on some of that religious salsa. It's like a circus for Christians. But the one thing you could never make fun of about Pentecostals was their girls. They had the prettiest church girls in the neighborhood. You knew their beauty was real because they didn't wear any makeup and still looked good. And I had married one of the the prettiest. Like with Sapo while I was growing up, I needed Blanca with me so I could feel valuable. No, I didn't want to mess that up.

·

THEN ONE day when I came home from work and was getting my books to go and meet Blanca at Hunter, I got a call from Sapo.

"Yo, Chino, whass up?"

"Whass up, man."

"So like, can you do me a solid? Like, you my *pana*, right? You know, like the day Mario DePuma jumped yo' ass at school? Who was there to save you from that fucken Italian horse? I mean, I know you didn't back down and shit but, like, he was fuckin' you up pretty bad."

"Sapo, I'm in a rush. Are you gettin' somewhere or just swimmin' laps?"

"Yo, I hear that. All right, you know that taped-up paper bag I left wi'choo lass night?"

"Yeah, but if you picking that up you gonna have to wait, bro. Because I have to go to class and meet Blanca."

"Oh, I'm touched, Jane and Joe Night School. How sweet."

"Whatever, bro. Look, I have to get off."

"*Pero, bro, no corra,* I call to ask ya if, like, could you drop it off for me?"

"What the fuck! Sapo, you think I was fucken born yesterday? Yo, I'm not going to do your dirty work, what the fuck. Me letting you keep that shit in my place is one thing, taking it around is another—"

"Hold your *caballos*, bro, like I wouldn't be askin' ya unless I knew it was somethin' easy and not out of your way."

"Yeah, well it's way out of my way. I have to go to class, man, I'll see you around." I was ready to hang up.

"Nah, wait! Bro, that's the beauty of it. You'd be droppin' those fucks right at Hunta. Yo, I swera-ma-mahthah. There's a guy in the library. You know where the library at Hunta is, don'cha?"

"Yeah, so?"

"Well, just put the bag in a backpack and he'll take it. It's no big deal. You'll lose the backpack but it's a cheap fucken bag anyway. My bro, you even know the dude. Tweety, remember him? Tweety from Julia de Burgos? Later on everyone started calling him Sylvester b'cause when he talked he gave you the weather. Remember him?"

"Ho, shit, that guy still alive?"

"Alive and spitting. Yeah, so Chino, come on. Some rich white nigga on Sixty-eighth Street ordered all this shit for a party in one of those penthouses by Park."

"I don't know, Sapo." I was afraid. Not of the cops but of Blanca.

"Yo, come on, man, one last favor for your *pana*, Sapo. You be just taking the sack to Tweety, bro. He's the one who's gonna be doing the real thing."

"So why don't you take it to Tweety? Look, I'll wait for you here to come pick—"

"I'm in the Bronx, Chino! You think I would've called you if I coulda come by? Fuck, man, you go to school or what?"

So, without telling Blanca, I did as Sapo had asked.

THE NEXT night Sapo knocked at my door and handed me fifty dollars, just for taking something to where I was already headed.

"Compliments of Willie Bodega, my man. For your backpack." Sapo slapped the crisp bill in my hand.

And that's when I heard the name Willie Bodega for the first time.

"Willie wha'?" I thought it was a funny name.

"Willie Bodega? You nevah heard of him? He's like the big Taino in this neighborhood, you know? Although only a few have seen his face."

It's important for me to remember that night, because once I heard that name it was never about Blanca or Sapo. As important as they were to me, it was always about Bodega. We were all insignificant, dwarfed by what his dream meant to Spanish Harlem. And in obtaining it, he took shortcuts and broke some laws, leaving crumbs along the way in hopes of one day turning around and finding his way back to dignity.

Willie Bodega Don't Sell Rocks.
Willie Bodega Sells Dreams.

I T was a night like any other. Blanca was laboring at the computer writing a paper for one of her classes and I wasn't. I was reading a book that had nothing to do with any of the classes I was taking. I knew that Blanca would soon get up from the computer and ask me why I wasn't writing my paper. I was ready.

"We only have one computer."

"I'm finished for tonight."

"So fast?" I thought I had it covered.

"Fast? I been at this paper for over a week. When are you going to start your work?"

"I'm researching even as we speak, see?" I showed her my book.

Blanca squinted at the title. She had her suspicions but let it go. Then someone knocked at our door. I went to answer it. It was Sapo.

"Yo, Chino, Bodega wants ta speak with ya." As always Sapo was Sapo and he said this not caring that Blanca could hear him. She strode to the door and stared at me, waiting to see what I was going to say.

"What does he want?"

"Bro, are you coming or not?" Sapo asked impatiently as if I was taking up his valuable time. He didn't look at Blanca and Blanca didn't look at Sapo.

Blanca pulled me away from the door. "Julio, who is this Bodega guy?" she asked, letting the door slam. Sapo waited in the hallway. He hated Blanca and he knew Blanca hated him right back.

"A friend."

"A friend of Enrique's, you mean?"

"A friend of Sapo is a friend of mine," I said, and Blanca shot me an evil look, then pointedly clasped her rounded belly.

"Blanca, please, I'll only be gone an hour or two. It's not like you're going to give birth any minute, you got months to go."

"Julio, we've gone through this already. When you leave with him," she loudly whispered, "I get these feelings, *Dios me salve.*"

"Blanca, no Christ right now, all right?" This upset her.

"What about your work?" Her voice got louder. "Weren't you studying or something?"

"I just finished." I don't know why I said those things to Blanca sometimes when I knew she could see right through me.

"You mean you want to hang with Sapo." She sighed and waved her hand dismissively. "Forget it. *Vete.* Act like a single man." She stormed into the bedroom to get on the phone with her sister, Deborah. Blanca called her sister only when she wanted to hear gossip or to complain about me. Deborah was the complete opposite of Blanca. She wasn't as pretty, wasn't Pentecostal, she cursed, drank Budweiser from the can, and got into fights. She was so much the opposite of her kid sister that from the time Blanca was ten and Deborah twelve, everyone called her Negra.

After the skirmish with Blanca I grabbed my denim jacket and headed out the door. When I came out, I saw Sapo waiting impatiently in the hallway. When he saw me he smiled, his big lips uncovering all his teeth. He was happy, as if he had won some duel.

"Let me tell you, bro, I always knew you were gonna marry that girl. And that's all right cuz she's fine, but you got to admit she's a bitch sometimes." His hand landed on my shoulder and he said, "Bodega is nice, man. You'll like the guy."

"What does he want with me?" I asked again.

"He didn't say. He just wants ta speak with you, thass all." We headed toward the stairs and Sapo squeezed my shoulder and then stopped. He took his hand off me, turned, and looked in my eyes to make sure I was listening.

"Bodega wants something from you, man. That shit don't happen often. Know what I'm sayin'?"

I nodded, and we walked down the stairs.

"Where does does Bodega live?"

"Bodega? Bodega lives in a lotta places. He has apartments all over the neighborhood. You got to have many places and juggle your place of dwellin' in order to create confusion. Only your closest of *panas* can know your exact whereabouts. All I know is he said he wanted to speak with ya and that he was goin' to be at his place on top of Casablanca. You know where Casasblanca is, don' cha? That fucken meat market."

"Yeah, I know," I said, and we walked out to the street.

From my place in the Schomburg projects on 111th and Fifth to Casablanca the *carnicería* on 110th between Lexington and Park is only four blocks. Regardless, Sapo led me to his parked BMW and we drove the short distance.

"There's this retard at the door yo'r going to meet. He's Bodega's cousin. Thass the only reason why Bodega has him around, b'cause you can't fire your own family. But the nigga is stupid, bro. So when we get there he is going to open the door and that nigga, bro, that nigga talks in songs. Like, he fucken grew up on radio. *Ese tipo está craquiado.*"

When we arrived Sapo parked the car right next to a fire hydrant. Outside the walkup some men had set up a table and were sitting on milk crates, drinking Budweisers in paper bags and playing dominoes. They had a small radio at their feet tuned to an old love song, *"Mujer, si puedes tu con Dios hablar pregúntale si yo alguna vez te he dejado de adorar."* Across the street, on the entrance wall of a project building, was an altar, meaning someone had just died. There were flowers, a forty-ounce Miller, pictures of saints, and pictures of the deceased, with six large candles burning in the form of a cross. Sapo led me inside the old tenement where the storefront butcher shop Casablanca had been been serving up meat to the neighborhood for years. We walked up three flights. Inside the tenement the walls were torn up, the stairs creaked, the smell was of old and decay; the only thing worse than the smell of a tenement is a pissed-up elevator in a project. If you look at the floors of an old tenement, you'll see layers upon layers of linoleum from different years. All in different colors. Sapo stopped at a steel door that looked like it was imported from Rikers Island.

A tall, big man with a baby's face and the shoulders of a bear opened the door. He was Bodega's cousin. He was slow, but only in intelligence. Later on I would find out that he was actually light on his feet, like a feeding grizzly. I guessed he was in his forties and was stronger than he knew. I mean, this guy could hug you and not know he was killing you. He was a child of AM radio's Top Forty heyday. Word had it he started to talk in song years ago, when AM radio broke his heart by going all talk. I figured Bodega kept him as someone to watch his back or at least to watch the door.

"*Oye, como va. Bueno pa gozar,*" Nene said to Sapo, who then introduced me.

"This is my main-mellow-man Chino. Yo'r cus asked for him."

"Chino, yeah, bro." Nene looked at me and extended his hand. I met it. "Hey, it's cool, bro. You a businessman, I take?" Nene asked me. I just shrugged. "You cool, Chino, because *any businessman can come and drink my wine. Come and dig my earth.*" And he let us inside. Sapo just shook his head and muttered curses under his breath every time Nene used a piece of a song. It was something Sapo had to tolerate, a clause he had to accept if he was going to work for Bodega.

Inside was nothing. Just bare rooms. I had never gone to Sapo's place, but I'd heard it was the same way. It had to do with not owning too many things because you never knew when you had to disappear for a while. You had to travel light and easy. Nene led us into a room with a desk, two chairs, and an old, dirty sofa with a *Playboy* magazine stuck in between the cushions. Standing behind the desk was a man in his forties with a goatee and the droopy eyes of an ex–heroin addict. His hair was curly and he was about five feet ten. He was talking on a cellular phone and when he saw Sapo and me he quickly smiled, cut off the conversation, hung up the phone, and motioned to me to take the seat in front of him. Sapo sat on the dirty sofa and pulled out the *Playboy.*

"Sapito, this is your friend?" Bodega asked.

"Yeah, this is my main-mellow-man, Chino. He's smart, Willie, yo he's smart. I useta copy off him when we were in school. Till I got tired of that shit." Sapo was excited. He was happy that I was there, as if he wanted me to be part of some crew. I saw Bodega scope me out and shake his head, as if he was disappointed. As if he had expected someone else.

"You a friend of Sapo, right?" He asked, knowing full well that I was.

"Yeah," I said, not really knowing how to answer.

"So check it out, Sapito tells me you go to college. That true?"

"What kinda question is that?" I said laughing, playing it off because I was a little nervous. I would have been scared, but Sapo was there with me and I knew nothing would happen to me.

"Yeah, man, I go to a public college, nothing big and fancy—"

"Yo, college is college and thass all that maras." Bodega then eyed me again up and down, then nodded his head, snapped his fingers, and pointed at me all in the same motion.

"You all right," he said, as if he finally approved. "So, check it out, Chino, right? It was Chino?"

"Yeah."

"So, check it out, Chino, you evah heard of Edwin Nazario?"

"Edwin Nazario? Is he related to the boxer who was going to fight Rosario, el Chapo?"

"Nah, same last name, no relation."

"Don't know him. Who is he?"

"He's a lawyer."

"I don't like lawyers, they're prostitutes in suits," I said, trying to be cool.

"Not my man Nazario. He's my brothuh, we share the same vision." Bodega pointed at his eyes as if he could see whatever it was he was going to tell me. As if it were there in front of him.

"I hear you," I said. I always say "I hear you" when I don't understand things or have nothing to add.

"Nazario, he's amazin'. Chino, he knows the law inside out, like a reversible coat. And thass just the beginnin'. With Nazario I intend to own this neighborhood and turn El Barrio into my sandbox." His cellular phone rang and he picked it up.

"I can't talk right now," he hissed, his droopy eyes flashing. "I'm in the middle of somethin', yeah . . . yeah, no no, at the botanica, *que pendejos son*, yeah . . . yeah . . . at the botanica." He put the phone down on the desk and looked at me.

"Like I was tellin' you, Chino, check it out, Nazario and I know that we are livin' in the most privileged of times since the nineteen-twenties, since Prohibition." I saw that Bodega was in no rush to get to where he was going. That night when I met him I didn't like him. It wasn't because he was some drug lord. Nah, to me that was no different than some Wall Street executive who makes a million dollars by destroying some part of the world. I didn't like him because he was a loudmouth who couldn't cut to the chase. Bodega was the type of guy who, if he was going to show you how to make paper airplanes, would first tell you how trees had to be cut down in order to make paper.

"B'cause men that made this country, men that built this country were men from the street. Men like me, men like you, men like Sapito there." He pointed at Sapo, who had his nose in the *Playboy*. "Men that used whatever moneymakin' scheme they could, and made enough money to clean their names by sending their kids to Harvard. Did you see that special on the Kennedys, on channel thirteen, Chino?"

"You watch channel thirteen?" I was surprised.

"Yeah, I watch channel thirteen. What you think, only kids and white people watch public television?"

"Nah, I ain't saying that. It's just that *eso está* heavy duty, thass all."

"Not only do I watch it but I'm even a member. So did you see that special on the Kennedys, Chino?"

"Nah, must have missed it."

"Yeah, well, that shit told the truth. Yo, *ese tipo era un raquetero*. Joe Kennedy was no different from me. He already had enough money in the twenties but he still became a rumrunner. Alcohol is a drug, right? Kennedy sold enough booze to kill a herd of rhinos. Made enough money from that to launch other, legal schemes. Years later he fucken bought his kids the White House. Bought it. Yeah, he broke the law. Like I'm breaking the law, but I get no recognition because I am no Joe Kennedy."

I wanted to ask Bodega what he was talking about but I just nodded my head and let him talk.

"Because, Chino, this country is ours as much as it is theirs. Puerto Rican limbs were lost in the sands of Iwo Jima, in Korea, in Nam. You go to D.C. and you read that wall and you'll also see our names: Rivera, Ortega, Martinez, Castillo. Those are our names there along with Jones and Johnson and Smith. But when you go fill out a job application you get no respect. You see a box for Afro-American, Italian-American, Irish-American but you don't see Puerto Rican–American, you just see one box, Hispanic. Now, you don't want to consider me an American, I got no beef with that. You want to keep me a bastard child, I got no beef with that, either. But when the spoils of the father are being divided, I better get some or I'll have to take the booty by force. East Harlem, East L.A., South Bronx, South Central, South Chicago, Overtown down in Miami, they're all the same bastard ghetto."

He paused for about a second and looked at me. For the first time I saw his eyes were a strange shade of pale brown, as if they had been dulled by some deep sadness that the years had turned into anger.

"I hear you," I said again. I was ready to excuse myself. At the first opportunity I was going to tell Bodega that I had to go home to Blanca because she was pregnant. That I hoped he would understand. That I would love to hang with him but I couldn't. But right that minute, Bodega slid open a drawer and pulled out a Ziploc bag the size of a Bible and said the magic words that kept me there that night.

"Yo, smoke with me, Chino."

I settled myself down and looked at the weed. That shit must be real good, I thought. When he opened the plastic bag, the aroma was like coffee and the seeds were as big as *quenepas*. Bodega then zipped the bag back up and flung it to Sapo.

"Sapito, roll us some."

Sapo smiled his huge smile and brought out his own *bambú*. He opened the bag, grabbed a handful of pot, and spilled it all over the

Playboy on his lap. He closed the bag and began to unseed the handful he had spilled on the magazine. "Ho, shit, I just realized," Sapo said, laughing, "I spilled all this pot on Bo Derek's face. Man, that bitch is still fine, she like forty and shit."

"Nah, she's wack. She was hot once, not anymore," I said, happy that the conversation with Bodega was stalled. As I watched Sapo, I hoped that Bodega would get down to the point. I wanted Bodega to just tell me what this had to do with me. But right then, it didn't matter as much because a nice joint was coming my way and since the day I had married Blanca, I hadn't had a good smoke.

"Nah, Bo Derek is still usable," Sapo said.

"Not like when she had those little *trensitas*. You know, when she had those little braids like Stevie Wonder. Back then she was fine. That shit should come back. White girls look fine with their hair like that," I said.

Sapo continued to smile. "You know, Iris Chacón in huh prime never posed for *Playboy*. Thass a fucken shame," he said.

"Now that," I agreed, "would have been worth paying for." Iris Chacón was my wet dream, as she was for many. When she danced, she prostituted your blood, masturbated your soul. She was a gift from the mother island to remind us of the women that were left behind, the girls that were not brought over to Nueva York and were left waving goodbye near *las olas del mar, en mi viejo San Juan.*

"But I don't care," Sapo said. "Iris Chacón or not, *yo las cojo a to'a'*. I take 'em all, from eight to eighty. Blind, crippled, and crazy." I laughed with him. Sapo hammed it up. "If they know how to crawl, they're in the right position."

I laughed. "Nigga, you're crazy."

"If they can play with Fisher-Price"—Sapo was on a roll, grabbed his crotch—"they can play with this device."

"Dude, shut up, get help," I said, laughing.

Just when Sapo was about to crack another snap—"If they watch *Sesame Street* they can"—Bodega came back to life. "So, Chino, like I was telling you . . ."

Sapo quieted down and I let out a deep sigh because I wanted to talk about something else. Even hearing Sapo's mad crazy snaps would have been a welcome relief. Bodega picked up on my boredom, smiled, and went right to the point.

"Nazario needs help. It would be good if he had you. You know, a smart guy, like an assistant, Chino."

"Hey, man, it's cool but I'm not interested in this business."

"Did I say anything about pushing rocks?" Bodega looked insulted. His voice sailed a notch. "I told you Nazario is a lawyer."

"Look man, I know you gotta do what you gotta do," I said. "I got nothin' against you or what you're doin'. I don't believe in this 'Just say no' shit because there ain't too many things to say 'Yes' to in this fucken place. But I can't."

"Nah, hear me out, Chino. Hear me out, don't interrupt me. Check it out. You know those three buildings on 111th between Lexington and Park, right in back of us and right in front of P.S. 101, you know, those newly renovated tenements?"

"Yeah, so wha'?"

"Those shits are mine."

"Yours?" I didn't believe him and looked at Sapo for confirmation. Sapo nodded.

"Those shits were condemned but look at them now," Sapo said. "It's like the fat girl no one wanted until someone took a chance on the bitch and put her on a diet, and now everybody's sweatin' her."

"But thass not all, Chino," Bodega continued. "I got a line of them that are being renovated on 119th and Lexington. And Nazario is working with his contacts in City Hall on getting me more. Housing. Housing, Chino. Thass how I'm going to do it. Thass the vision." The phone rang. He cursed at the air and answered it.

"Yeah . . . What botanica? You mean you fucks don't know what botanica? San Lázaro y las Siete Vueltas, what other botanica do you think? Now go!" Bodega hung up, shook his head. "Like children," he whispered to himself, "like fucken children."

Sapo kept rolling. Sapo could roll real good. A joint from him looked like it came out of a pack of Camels. I looked back at Bodega, who was still shaking his head. He muttered something to God or maybe to himself and continued.

"Like I was telling you, Chino, when Nazario acquired the first buildin', the cops would drive by and see Puerto Ricans workin' on tryin' to renovate a building. The cops would laugh. They said we had no ingenuity because we were Puerto Ricans. They would say things like, you guys ain't Incas, you have no Machu Picchus in San Juan; you guys aren't Aztecs, there ain't no pyramids in Mayaguez. You guys are Tainos, dumb mothafuckas. There ain't no ancient ruins on that island of yours cuz you guys can't build shit."

Bodega stopped, and held his index finger in front of his eyes. "But Nazario, he saw. He knew. He knew better." He moved his finger to his temple. "He's a lawyer, but he hustled. He can still hustle because he never forgot he is street. He hustled like all of us who started stealin' a hubcap here and a radio there until we owned the car. Nazario was hustlin'." Bodega cupped his hands around his mouth as if he was going to shout.

"'Yo! Anybody knows someone who's an electrician? A plasterer? A plumber?'" He dropped his hands and continued. "Nazario was in the street hustlin'. In Loisaida and in East Harlem. 'Yo! I'm tryin' to reno-vate a buildin' here! You know anybody who would do it for the love of his brother or at least for cheap?' And soon, the community answered him. 'Yeah, my brother is an electrician, he'll help out; yeah, my sister is a plumber; my cousin does roofin'.' And then, Chino, a blue plastic chute dropped down the side of the buildin'. Bricks began to fall. Pipes were cut. The roof was stripped. The buildin' was gutted. Like a fucken fish, it was gutted. And the cops stopped laughin'. And then Nazario was hustlin' again. Only this time it was with the fire marshal at City Hall. 'We haven't broken any fire codes. This building is safe. You can come see for yourselves.' And they came and they checked. And they declared the buildin' safe. And the fire department backed off. And you know what I did?"

"Wha'?"

"I placed fourteen families in the buildin', cheap rent, too. You know what that means, Chino?"

"You a sweetheart?" I said, smiling.

"Yeah, that too. But what it means is fourteen families that would riot for Bodega. Fourteen families that would take a bullet for Bodega.

Yeah, they ain't stupid, they know where the money is comin' from. They know who their real landlord is. They know what he does. But they're getting a slice, right? See, Chino, I see it as a grant. Just like IBM issues grants, like Mobil issues grants. Do those places really want to give money away? I don't think so. But it helps their image, it's tax deductible, and the government backs off some. In order for me to keep my slice, I also got to issue grants. But I take care of the community and the community will take care of me. They must, because their shelter depends on me." Bodega banged a fist on the table, then pointed a finger at the wall as if he were pointing at the people outside. As if he were pointing at the neighborhood.

"So if Doña Ramonita can't pay her rent, I take care of it. The community center needs a new pool table, I take care of it. Casita Maria's Peewee League needs new uniforms, I take care of it, bro. They all come to Bodega. The word is out. It's out all over El Barrio. Baby needs a new pair of shoes, go speak ta Willie Bodega. My daughter is getting married, and I need a big cake from Valencia, go see Bodega. My *fritura* stand in La Marqueta burned down, go see Willie Bodega, he'll help ya. Any shit like that. What I ask for is their loyalty. If something happens to me, people will take to the streets. Bro, there will be Latinos from 125th Street to 96th Street with congas and timbales twenty-four hours a day stopping traffic, overturning cars, setting fires, yelling, 'Free William Irizarry! Free that brother, that sweet, sweet brother! Free Willie Irizarry and lock up some fucken stockbroker!' I'm talkin' major riots here. Do you see what I'm talking about?"

As he asked me this I looked at Sapo again. He had finished rolling two joints. They were lovely: long, thin, white, like the fingers of a model. It seemed a shame to light them, but Sapo lit one up anyway. Toked it. Got up from the dirty sofa and handed it to me. I followed.

"One problem, Bodega," I said, holding the smoke in my lungs.

"Yeah?"

"Yo'r sellin' that stuff" — releasing the smoke — "to your own people."

"Fuck that!" He banged a fist on the desk again, only this time it was hard. I just ignored it and passed the joint to him.

"Nah, enjoy." He waved the joint away. *"To'a' pa' ti,"* he said, so I knew he couldn't be too mad.

"See, Chino, any Puerto Rican or any of my Latin brothers and sisters who are stupid enough to buy that shit . . ." He motioned with his fingers for me to come closer as if he was going to tell me a secret. I leaned toward him. Then he whispered, repeating, "Any Puerto Rican or any of my Latin brothers who are stupid enough to buy that shit, don't belong in my Great Society."

I wanted to laugh. Who did he think he was, Lyndon Johnson?

Back then, that night, to me he was a joke. I was surprised he had come this far. But I knew it couldn't have been pure luck. No one gets this far on luck. I was to discover that I was living in a rare moment when a personality becomes so interlocked with the era that it can't be spoken of in different sentences. Bodega was a lost relic from a time when all things seemed possible. When young people cared about social change. He had somehow brought that hope to my time. It was hard to define it at first because I thought no one could possibly believe any of that, not anymore. But Bodega didn't just believe it, he was actually practicing it. He had learned from the past and knew change couldn't just come from free love, peace, and brotherhood. Extreme measures would have to be taken, and all you could hope for was that the good would outweigh the bad.

"Great Society?" I repeated after him, shaking my head. "I don't know, Willie, that sounds like something out of the sixties, know what I'm sayin'? Something about declaring war on poverty and Spanish Harlem being a prisoner of war. Now, I don't know when that war ended, all I know is they never came looking to free us." I toked the joint again, laughing. I was about to get up and pass it to Sapo but I saw Sapo had lit his own joint. So I guessed this one was all mine. I smiled.

"Yeah, well I'm a throwback, m'man." Bodega returned my smile. "I'm glad you picked up on that, Chino." He was beaming. "You were just a puppy, Sapo was just a tadpole when the neighborhood was a joy. It was a joy because there was pride and anger and identity. The Black Panthers in Harlem were yellin', 'Power to the People!' Us here in El Barrio saw what they were doing up in Harlem. We began to ask ourselves, why can't we do some shit like that here? Somethin' had to be done, otherwise we were goin' to kill one another. So then came Cha Cha Jimenez, a cat from Chicago. He started speakin' about Puerto

Rican nationalism and soon formed the Young Lords. Us here in East Harlem took that movement and ran with it." Bodega began to pace the room with excitement. "The Young Lords were beautiful, Chino. El Barrio was full of hope and revolution was in the air. We wanted jobs, real jobs. We wanted education, real education, for our little brothers and sisters, b'cause it was too late for us. We wanted lead paint out of our buildings, window guards so our babies wouldn't go flying after pigeons, we wanted to be heard. But first we knew we had to get the community on our side. So what did we Young Lords do?"

"Wha'?"

"We cleaned the streets. Everybody, Chino, went home and got a broom, bought bags, rakes, Comet and Ajax for the graffiti walls, trash cans, and soon the community was for us. Soon they were cleaning the streets with us. No one feared us. They all loved us. Later we said to ourselves, hey, we didn't start the Lords to fuckin' clean the street. So one day we all put on our Sunday best and ambushed Gracie Mansion. To talk with Mayor Lindsay about jobs, education, housing, training programs. When we arrived at the gates of Gracie, Lindsay's aide said to us, 'Any complaints must be filed at City Hall.' We said, 'We're not here to complain, we're here to talk.' But Lindsay wouldn't see us. He could not believe that there were hoods in suits out by the gates who were not stabbing each other. Who weren't there to rob his house. Who had organized to make their neighborhood better. He couldn't understand that East Harlem, only a mile away from where he lived, had the capacity to see itself in the mirror and say, 'We need a change. Let's go and see the man.' Eventually, Chino, we all went home and did what Lindsay's aide had said. The next day we went to City Hall and filed our demands. And you know what happened the next month, Chino?"

"Nah, tell me," I said, knowing he was going to anyway.

"The next month, they hiked the subway fare from twenty-five cents to thirty-five cents." He shrugged. "So we waited, and we waited, and we filed and we filed. Finally, when we knew our demands weren't going to be met, when we knew Lindsay wouldn't get back to us, the sanitation department wouldn't even lend us brooms to clean our

streets, we had no choice but to take over the streets of East Harlem."
Bodega's cool was betrayed by excitement. "Those were the East
Harlem garbage riots of sixty-nine. We used garbage cans and thrown-
out furniture to blockade 116th Street from Fifth Avenue to First. And
Mayor Lindsay, the biggest fraud this fucken city has ever known, but
with enough charisma to charm Hitler, sent his fucken city officials
and his police goons after us. So we started stackin' guns inside a
church we took over by 111th Street and Lex. Thass right, inside a
fucken church. And we began preaching Que Pasa Power." Bodega
kept pacing around the room with the energy of a shadow boxer. "All
over the neighborhood, Que Pasa Power! Even old ladies started to
smuggle things for us, b'cause Mayor Lindsay's dogs would never think
of frisking them. Old ladies, Chino. Old ladies would do this for us
b'cause they knew, they knew where we were comin' from. Yo, it was
remarkable. Que Pasa Power was what was happenin'. *Pa'lante* was our
horse, a newspaper we pushed our ideas with." Bodega stopped pacing
and returned to his dirty desk. He sat down, facing me. "But just like
now, there was the eternal hustle." He looked at me quietly for a second. The sadness had returned, mixed with anger. "The eternal hustle,
Chino. The decision to either be a pimp or a whore, thass all you can
be in this world. You work for someone else or you work for yourself.
And when the Young Lords got too high and mighty they began to
bicker among themselves. Later they even changed their agenda and
became somethin' else. I was broken. Chino, bro, I left and knew that
the only way for me was to hustle. So I hustled enough heroin to knock
out all the elephants in Africa. And then I met ma man Nazario. He
was just gettin' out of Brooklyn Law School back then. And from those
days on, Nazario and me—" I saw some light in his eyes as if hope had
returned. He then joined his two fingers as if they were glued together.
"—Nazario and me, brothers. *Panas*. And now we've got bigger things
in mind. You see," he continued, "you either make money with me or
you make money for me. Thass what I tell my boys. Either way I win."

Bodega pointed at his eyes again. Then he laughed a little laugh.
"It's all a matter of where yo'r standing, where you comin' from. Willie
Bodega don't sell rocks. Willie Bodega sells dreams."

At that moment Sapo got up. He stuffed the *Playboy* in his back pocket, dropped the joint he had been smoking, carefully killed it with his sneaker, picked it up, and put the roach in his wallet.

"Yo, I'm going down to the bodega to get some beer," he said. "Anybody wan' anythin'?"

The Fire This Time

"BUILDINGS, huh?" I was a bit skeptical. "How do you escape the IRS? What do you tell New York City?"

"Ahhh, thass where my man Nazario comes in again. Yo, he's a genius. Nazario made up a legal management agency. It's supposedly owned by a Jew named Harry Goldstein, but you know who the real Harry Goldstein is? Thass right, me. The Harry Goldstein Real Estate Agency. I run the most humanitarian housing management company in New York City. B'cause, like I told you, Chino, if you take care of the community, the community will take care of you," Bodega said proudly, like he had found some truth only he knew about.

Sapo walked in with a forty-ounce Miller and a bag of chips. He pulled the *Playboy* out of his back pocket, opened his beer, and sat down.

"So if they need more heat I give it to them," Bodega continued. "They can't make that month's cheap rent? I give that, too. Something breaks, the super fixes it, quick. Complaints? Complaints, thass where you come in. Complaints would go t' you."

"Me?"

"Yeah, you."

"Why not Sapo? Why not have him work with Nazario?"

"Nah, nah." Bodega shook his left hand in the air dismissively. He looked at Sapo, who didn't look back. With the *Playboy* on his lap, Sapo was munching away contentedly, spilling crumbs on the pages. "Nah, nah, nothing against Sapito. But they know what he does. When I say they, I mean the community. I want someone smart and someone who has never worked a corner. And if he goes to college, all the better. A role model. Nazario the lawyer and his sidekick Julio College, both Ricans helping Ricans." He looked straight at me again, snapping his fingers just as he started to speak. "Both working together, getting buildings. Thass a big legal shit, but don't worry, Nazario will guide you through it all."

"I'm only half Rican, my father is from Ecuador," I felt compelled to tell Bodega.

"So what? You Spanish, this is your neighborhood. You grew up here, got beat up here, and I hope beat someone up too. Sapito tells me you used to paint R.I.P.s?"

"Yeah, so?"

"Thass good, bro. People remember you as someone who tried to make the neighborhood a better place. And that's good. And now they see yo'r in school and that's good too, bro. Just remember one thing, from an old *pana* who has been here longer than you, just remember, bro, that no matter how much you learn, no matter how many books you read, how many degrees you get, in the end, you are from East Harlem." He paused. Silence fell. I wasn't about to break it. I looked around the room, bypassing Sapo. There was nothing else to look at. A hole in a wall. A few roaches crawling nearby. Two windows with no curtains.

"So, man, like yo'r perfect, Chino."

"Perfect?" I asked, toking my joint, which was halfway finished now.

"Perfect to represent me. You and Nazario. B'cause, Chino, it gets bigga."

"Yeah?" I realized that my system was so clean that the joint had already taken effect. I wanted to laugh for no reason and a little vein in my forehead was throbbing.

"I mean, I plan on acquiring as many abandoned buildings as I can get my hands on. Renovating them and putting in people who I know will back me if I need it. Not particularly b'cause they love me but b'cause I am in charge of their well-being. They are dependent on me for their shelter. Where the city sees burned buildings I see opportunity. I'm talking about becoming the second-biggest slumlord after the City of New York."

My joint was turning into a roach. Bodega opened a drawer and handed me scissors. I took them and clipped my joint.

"See, Chino, I'm talking about property. I'm talking about owning the neighborhood legally. The way the Kennedys own Boston. But this ain't fucken Boston. This's New York City. Manhattan. Location is everything. I'm talkin' about ownin' a big chunk of the most expensive real estate in all the nine planets. Don't mara if what I'm after is the toilet seat. Wha' maras is where that toilet seat is located. From 129th Street down to 96th Street, from Fifth Avenue to First and after 116th Street, Pleasant, every neglected building, mine. The things I do, they're just a means to get me what I need, and when I'm done I'm going to be respectable and send my kids to Harvard, like Joe Kennedy. In a few years, why not a Nuyorican president?"

"What's with you riding Kennedy? Get off his dick already." With the help of the joint I felt confident enough to clown around.

"B'cause you gotta have a blueprint," Bodega said.

"Fuck the White House." I wanted to drop all this shit and just hang. "Let's skip Washington and target the Vatican. A Nuyorican pope is better. That way we'd have God on our side." I laughed as if the joke was funnier than it was.

"Oh, shit." Bodega looked at me closely and smiled. "Shit, you gone, bro. No more for you." He took the roach and the scissors out of my hand. He looked Sapo's way and said, "Sapito, Chino is Memorex. One fucken joint and the nigga is gone."

"Thass 'cause his lady don't let him smoke inna house. You should meet her, Willie. Fine, but a bitch," Sapo said in between swigs of his forty.

Bodega laughed. "If a man can't smoke a joint in his own house, who wears the pants in that fucken place?"

"Nah"—it was time to defend myself—"yo, that bitch does what I want. Blanca has no say." Of course they didn't believe me, but they let me get away with the lie. Because whatever you've heard about the

Latin woman needing to be saved from her sexist man is not entirely true. Keep your mouth shut and your legs open? That's a myth. My mother had my father on a leash and she never took Feminism 101. *Maria Cristina me quiere gobernar y yo le sigo la corriente para que la gente no crea que ella me quiere gobernar.* That's what it comes down to. And if you dare hit a Latin woman God help you, because you'll wake up with scissors in your back. Yeah, she'll go to jail for a good twenty years but you'll be dead forever. And if she isn't that violent, she'll get you, one way or another. I didn't know what Blanca had in store for me that night, all I knew was that it was getting late and she was already mad at me.

"Look, bro," I said, "I think I'll pass on this Nazario thing." Then I realized that I couldn't go straight home because I was high and Blanca would kill me in this condition.

"Come on, bro. Sapo told me you were busy and shit, with your job at the A & P and your night school. But, like, I want you around."

"Nah, I can't." I got up from my seat and kept shaking my head. "I can't, man. I hope this works out for you, but I can't. I'm mad busy."

"Thass it? You don't want ta think it over? Drive it around the block? Kick a tire? Spit on the windshield?" He stared at me hard, waiting for my answer as if I hadn't given it to him already. "Come on, think it over."

There was something honest in his dishonesty. Unlike Blanca, I believed it was dishonest people that brought change. It was paradoxical people like Bodega who started revolutions. All you could do with honest people was lend them money and marry their daughters. And as much as I loved Blanca, I'd never felt Christ was the answer either. He was taking too long to come. Spanish Harlem needed a change and fast. Rents were going through the roof. Social services were being cut. Financial aid for people like me and Blanca who were trying to better themselves was practically nonexistent. The neighborhood was ready to boil. You couldn't see the bubbles yet, but they were there, simmering below the surface, just waiting for someone to turn up the heat and all hell would break loose. The fire next time would be the fire this time.

Part of me really wanted to be there, to be part of it. But I had Blanca and the baby to think about and I wasn't about to throw that away. I was happy with Blanca. I had no idea what good deed I had done in my life to deserve Blanca, all I knew was that she was there. She wouldn't like me getting involved in any of this.

"Nah, it's cool. I wish you well, bro."

"Don't be like that."

"Nah, I got no time," I said, and extended my hand toward Bodega. He shook it. I was surprised to see disappointment in his eyes, as if I had had the upper hand all this time. I felt like I had something he needed, something he needed badly and didn't really know how to ask for. Something he had done a bad job in getting, or convincing me to give to him.

"*Mira*, Chino, you need somethin', anythin', come see me."

"*'Tá bien*, bro."

Sapo got up from the sofa and, without saying goodbye to Bodega, placed his half-empty bottle on the floor and headed out the door.

"Don't forget, you need somethin', anythin' . . ." Bodega broke off and looked at the ceiling, shaking his head as he whispered, "Thass a shame. A fucken shame." I guess he was saying this to me.

Nene was still outside the apartment waiting, keeping guard.

"Whass wrong with Sapo, bro? He like ignored me and just took off *with no direction home. Like a complete unknown. Like a rolling stone.*"

"Nice meeting you, Nene," I said, hoping to leave quickly so I could catch up with Sapo.

"Yeah, like, you know, Chino, it was nice meeting you too *and don't go changing to try and please me*," Nene said. I laughed, not because he could splice songs into his speech but because my system was so fucked up.

"So, *mira*, there's this party at La Islita, this comin' Saturday," Nene said to me as I headed for the stairwell. "Come, bro. You can bring your lady, Negra, right?"

"Blanca."

"Right, Blanca. Come, bro. My cousin always throws good parties there, lotsa beer and salsa."

"I'll try," I said and, a little high, I stumbled down the stairs.

When I stepped outside, the fresh air did me some good. It was early

spring and there were a lot of people out. The old men were still play-
ing dominoes, sitting on plastic milk crates, but the song on the small
box had changed. It was a late-sixties tune, 'Mangos Pa' Changó':
Cuando te fuistes con otro bajé a bodega pa' comprar mangos. I saw
Sapo smoking a cigarette by his black BMW and I went over to him.
Pa' luego hacerle una oferta a Changó.

"What's with you, bro?"

"Nah, man, get away. You got the cooties."

"Cooties? What the fuck. You think you still in the fourth grade?"

"Nah, don't talk to me, Chino. You fucked up."

"Why? Because I don't want to work with Nazario?"

Sapo looked at me and nodded as he took a long drag. *Pero no tenía
dinero. So mami, mami perdóname pero es que tuve que darle un holope
a alguien.* "Yeah, thass why. Bodega's been looking for a guy to work
with Nazario for some time. And I thought of you. You know, I built
yous up to Bodega. I told him, 'Nah, Chino is cool. You'll like him.
He's a cool guy and smart. He goes to Huntah.' Shit like that, and then
when he meets you for the job, you get all fucked up, laugh in his face,
and don't take the job. Do you know how that," Sapo said, jabbing a
finger in his chest, "reflects on me?"

"Sapo, all I know is, yo'r doing what you want to do. If you want to do
this then you do it. I ain't going to preach to you, bro. If you want to
leave that shit in my place it's cool. You want me to hold money for
you, I'll do that, too. But you know that in this business, the only thing
that counts is money. And Bodega might talk all this shit about helping
the community and shit like that but what it all comes down to is making money."

"Shit, I was there. He didn't lie to you. He said things about money.
He said he had to give some away in order to keep some. Money is
important. I don't deny that. But there are othah things involved here."

"Bullshit. This guy is talking a lot of dreams, bro. Clouds." As soon
as I said that I wished that I could take it back. I didn't yet know Bodega
too well, but I knew Sapo. Sapo was too smart to work for a guy who
only blew hot air. I knew that everything Bodega had told me was true,
because Sapo believed it.

"No, bro, there are diamonds in that dog shit he talks. I know. You still don't really know the half of it, bro. Why Bodega is really doin' all this. You don't know, so don't go fucken barkin' all this shit. Why can't you see things and say why not?"

"Ho, shit! What the fuck is this? Who are you, man?" This is all crazy, I thought. Bodega thinks he's Lyndon Johnson with his Great Society and now Sapo talks like he's Bobby Kennedy with this why-not stuff.

"Look, bro, all I know is when no one would gimme a job, Bodega did." Sapo got closer to me, like he always does when he wants me to pay attention. As if I'm deaf and can't hear well. "But I don't want to be some manager of a few crack houses. I wanna be part of history."

"Look, Sapo—"

"Nah, it's true. Bodega is going to own the neighborhood. Legally. And I want to be part of it. Maybe someday take it over when he's gone or somethin'. You too happy with your alleluia girl to understand."

"Hey, Sapo, come on, leave Blanca out of this."

"She's the real reason why you here, bro. *Pero no tenía dinero.* So *mami, mami perdóname pero es que tuve que darle un holope a alguien.*"

I didn't know what Sapo meant but I didn't press him about Blanca because back then I had no idea how important she was to Bodega.

"Nah, Sapo, yo'r my friend and you know that I won't lie ta you." I let what he had said about Blanca slide. "So you have a nice car and make good money, but Bodega, Bodega is the Man. Bodega has made a name for himself. You know about names, Sapo. When you get one it's only a matter of time before you have to prove who you are. And Bodega has the biggest name in the neighborhood."

"That's what I'm tryin' to tell you—" Sapo interrupted.

"Yeah, he might," I interrupted Sapo right back and he let me, because Sapo could've started shouting his point and drowned me out. "It's such a big name that it's only a matter of time before someone will wan a slice he won't wanna give up. I don't know much about this business like you do, bro, I only know that that's when things start to get sloppy. That's when dead bodies start appearing."

Sapo jerked back. He glared at me with the Sapo face that bites, that bites and leaves warts. When he spoke his voice was low and mean.

"Ya know, Chino, at least I admit I only think about myself. But you, you play it off as if you really care about other people when in fact it's always been you, you, and fucken you." He opened the door of his BMW and got inside. He turned on the ignition and, before he released the clutch, his tinted window slid down. His Sapo face was framed by the opening.

"Go home to your church girl. Go home and ask her about her aunt Vera. And, Chino, don't talk to me cuz you got leprosy, ma man." He tore out, leaving behind the smell of burnt rubber and the squeal of his tires.

We Needed More Space

T HAT night, I decided I'd better walk for a while because I couldn't go home to Blanca high. I walked down Fifth to Ninety-sixth Street, about half of the Museum Mile. I stopped in front of El Museo del Barrio on 104th Street and Fifth Avenue. Then I walked a block south and sat on the marble steps of the Museum of the City of New York. When Sapo and I were in the sixth grade we would play hooky by going there to play hide and seek, hang out. The museum was usually empty, especially during weekdays. Also, it could only afford one guard, and he was lazy. Once Sapo and I were running and we knocked a woman down. We laughed and kept running. When she complained to the guard we heard him say, "Were they touching any of the exhibits or something? No? Listen, lady, I'm not here to defend you. That's not my job."

After the museum got boring, Sapo and I would leave, cross the street, and spend the rest of the afternoon in Central Park. We knew Fifth Avenue was that part of El Barrio with rich people living in it. The buildings along Fifth were different from the project we lived in. Those buildings had doormen, huge glass doors, gargoyles on the walls, and air conditioners in almost every window. The people who lived on Fifth didn't travel past Madison Avenue. They always took cabs and you'd only see them walking when they were past Ninety-sixth Street, where El Barrio ends. When I was a kid, some residents had taken petitions to City Hall. They wanted Mayor Beame to declare Fifth Avenue from 110th to Ninety-sixth to be its own little neighborhood, separate from East Harlem, called East Central Park.

My mother used to work cleaning the homes of some of those people. One day when I was in the second grade I was too sick to go to school, and since Mami didn't want to miss work she took me with her. When I entered the apartment my mother was supposed to clean, I felt like I was inside the Museum of the City of New York. The place was huge. There were paintings and statues and mirrors and beautiful wooden things—nothing like where we lived. That was the first time I really saw the difference between those that had and those that didn't.

That night, after Bodega, after the walk, after I had remembered a few things, I went home hoping that Blanca was already asleep. I turned my key as silently as possible, and entered slowly. I crept into the bedroom and quietly changed clothes. I got into bed and didn't touch her because I knew she wouldn't let me and because I didn't want to fight. Blanca was in her second trimester and I found her incredibly sexy. I loved to make love to Blanca with her belly round as the moon. It was smooth and the feeling was of closeness. I wanted her to know she was still desirable and that I wasn't out there screwing other women. I wanted her to know I loved making love to her and that her body still excited me. Her breasts were full and her belly was so round and sex was great and different and screw all those men who won't make love to their wives while they are pregnant.

"Did you eat?"

"Sí, mami. I though you were asleep."

"You smell like marijuana."

"Sapo's always smoking that stuff, you know that, Blanca."

"When you speak . . . your breath," she mumbled.

I stayed quiet, moving my hand slowly over her stomach.

"Julio," she whispered after a little pause of night silence.

"What?"

"I never really liked your name, but now I kind of like it. What do you think about naming the baby Julio?"

"Whatever you want, Blanca."

"I like it," she said, turning around, placing her full stomach close to me.

"I'd like it to have your name if it's a boy and my sister's name if it's a girl."

"Why? I like your name, Nancy," I said, and she giggled.

"Nope. I want something biblical, like my sister's name, Deborah. She was a judge. The only woman judge in the Bible. I like her. I like that."

"Well, what good was it for your sister to be named Deborah when she turned out so bad that everyone calls her Negra?"

"Julio, my sister is not that bad, is she?"

"Of course not," I said, but I didn't mean it.

"Where did you go with Enrique?"

"Nowhere," I said, sliding my arm around her waist. She didn't say anything after that and I was happy.

Then I remembered something. "What about the name Vera?" If Sapo had told me to ask Blanca about this Vera, it had to be because we both had something to gain from it. I felt bad asking Blanca about her aunt; it was like me quizzing her on some betrayal that had never happened. "Vera, if it's a girl."

"No. No, no, no," Blanca said firmly.

"Isn't there a Vera in the Saldivia clan? You mentioned her, way back before we got married."

"Oh yeah, my aunt Veronica."

"That's her real name? Veronica. Oh, yeah, wait, I remember." It was about two years ago, before we got married. Blanca and I had been talking about those Latinos who Anglonize their names, from Juan to Jack, or Patricia to Trish.

"Yes, that's the one. We don't see her much. She sends my mother money for her birthday. That's the only time we hear from her. I gave my mother an extra wedding invitation for her to mail to her sister in case she wanted to make the trip, but she didn't come." Blanca yawned and stretched a bit.

"Is your aunt Veronica married?"

"That's why we never see her. She married well. Some rich Cuban she met. They live in Miami." That rang a faint bell.

"*Un cubano? Eso está* heavy duty. For a Rican to marry a Cuban he better be rich," I said, joking, because Cubans and Puerto Ricans never hit it off. The Arabs and Jews of the Caribbean. "But your aunt, didn't she live in the neighborhood once?"

"Yeah, supposedly she was going to marry this guy she was in love with, some street activist or something, but her mother made her marry the Cuban, at least that's what they told me."

"A street activist? You mean a Young Lord?"

"Yeah, that's what he was. I mean I was just being born, so I don't really know. But I heard the story." Nothing in Blanca's voice or body language indicated the name Vera meant anything to her. As it came to me, bit by bit, I understood more clearly what Sapo had told me earlier. Sapo believed in Bodega because he knew other reasons why Bodega was renovating the neighborhood. I started to believe a bit myself. I could picture Bodega in an Armani suit, all legal and respectable, his renovated buildings in the background, his name no longer Bodega but something else, something politicians want on their side, a commodity of goodwill. I pictured him finding her: "I've always loved you, Vera. Look at me. I fixed up everything, just like it was before."

I didn't ask Blanca anything; I could tell she was already feeling talkative.

"My *abuela* was right in making my aunt do that. I mean, the Cuban guy was rich and the street activist she had been in love with ended up in jail." In the dark I could feel Blanca smile. "You guys, we just turn our heads and you guys are in jail." She kissed me.

"Oh yeah, what about you girls?" I laughed. "We just breathe on you and you get pregnant."

"That's cheap. Your humor," Blanca said smiling, "sets Latin women back a hundred years."

"Tell me more about Veronica and the street activist."

"Who cares about her, I never even met her. Let's talk about you coming to church with me. In two weeks we'll be having a special guest speaker, an anointed." Blanca propped herself up on her elbow and clearly didn't feel sleepy anymore. She was done talking about her aunt, but it didn't matter because I already knew enough.

"An anointed? What's that?" I asked, letting her think I was interested.

"Someone who will one day, when he or she dies, rule with Christ in heaven for one thousand years," she said, excitedly squeezing my arm. "And this anointed is only seventeen!"

"Seventeen, huh," I answered, not caring the slightest bit. I just let Blanca continue talking about this seventeen-year-old anointed. I would throw in a well-timed "really" and "I hear you" and "yes, uh-huh." My mind was really on Bodega and what he had said earlier that night. About Vera and what Bodega really wanted from me.

In the dark I looked around our tiny bedroom. Our living room was even smaller, with the kitchen set in the corner. The rent was high for this matchbox and Blanca and I'd had our tuition raised last semester because of the new governor. We didn't want to take out loans and then have to pay off the government for twenty years. It was not a good way to start a professional career, in debt. So we were paying for all our studies at full tuition out of our own pockets. Then there was a baby on the way and we needed more space. And a way to save some money, too. Sitting there in the dark I saw some daylight. Bodega wanted something from me, so I would ask something in return. It was basic, simple street politics: you want something from me then you better have something I need.

Que Viva Changó

THE next day at work, I was pricing cans. I always liked pricing cans. It was better than straightening shelves because I got to use the sticker gun. When little kids were shopping with their moms, I would show off by pricing an entire box of cans real quick, and they got a kick out of that. Before I knew it they were asking me, "Yo, stick my hand." And I priced their palms, two for a dollar.

After work I decided to get something to eat before I went to school. I had two classes that night and Blanca had one. On my way to get some food, I saw Sapo's car parked in front of La Reyna Bakery. That bakery had been there forever. Half of El Barrio got its coffee every morning at La Reyna. Even though it was a small, dingy place, dark and crowded, people still went there because they made the best pastries, coffee, *rolitos* (flat oven bread with butter), *empanadas*, and *sanwiches cubanos* among other things.

Inside I saw Sapo, yelling his order just like the rest of the customers.

"*Dame un flan* and three of those little cakes!" La Reyna was like those pits on Wall Street, everyone screaming what they wanted, things happening fast.

I walked up to Sapo. "You still angry at me, bro?"

"Nah, I ain't angry at you. You still my *pana*. *Dame un flan* and three of those little cakes! So wha' choo doin' here, bro?" he asked.

"Same as you."

"Better start yellin' then, before they run out of cakes, bee."

"Sapo, did Bodega want to see me because he wanted me to work with Nazario or because he wants me to get Blanca to invite her aunt to New York?" He turned and hustled me outside.

"Wha' the fuck's the mara wi'choo? You know how many people are in there? You don't mention shit like that in public. These people may have a lot of hair, but they all think they're Kojak and like to ask questions." A guy came out of the bakery and handed Sapo his order. Sapo gave him five dollars and told him to keep the change.

"Take a ride with me, bro," Sapo said.

"Yo, I got class tonight . . ."

"Class, class, you always have class. You got a lot of fucken class, you know that, Chino?"

"Fuck you."

"So, *mira*." Sapo took out his car keys and opened the door. "I drop you off at Hunta, cool?"

"Yeah, that's cool. It's better than paying a fare that ain't fair." I was happy to save myself a buck fifty and I decided to get something to eat later.

"Yeah, I knew you'd like that. You're like the fucken Green Hornet, you like to be driven. But don't get used to it, cuz I ain't Kato and you the one that looks Chinese."

"Yo, that show was wack," I said. "The action scenes always took place in the dark. Bruce Lee looked dope in that chauffeur outfit, though."

Sapo nodded in agreement. "This won't take long, Chino, but I hafta pick up Nene." Keeping one hand on the steering wheel, Sapo dug into the paper bag and pulled out one of his little cakes. He swallowed it whole and then dug for the second one.

"It's cool if it doesn't take too long. You know I—"

"Have class. I ain't deaf. I heard you the first time. So, you want t'know about Bodega?"

"Yeah."

"Why don't you ask him yo'self."

"You my *pana*, bro, and I wouldn't know where to look for him anyway."

"Yeah, thass true, Bodega only lets himself be seen when he wants ta be. Yeah, so check this out, Bodega did want you to get Blanca to ask her aunt to come to New York. That don't mean he didn't want you to work with Nazario, cuz he did." The third little cake was downed just as quick.

"So why didn't he just come out and say what he had to say."

"What, you wanted him to get all romantic and shit? Cut the dude some slack. See, Chino, you got it all wrong. Bodega believes ever'thin' he told you about. But he's also in love with some bitch from his past. Or he's still in love with the past. I don't know which or both or what the fuck. All I know is I'm going to ride his dream like a magic carpet. Cuz, Chino, it don't take a genius to figure out Bodega is where I want to be and he knows what the fuck he's doing. Know wha I'm sayin', *papi*?"

Then we spotted Nene sitting on the stoop. Sapo pulled over and I unlocked the door so Nene could get in.

"You know each other, so I'm goin' to start on my flan." Sapo took out a plastic spoon and began to eat his flan, which floated inside a white carton filled with sugary syrup.

"Yeah, I know you, Chino," Nene said, recognizing me.

"How you been, Nene?"

"You know me, *I'm just a soul whose intentions are good.*"

Sapo finished his flan real quick, his big Sapo mouth engulfing every spoonful. But when he started the car, Nene got nervous, and seeing him nervous made me nervous.

"Yo, Hunta is on Sixty-eighth Street, bro, you going uptown."

"This won't take long, Chino. Nene and me have to do somethin' real quick." I knew something was up. I wanted to tell him to let me out, but I stayed because I needed Sapo to set up a meeting with Bodega, so I could make a deal with him. I was hoping that it wasn't too late. Maybe Bodega had found another way to contact Vera. I didn't know, so I had to stick around and have Sapo talk to Bodega on my behalf as soon as possible or my chance at making a deal would be over.

Nene was sweating. "You sure about this, Sapo?"

"Yeah, I'm sure about this. Your cousin wants this done."

"Yo, where we going?" I asked.

"*Pa' viejo*." Sapo laughed.

"Yo, I got class."

"Why don't you fucken put that shit in the news. I heard you the third time."

And I didn't bother to say it again.

Sapo stopped his car in front of the poultry house on 110th and Second where you could buy live chickens, turkeys, geese, and ducks. It smelled like a zoo and you could hear the fowl cries blocks away.

Sapo and Nene went inside while I stayed in the car. A few minutes later, they came out carrying a large box with holes punched in it. Carefully, they placed the box on the backseat and Nene slid in next to it.

"This fucken thing is going to stink up my car, man." Sapo spat out the car window.

"What the fuck is that, bro," I said, laughing. "I thought you ate your flan already. Like, if you still hungry I can spring for pizza."

"Nah, this is for Doña Ramonita at the botanica," Sapo answered, through gritted teeth.

"It's watching me, Sapo. It's watching me." Nene was looking through the little holes. "It knows this is the end."

"Of course it knows. You think it's stupid enough to think we got him for a fucken pet?" Sapo took off.

When we reached the botanica on 116th between Park and Madison, San Lázaro y las Siete Vueltas, Sapo parked his car and asked me and Nene to carry the box. "I put in my time," he said.

Doña Ramonita was a heavy woman with strong African roots from Puerto Rico's Loiza Aldea. With her hair pulled back in a pink bandanna and her hands on her hips, she looked like Aunt Jemima from the pancake boxes. She was standing next to a life-sized statue of San Lázaro with all his boils and diseased skin. Incense was burning all around the botanica and the shelves were crowded with teas and potions and smaller saints. On the walls were cheap religious pictures depicting the Devil being slain by the angel Michael. In those pictures, the Devil is always painted completely black with horns and a tail; Michael is always rosy and winged with a sword he twirls like a baton.

The botanica also doubled as a pawnshop. It was a place that knew hunger and desperation. A place you could find things hocked out of a deep need for something good or bad. There were wedding rings, baby bracelets, radios, televisions, necklaces, engraved watches, old-fashioned spoons and knives, scarves, pins, coins, and other junk that was left behind for Doña Ramonita to resell. Popular items were the boxes on the floor filled with Spanish LPs from past decades, old mambo and salsa records, plena, bomba, Latin hits our parents would dance to. A few secondhand mint-condition musical instruments like trumpets, trombones, congas, and tambourines were on display inside a glass case, their price tags sticking out like a tag on a dead man's toe.

"Doña Ramonita," Sapo said, "Willie Bodega would like you to make an offering to Changó on his behalf. This is for him," Sapo said, pointing at the box Nene and I had placed on the floor, "and this is for you. It is the favor you asked Willie Bodega for." He gave her a wad of twenties. She didn't count them or say anything, just took the money and stuffed it inside her bra. Nene stared at her and started singing softly, *"I got a black magic woman. Got a black magic woman."* Like most of the neighborhood she knew Nene was slow and paid him no mind. When she went over to the box and opened it a goose flapped its way out and started to walk around nervously as a few customers looked on with admiration.

"*Mijo*, this animal is perfect. It is important that the sacrifice be healthy. Changó will be very happy," she said, and then went behind some curtains to the back of the botanica, leaving us with a scared bird wandering around.

"You know, Sapo, I can report you to the ASPCA." I laughed.

"Shit, I could care less about this chicken, my car stinks now." Sapo spat on the floor.

"It's a goose, bro, not a chicken."

"Who the fuck are you, Old MacDonald? The shit stunk up my car. If it was up ta me I'd wring its neck right here."

Nene stopped singing and stared at the goose. I detected some pity on his solemn face. Then Doña Ramonita emerged dressed in white, with a rosary wrapped around her waist and some beads dangling down her side. She was carrying a leash and three small jars of lightly tinted water.

"*Díganle a* Willie to wake up tomorrow at sunrise. Make sure that his window has a clear view of the sun, *si no que vaya al rufo.* He must take off all his clothes and then turn himself seven times to the right as he pours the water from this jar, the first jar, on himself. Then he must turn seven times to the left as he pours the second jar. The third jar I will keep and pour on the sacrifice, also at sunrise."

"Wait. What if it's cloudy?" Nene piped up, "I know it's *hot town summer in the city* but it could rain tomorrow."

"He must wait then, till the sun comes out. I will wait with him too." Then with deft precision she cornered the goose, leashed its head, and dragged it to a corner where she tied it to a table. "I will pour the water at sunrise, turning the sacrifice seven times." Doña Ramonita paused and looked at the three of us carefully, making sure that all of us heard what she had to say. "But I can tell you now," she said, her eyes panning left to right, from Sapo to Nene to me, "I have seen the woman he is after. I have seen her in dreams. She is coming from a hot place. A warm climate, almost like Puerto Rico *pero eso sí,* the woman he is after is coming with a lot of trouble. As if she is the daughter of Changó himself."

Doña Ramonita was right. Vera would arrive, fading in and fading out of the neighborhood as if in a film. A character so out of focus that it was hard to know when you had her just right, and when you did, the film ran out. It didn't matter that the show was over and everyone was going home disappointed, only that you felt responsible for the movie being bad. You knew you weren't the filmmaker, but you were the one who dragged everyone to see it. With Vera it would be the whole neighborhood that got cheated. Many were at fault, and I was among them.

As we walked out of the botanica and headed toward Sapo's car, Doña Ramonita reappeared, shouting.

"And tell Willie he has to buy new clothes! All in white. Changó's favorite color is white. Willie will need a lot of white!" she yelled. Sapo nodded to assure her he would relay the message. She then bowed her head ever so slightly and slowly went back inside her botanica.

Sapo opened the car door and a terrible odor rose from inside. "Fucken shit." He opened all the doors and pressed a button to slide all the windows down. He took out a cigarette and the three of us waited outside the car for the smell to clear.

"I feel bad for that bird, you know," Nene said, "but you know, at least he gets to meet the spirit in the sky. *Thass where I want to go when I die. When I'm old and they lay me to rest I want to go to the place thass the best.*"

I felt this was as good a time as any. "Sapo, I have to speak with Bodega again." Nene kept singing.

"'Bout wha'?"

"Tell him I can deliver Vera. That's the woman he's after, right? Blanca's aunt?"

"Wha'? Now, Chino—" He took a long drag on his cigarette. I knew his loyalty was to Bodega but Sapo was still my friend.

"Tell him I know where she is and I can reach her. All I want from him is a two-bedroom apartment in one of his buildings. Tell him I got a kid coming and I need the extra room."

"Fucken shit, Chino." Sapo was mad. He flung his lit cigarette on the pavement with so much force, it made a stream of sparks. "Why the fuck didn't you tell me this before I put the fucken chicken in my car!"

For Being a Cabrón

I F there was one person who was going to know where I could find this Vera, it was Blanca's sister, Negra. Although I didn't know yet if Bodega would agree to my deal, I figured it wouldn't hurt to pay Negra a visit. We weren't really friends but we were family.

Negra and her husband lived in the Metro North projects on 100th and First. These projects face the East River and have million-dollar views. On the Upper East Side an apartment facing the East River would be priceless, but this is Spanish Harlem, where most rents are subsidized by Section Eight. Regardless, the panoramic scenes are the same from any neighborhood: red-orange sunrises, blue-black moonlit nights. In the wintertime, when the East River freezes, the views are staggering. The ice acts like a mirror and the world seems to have two sunrises and at night two moons, one in the sky and one on the ice. During storms, you can see huge waves pound the FDR Drive, sometimes reaching all the way to the highway itself and washing up against the cars. Above the East River the cloud formations are ever-changing, and when a dying hurricane is about to hit the city you can see how the waves and the clouds synchronize their gyrating motions, like Jupiter's red eye.

Negra was lucky. She lived on the twelfth floor facing the East River. I took the elevator, punched 12, and tried not to step in a puddle of piss where vials were floating. As soon as the elevator door opened, I could hear Negra yelling. I reached her door and knocked hard. Soon she peered through the peephole and opened the door.

"*Que me lleven.* I don't give a shit!" she yelled. She was smoking a cigarette, taking long, angry drags.

"What happened, Negy?" I asked, as she sank into the sofa and continued to smoke.

"Ayy . . . ayy . . . You're crazy, Negy." I heard a faint moaning coming from the kitchen, where I found Negra's husband, Victor, sitting on a chair and holding his stomach with one hand. There was blood on his shirt and on the floor.

"That bitch is crazy, man. That bitch is crazy."

"Victor, let me look at that shit." I knelt down and gently moved his hand away.

It was a small but deep gash. "That shit is nasty, bro. How'd that happen?"

Negra rushed into the kitchen and began to yell. "That's good for him, Chino! For being a *cabrón!*"

"She's crazy, she's . . . fucken crazy . . . Chino," Victor responded weakly. He was leaking blood slowly but steadily.

"Look, Negra, we have to get him to Metropolitan."

"He doesn't want to go!" she yelled, and then lit another cigarette.

"Ayy . . . *ayy* . . . *ayy* . . . *coño.*" His moaning made Negra angrier and she erupted.

"Chino, I'm doing the laundry, right!"—she took a violent drag— "and I find in his pocket a movie ticket stub for *Donnie Brasco*"—she blows smoke—"I know, I know what he's been up to. But to make sure I ask him while I'm cooking, does he want to go to the movies tonight after dinner?"

"Thass a lie, Chino, she's lying, *ayy* . . . *ayy* . . . *Dios Mío.*"

Negra yells at Victor to shut the fuck up and then continues. "So I asked him, '*Papi*, you want to go to the movies?' He says, 'Sure, why not.' I say, 'I want to see *Donnie Brasco.*' He tells me, 'All right, let's see that.' I say, 'Unless you've seen it already with your buddies Mike and Nando.' He says, 'No, I haven't.' I say, 'Are you sure you haven't seen it?' He smiles and tells me, 'No, I haven't gone to the movies since I went with you.'" She stopped and stared at Victor. "So I showed him the stub, Chino. I told him this was in his shirt pocket. Thass right, you didn't see this with Mike or Nando or with me because this is a movie you took another woman to see!"

"She's crazy. I . . . I always like Al Pacino . . . you know that, Chino. Right? Right? Tell her, tell her I always liked Pacino." In pain, Victor was begging for help.

"I'll tell her on the way to Metropolitan, man. We got to take you there quick, bro," I said, and knelt down to check his wound again. He shrugged me away. I turned back to look at Negra.

"Negy, he needs to go—"

"He doesn't want to go!" she shrieked.

"What about calling an ambulance, then!" I shouted back. Everyone was angry now and I wasn't about to be left behind.

"Nah . . . nah . . . I don't want anyone called," Victor said.

"*Que me lleven.* Die. Bleed to death then!" she said, lighting another cigarette and stomping back into the living room.

"Chino, come closer," Victor said, "You got to . . . take me . . . to Mount Sinai," he whispered.

"But Metropolitan is two blocks from here." It made sense to go there, because Mount Sinai was all the way west on Fifth Avenue.

"Nah, cuz Negra might wanna come too . . . and . . . and . . . Negra can't come to Metro . . . see . . . my girl . . . she . . . she works at Metropolitan . . . emergency room . . . an' this is her shift."

"Wha?"

"Not so loud . . . *ayy* . . . man, I feel dizzy." Right then Negra walked back in. Her face seemed less angry and I thought I even detected some remorse. She joined me, kneeling next to Victor, and started to coo, whispering that he should let us call the paramedics, brushing his hair back lightly. I knew that Victor would never agree to that because the ambulance would drive him to the nearest hospital, Metropolitan.

"Help me, Chino," he pleaded. I knew it wasn't just his health he was worried about.

"Negra, I'm taking Victor to the hospital. Get me a towel." She jumped up and raced out to get me one.

"Vic, I'll take you to the hospital but you got to let me put a towel around you, okay?" I knew he was reluctant to pull his hand away from his stomach, but he agreed, nodding his head and grimacing in pain. Negra ran back in with the towel.

"I'm coming too," she said.

"You're . . . crazy . . . I don't want you near me!" Victor yelled at Negra, more out of pain than anger.

"I don't want you . . . coming . . ." Victor glared at Negra. "Chino will take me."

"Yes, I'll take him," I repeated, helping Victor to his feet.

"See . . . Chino . . . will take me," he moaned.

Negra agreed and even seemed sorry. She touched her fingers to her mouth, mumbling worried words as she opened the door. I was holding Victor with one arm around his shoulder and one arm around his stomach as we made our way out of the apartment. Negra walked out too and called the elevator. She got in with us and caressed Victor's face. She kept telling him she believed him and that she was sorry. Once outside the building, Negra flagged a gypsy cab. Victor and I got in. He collapsed in the taxi, moaning a bit. Negra tried to kiss him but Victor turned his face away from her, so she pulled back. We drove off, leaving Negra standing at the curb shouting to us, "Call. All right? Call me."

"Metropolitan Hospital," I said to the driver, but Victor summoned a bit of reserve energy.

"Nah, nah, Mount Sinai Hospital," he said and the driver took off.

"Why, Victor? Negra's not coming with us."

"I know . . . but my girl at Metro would want to know how this happened . . . and she don't know I'm . . . married."

"Thass fucken great, bro. You dying and shit and you're worried about some bimbo knowing you married. Thass great, man." I looked out the window and thought, to each his own. Victor and Negra deserved each other. But Blanca and I were far from perfect either these days.

"When they ask me to fill out the form, what do you want me to put down, Victor?"

"I fell on it . . . write that I fell on it."

.

WHILE VICTOR was being attended by an emergency-room doctor, I phoned Negra.

"When you filled out the form, what did you put?" was her first question.

"That he fell on the knife."

"Thass good." I heard a sigh of relief. "You know, Chino, I never meant to throw it at him, it just flew." Like I believed that.

"Can you call Blanca and tell her where I'm at?" I didn't really have to ask this of Negra, I could have called Blanca myself, but I needed some fill-ins for my next question.

"I'll call Blanca for you, Chino."

"And another thing, Negra, I need to find your aunt Veronica. The one who calls herself Vera."

"Why?" There was a dip in the middle of that *why,* to let me know that she knew I had something to hide. I let her have it.

"I didn't ask you why the knife flew out of your hands, right? I wrote on the form that Victor fell on it. Victor wanted to tell the truth. Victor wanted to tell the doctors that his wife threw it at him. You know what that means, right? The doctors would have to report the incident as a possible crime, right? But I convinced him not to. I said you know she still loves you, so why would you want to send the cops to your house? So, *mira,* you owe me. You owe me big." I paused and waited for Negra to say something. She stayed quiet, so I continued, calmer and slower.

"All I'm asking, Negy, is if you have any information about some aunt of yours. That's all I'm asking."

"Why not ask Blanca?" She was too smart to fall for this. Negra could always see an opening where she could get back her leverage, regain the upper hand. She knew I was asking a really stupid question with an obvious answer.

"You know your sister, all she knows is school and church." I was proud of my quick reply. I hoped Negra would buy it. There was no response for a little while and I could just picture Negra mulling this over as she lit a cigarette.

"*Tía* Veronica?" She exhaled, and I could almost smell the smoke. "She lives in Miami."

"I know that already. Where in Miami?"

"That shouldn't be too hard to find out. I'll ask around. I'll find out. Okay?" Pause. "And Chino, thanks for taking Victor, all right?"

"Yeah, all right. Just get me her address. And listen, they're going to keep Victor overnight for observation. So you can come and pick him up tomorrow, okay?" I was ready to hang up.

"Okay. Hey Chino!" she said loudly, bringing my ear back to the phone.

"I'm still here, but make it quick."

"Does Victor really like Al Pacino?"

"He loves him."

·

I DIDN'T want to alarm Blanca, so before I got home I buttoned up my denim jacket, which only had a bit of blood smudged on the sleeves. When I got to our building I walked up the stairs, took my keys out, and opened the door.

Blanca was waiting, furious. "Why didn't you tell me?" she demanded, waving a piece of paper in my face. "I had to find this under the door, Julio?" I looked at the paper in her hand. It was a lease. The Harry Goldstein Real Estate Agency, two bedrooms for half of what we were paying the City of New York to live in a one-bedroom in one of its projects.

"I wasn't sure we'd get it. I didn't want to get your hopes up." Bodega hadn't wasted any time.

"I'm so mad at you, Julio, keeping me in the dark! After all we've talked about, after I asked you to tell me everything you're up to, you kept me in the dark."

"I kept you in the dark? I get us a better place to live and I kept you in the dark?"

"You know that's not what I mean. You do things as if you were still single. As if my two cents means nothing. As if you—" She stopped and took a deep breath. She lowered her head and asked the Lord for help. When she raised her head to look at me again her face was red and her eyes were wet from the hurt that dries your throat and hurts when you swallow.

"I'm happy that you got us this apartment, Julio. I'm actually very happy. It was a good thing. But you didn't ask for my input. You just went and did it. Do you understand what I'm saying?" I nodded.

"Nancy"—I called her Nancy when I wanted her to know that I wanted to clear things up without fighting. Sometimes it worked, sometimes it didn't, but it was always worth a shot."Nancy, I'm new at this married thing, all right? You know I love you but I've been used to doing things alone all my life without consulting anyone. But I'm trying, Nancy. All I know is that I try. At times I forget to tell you things and just play it by ear. If I'd asked Housing for a two-bedroom they would have just placed us on a five-year waiting list. After five years the rent for a two-bedroom would be even higher and we'd still be living in a project. So when the chance came around to get something better, I took it. You know how fast applications go, Nancy. So I just filled it out and hoped for the best." I didn't know what else to say.

"I'm not saying this wasn't a good thing, Julio. Just tell me what you are planning, all right? If you filled out an application just tell me where."

"Why? As long as it's a better block—"

"Because I want to know!" Her face got angry again. "Besides, did you ever think that I might not want to live there? Did you ever think of that, Julio? What if I don't like the block, the building? From here on out I better not get secondhand news, all right?"

"Yeah, all right," I said.

"We'll talk about moving tomorrow, okay?" Then she gently kissed me hello, since she hadn't when I'd walked in. She thanked the Lord again and hugged me. Her eyes fell on the bloodstain on my sleeve.

"What's this?"

"Ketchup. I was eating fries," I lied. She bought it.

Then Blanca, placing her hands in the small of her back, slowly sat down on the couch. She took a pillow and positioned it behind her arched back. She pressed her hands against her swelling belly and focused her eyes straight ahead, on nothing in particular. I knew she wanted to ask me something and was debating whether to ask me now or later.

"Do you know anyone who wants to get married?" she finally asked.

"Why?" I went into the bedroom to change.

"Well, there's this sister . . ." When Blanca said "sister" or "brother" that meant it had something to do with her church, which made me nervous and angry at the same time.

". . . and she needs to get married."

"Aren't there any men in your church?"

"No, there aren't. Most of them are married or teenage boys. And if they're single and old enough they want a young sister who's beautiful and a virgin. It's the worst thing."

"I like it when you knock your church."

"No one is perfect, Julio." She didn't appreciate my comment. "The church is full of imperfect people. Noah was a drunk, but God gave him the ark. David committed adultery with Bathsheba but God made him king. Peter denied Christ, but God—"

"I get your point. So what you're telling me is, because this sister is not that young and who knows if she's a virgin, no brother will take a chance on her?"

"Yes. They say they want a wife that's spiritual and wants to serve God. That's all they say they want. But when a sister shows up who's not that young or pretty it doesn't matter how spiritual she is."

I started laughing. I could hear Blanca laugh a little and get up from the couch.

"Yes, it's funny," she said.

"Don't worry," I told her, "let her wait, a brother will come."

"That's the problem. She doesn't have time, she's illegal. She's going to be deported." Blanca joined me in the bedroom. Her face glowed by the light coming from the lamppost outside the window. I gave her a little kiss. She smiled a little.

"This girl," I asked, "is she from some country where they persecute Pentecostals or something?"

"Of course not. What day and age do you think we're living in? No one's throwing us to the lions anymore. She's from Colombia."

"So let her go back to Colombia, then. You always say the most important thing is to serve Christ. If Christ is everywhere, He must be in Colombia, too." I lay on the bed and stared at the ceiling. It stared at me back. Enough of this, I was thinking about Vera and Bodega. Where could I find this woman and fulfill my part of the deal with Bodega? I hoped Negra could help.

"That's not the point. She's very nice. And she wants to do so many things. She wants to learn English and go to school. She wants to do things she could never do in Colombia. I know Immigration won't come knocking at her door and drag her back to Colombia. They'll just make it hard for her to ever better herself. Isn't that what it's all about, Julio? Isn't that why we're going to school and talking about buying a house someday?"

Of course it was. But those who travel the farthest are those who travel alone. And we had a kid coming, there was no time for this. It was bad enough I had to get mixed up with Bodega just so we could have a better place to live, a cheaper place, and save some money, too.

"Blanca, we have our own problems," I said, making believe I was trying to go to sleep. Blanca sat carefully on the bed next to me. I knew she was thinking again. I wondered why she had so much interest in this girl from Colombia. I knew Blanca was kind, but getting someone a green card is tough. Especially since Blanca had cut herself off from the street. There was no way she could ask around, put the word out on the street wire, because the street was never her playground. Her only source was the church, and if that community lacked what she needed, she had no other options. All her life, her parents had kept her sheltered by religion. Sheltered by the fear of God. When Blanca grew up she never shook it but embraced God even more, and now she needed something her church couldn't deliver—some sucker to marry a girl from Colombia. Blanca had probably already asked around dozens of congregations without any luck. Now she needed another outlet. And she didn't want to get caught up in the petty politics of the streets. She didn't want to owe anything to anyone. She wanted to help this girl on her own.

"Maybe I should ask Negra," she whispered as if to herself.

"Blanca, why are you doing this?" Blanca knew as well as I did that once you asked Negra for a favor, you'd better be ready to pay up. Considering the magnitude of what Blanca would be asking, if Negra or anyone Negra knew could deliver, the payback wouldn't just be a bitch but a house full of whores.

•

FROM THE time they were little, they had been polar opposites. Negra hated the church, couldn't wait to leave her parents' house and rip up her Pentecostal roots. Negra was the type who smoked joints at midnight in the bathroom, keeping the window open so her parents wouldn't smell anything. The one who sneaked out of her house wearing tight jeans under a long skirt. She would leave the skirt at some friend's house where she could get it later, then sneak back home, skirt and all. She loved boys. And it was no surprise to her parents when she met Victor at Corso, a dance club, and left their house, unmarried. Negra never looked back.

Negra's reputation for information was made at the time of Popcorn's murder. Popcorn was the neighborhood's only openly gay man. He was great, always full of life. Always laughing and joking. He had a beautiful mane of long black hair and wore tight jeans, makeup, and Hawaiian shirts, and he carried a knife in his back pocket. When some guy would make fun of him he'd laugh and say, "The only difference between you and me is what we do in bed." So now that guy had two choices, fight Popcorn or say something tough and funny and walk away. Everyone knew it was better to walk away because if Popcorn was for real and you lost the fight, the entire neighborhood would know you got your ass kicked by a homo, and if he was only bluffing, then there was no glory in it—anyone's little sister could beat a homo. Popcorn played this card to the fullest, carrying his knife in his back pocket like a second bulge. So everyone laughed and left him alone and he didn't care because everyone said cruel things to everyone in the neighborhood. The first rule of the street: "Not everything that snaps at you is trying to threaten your manhood."

But then one day Popcorn was found stabbed to death on the roof of his apartment building. He used to climb up there to sunbathe. Nobody knew why he had been killed. The cops were lost. They asked questions for a week. That's what they do when someone is killed in Spanish Harlem, they investigate for a week and if the media and the community don't make a big deal of it, they leave it unsolved. They figure, who cares, we made an effort, we'll keep our funding clearing important cases. But Negra knew who had killed Popcorn. She didn't tell the cops. She just told the entire neighborhood and eventually someone must have tipped off the cops.

A girl named Inelda Andino had killed Popcorn. Negra's explanation was simple: "She was always jealous of his hair. Popcorn had the best hair in the neighborhood and that girl was shallow. So shallow, I've stepped in deeper puddles." Later, Negra was proven right when the knife was found in Inelda's mother's apartment with Popcorn's credit cards and I.D. It had been one of those fights where one party is so enraged, so blind with anger they have to kill the other. In Popcorn and Inelda's case, it had been a heated argument about who had better hair.

No one ever questioned Negra. The cops thought the person who had tipped them off deserved the credit, but the neighborhood knew better. The neighborhood knew Negra.

•

I RUBBED Blanca's back. "Why would you want to owe Negra anything?"

"Because I want to help this girl," she said.

"Blanca, even if you find this girl someone to marry, it's not that easy. She might still get deported. You think Immigration is that stupid?"

"Yes, they can be. Trust me. All we have to do is find someone who will marry Claudia then—"

"Claudia? Is that her name?"

"Yes, Claudia," she continued, "then have a lease signed with both their names on it. An apartment with pictures, maybe, because Immigration does send someone to inspect. But that doesn't mean they really have to live together."

"And how do you intend on getting all this? It's hard finding a husband and a place. You don't just add water."

"That's why I'm asking you. Look, it can be anybody. He can even live with his parents—"

"Oh, please, let's go to sleep."

"Just promise me you'll ask around." In other words, Blanca was telling me it was okay to ask my hood friends.

"Fine. I'll ask around." Blanca got up from the bed and bent over to kiss me. I kissed her back. As she went into the bathroom to brush her teeth, the phone rang.

"That's your sister!" I yelled from the bedroom, knowing the only one who would call that late was Negra, wanting to tell Blanca about what had happened with Victor. Blanca went into the living room and picked up the phone. I could hear her voice, worried and excited at the same time as she asked about Victor's condition. Blanca laughed and then preached to Negra about fidelity, which meant Negra was thinking of getting back at Victor in yet another way. I didn't care, I was happy this thing with Blanca about this illegal girl hadn't turned into a huge fight.

As she spoke with Negra, I listened to her sweet, earnest voice in the darkness of the bedroom and I felt happy. I didn't know what I had done to deserve Blanca but I wasn't about to ask. I was afraid fate would backtrack and look for errors and take Blanca away. I was just happy she was there with me. Her voice drifted from the living room to the bedroom, light and sweet, like she was still fourteen and at Julia de Burgos. I remembered those springs when she would wear thin cotton dresses to class and make me moan and ache in Spanish Harlem. Or wear her tight skirts while carrying her Bible. And when she sat in the library, she'd cross her legs and let her sandal dangle in midair as she read and played with her hair. I'd watch her from across the room and tell myself that she had no idea how beautiful she looked.

"Negra wants to talk to you," Blanca yelled from the living room, yanking me back to the present.

"Me?" I yelled back.

"Yes."

I got up, went to the living room, and took the phone from Blanca.

"You're in luck," Negra said.

"You got something already?"

"She's coming to New York, Mami told me. Her old elementary school is going to name the auditorium after her." Negra was laughing.

"No, get out? They do that?"

"Yep."

"What if she doesn't show up?"

"She'll show up, all right. From what Mami tells me, that woman is so stuck up, one day she is going to wake up a mirror. Loves attention. I hate her already."

"Listen, Negra," I whispered, looking behind me to make sure that Blanca was nowhere in earshot, "don't tell your sister any of this, okay?"

"Why?"

"Why nothing, I just don't want her to know, thass all."

"Why not, it's her aunt too."

"Just shut up and don't tell her."

"I don't know, Chino." I knew she wanted something. She had already paid me back by getting the information and now she wanted me to owe her.

"Trouble in paradise, Chino? Why don't you want Blanca to—"

"Fine, I owe you." I gave it to her. "What do you want?"

"I don't know yet."

"Negra, I got to get some sleep, so think real quick or let me slide for another day."

"All right, I'll let you slide but you still owe me."

"Fine," I said, and hung up knowing I was going to regret that.

No Pets Allowed

THE following day Sapo gave me a call.

"Whass up, *pana*? Like, can you do me a solid? Like, you my main-mellow-man. Remember the day the entire CIA crew wanted to jump yo' ass b'cause you were wearin' a sweatshirt with their colors? Or like the other day when I got to Bodega to send someone to slide a lease undah yo' door?"

"Sapo, *mira*, tell Bodega thanks. Tell him I have what he wants."

"In a minute, in a minute. So, like, can you do me a solid?"

"What do you want? Do I have to kill anyone?"

"Bro, you can't kill a fly. At times I think yo'r softer than yo'r alleluia wife. Like if they mug you, you'd ask the robbers if they need a ride home. So, Chino, like, I have a shitload of stuff, can I leave it wi'choo, Chino? You know you the only guy I can trust, right?"

"Of course."

"Second thing."

"Wha'?"

"Bodega wants ta see yah."

•

SAPO MUST have arrived at around 10:30 that night. Blanca and I were walking back from the subway after our night classes at Hunter, commiserating about how much work we both had. I spotted Sapo's BMW parked outside the building. Blanca stared at me a little while, then said, "Julio, why? Let's just go to sleep." That's all she said, but I knew I couldn't get out of it. I had to go. No matter what Blanca would say or how angry she would get, I had to do my part. Fortunately Blanca was in good spirits that night, and when I motioned my head toward the car she just sighed.

"You know, Julio," she said, "the lease says no pets allowed. So when we move he can't come over anymore." She kissed me and told me to get something to eat. I gave her a hug and could smell the shampoo in her hair, something like peaches. I let go, watched her walk inside, and went over to Sapo.

"No fits? Whass the world coming to?" Sapo said as I started to get in his car. "Wait, Chino, can you like take this upstairs." He handed me a nice fat eight-by-eleven envelope, all taped up. Sapo always taped them up really nice and tight, because that way he'd know if someone messed around with his stuff. I took no offense. I knew he trusted me. I ran the envelope upstairs, into the kitchen and slid it to the bottom of a giant-size half-empty Apple Jacks cereal box. Blanca saw me and just shook her head but didn't say a word.

"Hey, who said that cereal prizes have gotten cheap?" I said, walking over to where Blanca sat on the sofa. "Junkie Flakes, they're grrrrreat!" I even did the tiger imitation.

"It's not funny, Julio." She carefully got up, and walked into the bathroom. "Try not to be home too late," she said, closing the bathroom door.

"All right, Blanca," I said to the shut door. I put the box on top of the fridge and went back downstairs.

"Thanks, bro," Sapo said, opening the car door for me. "You know, I got some girls comin' and I can't have that shit around. The girls I'm having ovah are born thieves. They can steal the nails from Jesus Christ and still leave 'im hangin'."

"Where's Bodega tonight?"

"Taino Towers. Fortieth floor. Got the best view in the neighborhood." And we took off.

•

THE TAINO Towers on 124th and Third took up an entire city block. There were four towers, one on each corner. Four towers of cheap, ugly white concrete. Forty floors of cheap windows and a lobby with a guard who slept most of the night. At the base of each tower were businesses ranging from supermarkets to dental offices. I hate towers. The taller the building, the more people you place on top of one another, the higher the crime rate. They're mammoth filing cabinets of human lives, like bees in a honeycomb, crowded and angry at paying rent for boxes that resemble prison cells.

Bodega rented an apartment on the top floor of the tower facing the East River, mostly for the view—he had enough other places to live in. When Sapo and I arrived downstairs the guard didn't ask who we were visiting. "I'm not a doorman," he sneered. We took the elevator up, and knocked on 40B. Nene opened the door.

"Hey, Sapo and Chino. Whass up, like *I want to take you higher.*" He let us in.

"Tell yo'r cus Chino is here," Sapo said.

"Oh, man. Wait, like, Nazario is with him. They been talkin' for a long time."

"'Bout wha'?"

"I don't know, Sapo. You can wait for him, but . . ."

"Anythin' else you know?"

"They keep mentionin' this guy Alberto Salazar."

"Who's that?"

"I don't know, Sapo. I just know it's bad. *There's somethin' happenin' here, what it is ain't exactly clear.*" Just then Bodega and Nazario stepped into the living room.

And that's when I first met Nazario, or better yet, when I realized who he was. I had never spoken to him or even known his name, but I'd seen Nazario's face a few times around the neighborhood. He was a tall, confident man in his forties who walked the streets wearing expensive suits and alligator shoes but was never mugged. Now I knew why. It was Nazario who represented Bodega around the neighborhood. Nazario, with his clean-shaven face and the good looks of someone who never in his life has been in a street fight, went around spreading favors for Bodega.

"And he didn't take the money?" Bodega was asking Nazario.

"No, he looks like a good man. Just doing his job. I don't know, Willie, this could be bad."

When Bodega saw me he started to smile. But then his lips froze when Nazario said, "*Willie, esto está serio.* This guy has something." Bodega walked over and introduced me.

"This is Julio," he said to Nazario. "He's in college."

"Under our program?" Nazario asked Bodega. Bodega shook his head no. I didn't know what Nazario meant at the time, but later I would. Still, Nazario looked happy. "That's great!" he said as if it was the best news he had heard all day. "When do you graduate?"

"Next year," I said.

"Good. That's one more professional in East Harlem. Soon," he said, smiling at me, "we'll have an army of them. An entire professional class in East Harlem and no one will be able to take this neighborhood away from us."

"Sounds good," I said, thinking to myself that these guys talked a lot of dreams. But soon enough, I'd start to believe in them too.

"Sapo," Nazario said, walking past me but stopping a moment to pat my shoulder on the way as if to say, good job, "Sapo, we have to talk." Nazario and Sapo walked out of the apartment and into the hallway. Bodega drew me into the kitchen.

"You drink beer, right?"

"Yeah."

He opened the fridge and handed me one. "When you moving?"

"I haven't talked it over with my wife yet, but soon."

"That's good. Listen, you have anythin' for me?" He sounded embarrassed. "I don't want you to think," he said, looking at the floor, avoiding eye contact, "that I didn't mean what I said a few days back. That I'm some weak fuck who—"

I cut him off. "Hey, it's cool. Say no more. Look, Vera is coming to New York."

His body quickly straightened up. "You spoke to her, Chino?" He was like a kid. He pulled up a chair and sat in front of me.

"I haven't spoken to her, but I know she's coming next week. Her old school. P.S. 72, you know, on 104th and Lex, is naming the auditorium after her. So you can speak to her then."

"Will she be comin' alone? Did she sound happy?"

"I didn't speak to her, bro," I said, but it was as if he hadn't heard me at all. Bodega kept asking me questions and for a minute there I thought he was going to ask me what he should wear. Then Nazario walked back inside alone. He saw Bodega's face, saw it wasn't the same person.

"What's with you?"

"Not'en'," Bodega said.

"Sapo's waiting."

"Tell him to go home."

"What! No, Willie, this is serious."

"Tell Sapo to go home," Bodega repeated.

"Willie, come to the other room." Nazario beckoned with his hand for Bodega to join him so they could talk in private. Like usual, I took no offense. The less you know the less trouble you'll get into.

"Nah, Chino is good people," Bodega said, letting Nazario know that I could stay.

"It was good meeting you." Nazario didn't care. He extended his hand toward me and smiled that cold smile. "Can you excuse us?"

"Sure, and it was nice meeting you, too," I said. "I got to go anyway."

"I'll speak wi'choo soon, all right, Chino? Sapo will get in touch wi'choo and let you know where to meet me, all right?" Bodega said, making triumphant fists in the air as if he had won some showdown fight. I nodded and walked to the door. Nene was sitting on the sofa listening to the radio. He got up and opened the door for me. I could hear Bodega and Nazario in the other room arguing and, sure enough, the name Alberto Salazar kept coming up.

Nene was waiting for me at the door.

"Man, you must be doing some serious work for my cus. He calls you a lot. Me, you know I'm just Nene. No one listens to me, you know, but I function anyway. And sometimes I say dumb things, you know, b'cause I'm Nene. Things that you know people don't get, but I know you get them, right, Chino?"

"Yeah, I get them," I said, because I didn't want to leave him hanging.

"I know I ain't all that bright. *I don't know much about history, don't know much biology,* but Chino, I know my radio, you know. Ask me, ask me anythin', anythin' 'bout my music."

"All right," I said as I walked to the door, "Who sang 'Everybody Was Kung Fu Fighting'?"

"Those cats were fast as lightning, huh! Here comes the big boss." Nene sang a line and then answered me, "Thass kids' stuff, Chino, that guy Carl Douglas. A one-hit-wonda type of guy." Nene put out his palm and I gave him five and walked out the door. Out in the hallway I waited for the elevator and Nene stuck his babyface and body-of-a-bear out the door. "Chino, you all right, bro, *you ain't heavy, you're my brother.*" I smiled back at him again and took the elevator down.

I looked for Sapo's car that night but didn't see it. That was okay, because it was a hot spring night and El Barrio had turned into a maraca and all the people had come out transformed as seeds. Like all ghettos, Spanish Harlem looks better in the dark when everything broken and dirty is hidden by darkness and the moonlight makes everything else glow like pearls. That night the people were jamming, shaking, moving. Hydrants were opened, women were dancing to salsa blaring from a boom box on the cement. They danced with one eye on their partner and one eye on their children playing hopscotch, scullies with bottle caps, or skipping rope. Teenage girls in tight jeans flirted with guys who showed them their jewelry and tattoos. Old men played dominoes as they drank Budweisers wrapped in brown bags. I walked home happy. I even said hello to a rat that crossed my path, running from one garbage heap to another. "Hey, dusty guy. Where you going, eh?" I said when it poked its head from a plastic bag. I was happy. I was keeping my part of the deal. At the time, I didn't care about this Salazar. It was almost over for me. All I had to do was take Bodega to Vera and I was gone. Once I'd done that, I could continue my life with Blanca in total clarity. We'd be living in a better place, clean and newly renovated. More important, I'd be able to talk to my wife again without hiding anything between parentheses.

Underground Economy

EARLY the following Saturday morning, Sapo knocked at my door.

"Yo, Chino, bro, like Bodega wants ta meet you at El Museo del Barrio."

"Like, now?" I asked.

"Yeah, now, bro. *Ahora*. As we exist. As the planets are circlin' the sun."

"But El Museo hasn't opened its doors yet."

"They'll open them for Bodega, don't worry. He like gives them crazy cash. It's a waste of money if you ask me, kid." Then he spat. "But as long as it's not my money."

"Wait, you're sayin' Bodega gives money to the arts?"

"Bodega does with his money what he wants. I do with mine and you do with yours," was all Sapo told me. I invited him inside.

"Come in. Let me wash up. Blanca's asleep."

Sapo was bemused. He walked in and started to look around. "Like I ain't never been all the way in here and I haven't exactly missed much."

"Why does Bodega want to see me anyway, I already told him when Vera is coming. Like, I'll be there when she arrives." I headed toward the bathroom.

"Fuck should I know. I'm like the fucken I.R.A. I just follow orders."

"Bullshit, *pana*, you know more than you let on." I brushed my teeth real quick.

"Withholdin' info is an advantage."

"Yeah? So are you goin' to tell me how Bodega got all this power or, like, you going to have an advantage?"

"No advantage there, Chino. Thass no secret. Anyone in El Barrio from the university of the street knows that the Italians controlled the neighborhood. They ran the numbahs, they ran the drugs." I heard Sapo sit down on the couch and turn the TV on. I wasn't worried about Blanca waking up, because she slept like a rock. "So like there were places you could burglarize and then there were places, Italian-owned, Chino, that you didn't fuck with."

"Yeah, thass right. There was that restaurant, that big fucken mafia joint?"

"Mario's," Sapo said.

"Yeah, that was it."

"Yo, that fucken restaurant had a three-month waitin' list cuz it took that long to screen its guests in case they were FBI-connected, know what I'm sayin'?" I heard him opening the fridge. When I came out of the bathroom, Sapo had a bowl of Coco Puffs and was sitting in front of the TV watching cartoons.

"Like this won't ruin your rep."

"Nah, cartoons are dope," he said. I went to the bedroom to find some clothes and mull over what Sapo had told me. And he was right, it was nothing new. The Italians ran the show. When I was a little kid, Spanish Harlem was different. Many Italians were still around. There were Italians-only social clubs where you'd see pink limos parked in front of pumps. There were racially segregated tenements that never rented to blacks or Latinos. The Dime Savings Bank on 105th and Third always had a special window where Italian men wouldn't have to wait on line like everybody else.

"So what happened with the Italians, bro?" I asked Sapo when I came out, dressed.

"Fat Tony Salerno, evah heard of him?"

"Nah."

"Nigga was this big don."

"Yeah?"

"The nigga was indicted on charges of racketeerin'. The judge posted bail at two million and his boys ran down to court and paid it in cash. Now thass serious money."

"Yeah, yeah, yeah. Now I remember. That was on the news. That nigga had to sell some of his tenements to pay for all his lawyers' fees. But he still got sentenced to a hundred and seventy-five years."

"Thass right, and after that the Italians weren't so sacred. And with the big white shark outta da way, you had all these little guppies jockin' for power."

"And Bodega won?"

"With Nazario's help. Yo, like, I took all your milk," he said, getting up and placing the empty bowl in the sink.

"Thass wild, bro, Bodega won."

"Yeah. Now, like, you ready? Cuz I got things to do and Bodega is waitin' for you."

As we walked out Sapo yelled toward the bedroom, loud enough to wake Blanca, "*Bendición!*" then he laughed.

"You crazy, bro. What the fuck, she ain't your mother," I said as I quickly locked the door and ran downstairs.

We got into Sapo's car and rode down Fifth Avenue.

"Yo, Sapo, you know anyone who's hard up to get married?"

"Girls? Plenty. Guys? None. Why you ask?"

"Blanca is trying to get some girl a green card."

"Get the fuck."

"Yeah, so if you know someone—"

"Well, I know this sad junkie. We can make him go cold turkey for a day or two. He'd do anythin' for a fix."

"No junkies, man, she'd be better off in Colombia."

"Then what the fuck do you want? Where you think you livin' at? You think you gonna find some gay mothafuckah who has to marry some bitch or his rich father will disown him? I don't think so. If she wants to stay in the country, she bettah take the junkie."

"Never mind I asked." That was stupid. Why did I even try?

"Nazario might help, nigga knows everythin'," Sapo advised. But I shook it off. I was already tangled up with Bodega. I didn't want to get mixed up with Nazario, too.

·

SAPO STOPPED the car in front of El Museo Del Barrio and I got out.

"Yo, I'll see you like layra, Chino."

"See you, man."

"One last thing," Sapo said. "Like, I'm gonna ask you a fayvah."

"So what else is new? I still got your shit in my house, you need that back?"

"Not yet, Chino. What I'll need from ya is somethin' small. Real small. Like the day you just wanted me to walk wi'choo cuz some niggas were eyein' you bad, 'membah that?"

"Yeah, I remember."

"Well, it'll be even smaller than that."

And Sapo took off.

I walked to the side of the building where the entrance was that month because the front entrance was being renovated. It was locked. I pounded on the door and a guard walked over and stood by the glass doors that separated us.

"The *museo* is not open yet," he yelled through the glass.

"Wait, I'm s'posed to meet someone here."

"Who?"

"Willie Bodega," I said, and he looked around. He went back inside to check on this. I looked across toward Central Park. It was a beautiful day, the blue jays were making noise, the trees were getting back their leaves. I was thinking of maybe later taking a walk in the park with Blanca, when the guard returned.

"Sorry about that." He had a smile on his face and started to unlock the door. "You know that I shouldn't let anyone inside yet. But since you're a friend of Willie, I'll let you in, okay." He shook my hand, nearly pulling me inside. He pointed to where I could find Bodega.

I saw Bodega standing in front of a painting by Jorge Soto, a large canvas portraying a transparent Adam and Eve, with blood running through their bodies as if they were subjects in an anatomy textbook. I stood next to Bodega. Even though he knew I was there he kept studying the painting.

He didn't greet me, just pointed at Adam. "This man right here, he had it all. Could even talk with God. But it meant nothin' to him without her."

"I hear you," I said. "So, like, Bodega, I already told you Vera is going to be here next week. I'll be there wi'choo when she arrives. So why you wanted to meet me here today?"

"B'cause, Chino, I'm going t' ask you for somethin' when Vera comes and I thought you should know me. Besides, I'm gonna marry her this time, and that means we're gonna be related. And you're good people."

"Wha'? You gonna wha'?"

"Marry her, of course. What'd you think I went through all this for?"

"Look, man, what you want to do with Vera is your thing, I'm just keeping my part. But, like, Vera is already married."

"I know that," he said, and his mood changed. He gazed at me with the confidence of someone who has marked the deck.

"That doesn't matter to you at all?" I asked. "What if she doesn't want to leave her husband?"

"Of course she'll leave that *pendejo*. She never wanted to marry him in the first place. It was her fucken mother who pushed her." He slowly walked away from me to stand in front of another painting. It was titled *Despierta Boricua* and depicted a Taino Indian tied to a New York City fire hydrant.

"So much was promised to us when we left our island," he said softly as he looked at the painting. "They gave us citizenship and then sent us to the garment district. I'm going to make sure they make good on their promises."

"Did you ever meet Vera's husband, Willie?" I asked.

"Meet him, no. But I knew his family was one of the people that escaped Castro in fifty-eight. No shame in that. But his family was rich 'cause they had supported Batista with a shitload of money they had siphoned off the people of Cuba." His eyes left the painting and looked at the floor. The tiles were beautiful, new. El Museo del Barrio had just gotten a face-lift. The floors were shining, the walls a cool, soothing

white, and the titles of the paintings were written in Spanish, with the
English translation as a secondary thing. It felt good to be there. El
Museo del Barrio was the only museum where I could look at the
paintings without having a guard follow me from wing to wing. At the
Met I got suspicious looks. First the guards checked my shoes to see if
they were once alligators. When they saw my worn sneakers, they
treated me like I might pull a knife from my back pocket and go slash-
ing Goyas.

"See, Chino, back then, politics was all I knew. I tried to explain to
Veronica who this guy she was gonna marry was, the reason he was
rich. I was telling her he was not a friend of the people right up to the
night before the wedding. Do you know what she said?"

"Wha'?"

"She said she loved me. She said that she didn't care if I didn't have
any money. The problem was, she said, I didn't have any vision of how
to get it. She said she wouldn't mind being poor for a few years, but
since I only had a vision for political stuff, I was going to be poor for the
rest of my life. And then her mother came out and yelled for her to get
back inside. Her mother looked at me like I had leprosy. So I left thinking, Shit, that bitch don't deserve me. I thought the Young Lords were
gonna succeed and that she had missed her chance at history. But a
couple hours later, Chino, I was in tears and not that much mattered."

I didn't say anything and silence overtook us. I guess if I had been
old enough back then I would have felt the same way he did. Back then
when Bodega was a teenager, the Young Lords were an urban guerrilla
group that had its origins in Chicago, but they made all their noise in
El Barrio. They wrote up a manifesto called the "Thirteen Point Program and Platform." The first point was to free Puerto Rico from the
United States. The second point was for all Latin countries to have self-
determination. They wanted better neighborhood programs. They
launched food drives, clothing drives, health-inspection drives, door-
to-door clinics. They were many, they were young, they were educated,
and they were armed. They took over a redbrick Methodist church at
111th and Lexington and made it a conference center by declaring it
the People's Church. The Young Lords party was also ahead of its time;
point number five of the manifesto stated, "Down with Machismo and

Male Chauvinism!" This was due in part to the fact that half of the central committee was composed of women who, along with the men, developed strategies and carried guns.

I listened as Bodega described how he would preach these points to Vera. Telling her that Latin women were undergoing a revolution and that this would force the Latin man to change his ways and reinvent himself. Bodega wouldn't preach these points eloquently but he would speak of them with so much passion and street intellect that Vera fell madly in love with him. She liked his ideas, his conviction, his optimism. Bodega would invite her to rallies, to the Lords' headquarters at 202 East 117th, to Marxist education classes, to urban military tactics classes, to food drives. Veronica would attend and at times even help out with breakfast programs and clothing drives, but what Veronica really wanted was for Bodega to find a real job and marry her.

"How old were you back then?" It was the only thing I could think of saying.

"I don't know, let me think. Seventeen, I was seventeen."

"So you left Veronica. You were angry at her and everybody. Then what happened?" We both began to walk around El Museo.

"Crazy shit. Some crazy shit. It was, like, three in the morning. I climbed up the fire escape to her room. I tried opening the window but there was a gate. So I tapped on the glass and Veronica woke up thinking it was a thief and I scared her half to death."

"That was smart, bro. Couldn't you wait till morning or something?"

"Nah, I couldn't, b'cause she was getting married the next day and if her mother had woken up, you know, it would have been over. So I almost gave Veronica a heart attack until she realized it was me. She knew I could never hurt her. And she was a little scared, but it wasn't because I was there, it was cuz she was marrying some guy she didn't love."

"You sure she didn't at least like his money?"

"Didn't I just tell you, she said she didn't care that I didn't have money, what bothered her was that I had no vision of how to get it."

"Yeah, thass right, you told me she said she didn't care that *you* didn't have any money, but you didn't say that she said she didn't like the *Cuban's* money. See the difference, bro?"

"Nah, I don't," he barked, "and what the fuck do you know anyway?"

"Look, bro, like you said, we are going to be related, right? So, like, do you want me to lie to you or do you want me to tell you what I really think?" My voice was respectful but loud. "All I'm telling you is that Veronica never said she didn't want this guy's money."

Bodega left my words hanging and walked away toward a small wing that had an exhibition of wooden religious figures. The Three Kings on horseback on their way to meet El Niño, with everything and everyone made of wood and colored with house paint. The wood was old and the paint was cracking, giving the Nativity scene a poignant look of absolute poverty.

"You understand me?" I walked over to him and realized that all this time we had been talking, never had we looked each other in the eyes. All this time, when we'd spoken we'd looked at the artwork. It was a good way to relieve tension and just talk.

"When you moving?" Bodega asked me. I had hit a nerve. Veronica was something sacred.

"Tomorrow."

"Thass good."

"Look, Willie, you said you wanted to ask me something. What is it you want to ask me?"

"Not yet, Chino, not yet." And Bodega finally faced me and looked in my eyes. "But it's something good. Don't worry."

.

THE NEXT day Blanca and I rented a U-Haul van and got family and friends to help us move. Negra and Victor pitched in. Victor had recovered but was still weak so, like Blanca, helped only with the light stuff. During the move Negra and Victor were acting as if they were on their second honeymoon, all kissie-kissie and lovey-dovey.

"Victor, honey, watch it with that, don't hurt yourself."

"Negra, *querida*, be careful. Let me help you with that, baby."

For two days Blanca and I lived out of boxes until we had the time to fix things up and put everything in order. Then, just two days before Vera would arrive in New York, I got home late and tired. The house was dark. I figured Blanca must be with Negra or one of her friends or still at church. I fried myself a burger and got a *malta* from the fridge.

After I ate, I decided to study and flipped on the television for background noise. That's when I heard about the dead body. The English news channels didn't make a big deal out of it, to them Alberto Salazar was just a Latin reporter for a small newspaper. Just another dead Latino tonight. It only got a blurb. But I needed to find out more, in case Alberto Salazar was the same guy I had heard Bodega and Nazario talk about that night at the Taino Towers.

So I finished my drink and switched to channel 47, hoping they would give one of their own more news time. I wasn't disappointed.

The report said Salazar's body was found in the East River. He had been a reporter for *El Diario/La Prensa* working on an investigation of a drug lord in East Harlem. Salazar had been a big man, six feet two, 260 pounds. As the camera panned an empty pier, still wet from the afternoon rain, the Spanish newscaster reported that there was evidence of a struggle. In addition to the gunshot wound, Salazar had suffered a serious bite to the shoulder. That's when I knew who had killed him.

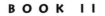

BOOK II

BECAUSE A SINGLE

LAWYER CAN STEAL MORE

MONEY THAN A HUNDRED

MEN WITH GUNS

These dreams
These empty dreams
from the make-believe bedrooms
their parents left them

PEDRO PIETRI
— "Puerto Rican Obituary"

My Growing Up and All That
Piri Thomas Kinda Crap

SAPO was different.

Sapo was always Sapo, and no one messed with him because he had a reputation for biting. "When I'm in a fight," Sapo would spit, "whass close to my mouth is mine by right and my teeth ain't no fucken pawn-shop."

I loved Sapo. I loved Sapo because he loved himself. But by now you know it was never about Sapo. It was always about Bodega. And to this day it continues to be about Bodega. Bodega had an unforgettable blend of nobility and street, as if God never made up his mind whether to have Bodega be born a leader or a hood. Bodega did something to the neighborhood, something with staying power, like a song that no one could possibly like but you, because you heard it at a time when your heart was breaking.

But after Alberto Salazar was found dead no songs were played. No one thought of love or anything. The neighborhood became a tomb. Mute as an Egyptian. Every member of the street wire from the pimp to the junkie to the hooker talked like an Italian: "I ain't see not'en'."

Blanca had seen the news on TV. My guess is that at first Blanca thought that what had happened was a terrible thing. Then later, when things were going around about Salazar knowing things he shouldn't about some drug king, I figured she must have felt even worse, that

Salazar was a good man, God be with him. At some point she no doubt heard that Salazar was investigating Spanish Harlem. I figure it was then she really got suspicious. And when the newscasters mentioned the chunk of flesh missing from Salazar's shoulder, memories must have rained down on Blanca like parachutes. She'd been an eyewitness to one of Sapo's bites. It had been a gruesome display of hate and anger and Sapo, as only Sapo could, presented it with showmanship.

·

BACK IN Julia de Burgos Junior High, back in the days of my growing up and all that Piri Thomas kinda crap that I will spare you from, there was the English teacher, Mr. Blessington. He kept telling us boys we were all going to end up in jail and that all the girls were going to end up hooking. He would say these things right out loud and the administration wouldn't do anything. I hated Blessington and he knew it. He looked at Blanca with the eyes of a repressed rapist. He thought he was smooth but what he came out looking was creepy. He'd come to school in a suit and tell us that a man with a suit is a man that is valuable and that a man without a suit has no worth. He always did Robert Frost poems with us, which were all right, but after a while we started to hate Robert Frost. Blessington thought he was doing us a service, and that was his error. He was one of those upper-middle-class people who think highly of themselves because they could be making money or something, but no, they have taken the high road and have chosen to "help" poor kids from the ghetto.

On the other hand the science teacher, Jose Tapia, was always lecturing us on how fortunate we were because we were young and Latin. His speeches were at times so fiery and full of passion that every year the principal would try to make Tapia the gym teacher, in hopes of cutting down Tapia's influence over us. But as a science teacher Tapia was state certified and was appointed to our school so there was no way for the principal to get rid of him.

And he didn't want to be called Mr. Tapia, simply Tapia.

One day when Sapo and me were in the eighth grade, Tapia told us, "You speak two languages, you are worth two people." Sapo retorted,

"What about the pope? He speaks like a hundred languages, but he ain't worth jack." The class was rolled.

"Sapo, do you think the pope would be the pope if he didn't know his hundred languages?" Tapia asked after the laughter died down.

"Nah, if he didn't speak a hundred languages he'd still be pope, because he's white. All popes are white. I ain't never seen no black pope. I ain't seen a Spanish pope, either."

"Hey, Tapia," I said, "I never even seen a black nun." Of course we were just stalling. The truth was we hadn't done our homework and wanted to kill time.

"Or a Chinese nun. All I've ever seen are white nuns," Edwin jumped in, so I figured he hadn't done his homework either. "You can't have a black pope if there are no black nuns." I hated Edwin. When he borrowed a pencil he never gave it back and when school was almost over, he always borrowed loose-leaf paper because he didn't see the point of buying a new notebook.

"Yeah, a black nun!" Sapo shouted in agreement.

"Julio, can you shut him up?" Blanca whispered to me. I always sat next to Blanca. I would leave my science book at home on purpose so I could use the excuse of sharing hers. Tapia understood this and, even though we had assigned seats, would always let me move.

"No," I whispered back at Blanca. "Sapo has a point."

"The point is Sapo hasn't done his homework."

"I haven't done mine, either," I said.

"Then this book"—she pulled the science text we were sharing toward her side of the desk—"does you no good."

"Look, forget about the pope," Tapia continued. "I don't care about the pope. The pope is not one of my students. The pope has a good job and there are black nuns and Chinese nuns, too, but that doesn't matter. All that matters is you. I care about you. And I played the same games when I was your age. If you haven't done your homework just tell me." Hands shot up.

Tapia sighed loudly. "Edwin, you didn't do your homework?"

"Yeah, I did."

"Well?"

"Well, I did it, I just didn't bring it." The class laughed and Tapia looked at his roll book.

"All right, Edwin, you live on 102nd and Third. That's three blocks from here. You better get your homework at lunchtime or you'd better have it done by then." Edwin nodded his head.

"Sapo, your homework?"

"I didn't do it."

"Why didn't you do it?"

"Because Mr. Blessington told me I was going to end up in jail, so why waste my time doing homework?" We all laughed.

"Sapo, don't you want to prove Blessington wrong?"

"Nah, I'd rather not do my homework."

Tapia got upset. He threw down the roll book and began to yell at us. "I don't care what Blessington's been telling you! If you are here it is because you want to be, right? Otherwise don't even come to school, just stay on the street. You can make more money selling pot on the stairwells than coming to my classroom, but if you come—and I want you to come, I like having you here—all I ask is that you make an effort! That's all I ask. Don't give me this nonsense about what Mr. Blessington is telling you. You guys are smart enough to know that it's up to you to become what you want to be. So why even listen to him? I've heard what he says. It's all nonsense." Tapia pointed at one of the girls. "Rita Moreno, she was once like you, is Rita Moreno hooking?" Tapia then pointed at one of the guys. "Reggie Jackson, he was once as young as you, he's half Puerto Rican, is Reggie in jail? They worked hard. That's what you have to do. Just do your work and don't pay attention to Blessington."

So we all quieted down and did our work, even Sapo, although he copied off me. Sapo always copied me but it was no big deal. The next period was English and we hated it because it was Blessington. I was in no mood for Robert Frost, that white-assed crusty old man from some cow state. But I couldn't say that to Blessington. Instead, as politely as I could, I asked, "Mr. Blessington, why do we always do Robert Frost, why can't we do someone else?"

"Because Robert Frost," he said, slowly shaking his head in disbelief as if I was asking something real stupid, "is a major American poet."

"Well, I heard that Julia de Burgos was a poet; why don't we do some of her poems?" I said, and the class jumped in with me.

"That's right," Lucy, Blanca's Pentecostal friend whom we used to call Chewbacca, chimed in, "why did they name the school after her? She must have been important."

"Yeah, they didn't name the school Robert Frost Junior High, why we always reading him?" someone else asked. Truth was, I was happy we were killing time. I wanted those forty-five minutes in his class to fly. I wanted to keep this discussion going for as long as possible.

"If any of you have noticed since September," Blessington pointed out, "this is English class, not Spanish. Julia-day-Burgos"—he pronounced her name with a thick accent—"wrote only in Spanish."

"But maybe she wrote in English too. I write in Spanish and in English sometimes," Blanca said to him. Every time Blanca spoke Blessington would leer. It was one of those cartoon monster smiles, where the monster rubs his hands as he thinks of something dastardly.

"Listen, you people"—he always called us you people—"Julia-day-Burgos is so obscure it would be hard to find a single poem of hers. In any language." I turned to Blanca and, whispering, asked what *obscure* meant. Sapo was quietly drawing all this time. He drew terribly, but it never stopped him. He mostly did it because he was bored. But I knew he was listening and could jump in any minute.

"But if she is so unknown," I said confidently, emphasizing the word Blanca had provided to let Blessington know that I knew what *obscure* meant, "then I agree with Lucy, why did they name an entire school after her? Why not after someone famous?"

"Finally, a good question," Blessington said, adjusting his tie and buttoning up his blazer. "I'll tell you why: because the people in this district are simpletons, that's why. District Four has no idea what it's doing. The name they chose for this school was probably the worst name they could choose. Why, we teachers didn't even know who she was when they renamed this place."

"Mr. Tapia did," Sapo piped up, leaving his drawing for a minute. We all knew what Blessington was saying was that none of the white teachers knew who she was, and they were the only teachers that mattered.

"Oh, him," Blessington said in a tired voice. "Him again. Well, I heard he's a good science teacher," he said with a smirk, "but we're in English now. You people need to get on with today's work." And it was all right with me because we had chopped off at least fifteen minutes of the period. Blessington then went to the board and wrote, "Analogies Between Frost's Poems and New York City." I turned around and asked Blanca what *analogies* meant. She told me. I laughed.

"What similarities?" I called out. Blessington was upset now.

"End of discussion," he said. "Get out your homework." Blessington walked over to Sapo's desk.

"Enrique, where's your homework?" Blessington asked.

"I'm going to jail, so why bother, right?" Sapo kept drawing. "Yo'r the smart guy here, right, can't you figure that out yo'self?" The class went "Oooooh," which Blessington took as a challenge.

"You'll be lucky to even make jail," he said to Sapo.

"Why you snapping at me? I said you were right."

"I know I'm right. I'm doing all you people a favor. I say these things to you so you can maybe prove me wrong. Now, it's sad to say, but I've yet to see one of my Puerto Rican students, just one, prove me wrong. And I know it's not going to be Sapo here." Blessington then leaned over and took Sapo's drawing from him and crumpled it in his hands. Sapo got so mad, he shot straight up from his seat and thrust himself at Blessington so they were face to face.

"Thass right, I won't prove you wrong b'cause I'm going to jail for jamming your wife." The class was silent because that wasn't a snap any longer but an insult. They stared each other down for a second or two before Sapo turned around and headed for the door. "Where do you think you're going?" Blessington yelled, and went after Sapo, grabbing him by the shoulder.

"Don't touch me, man!" Sapo yelled, but Blessington didn't listen. I got up from my seat and went over to Sapo.

"Yo, take a chill pill," I said to Sapo. Blessington yelled at me, "I can handle this. Sit back down!" He didn't let go of Sapo. Sapo started to pull himself away and that's when Blessington made the mistake of putting Sapo in a headlock.

"Yo, you choking him!" I yelled, but Blessington kept at it, all the while cursing at Sapo. Blanca and her friend Lucy started to run out of the room to get the teacher next door. Blessington released Sapo and went after Blanca. And that's when Sapo jumped him from behind. Sapo crawled on Blessington as if Blessington were going to give him a piggyback ride. Before Blessington could shake Sapo free, Sapo dug his teeth into the base of the teacher's neck. Blessington screamed; the blood spurted out, running down his back and staining his white shirt collar crimson. Sapo scrambled off Blessington's back as Blessington fell to his knees, pressing the wound with his hands. Then Sapo came around and grabbed Blessington's face in his hands and pulled it toward his own. Sapo spat out a chunk of Blessington's flesh, bouncing it off Blessington's left cheekbone. Covered in blood and saliva, Blessington's eyes were frozen in disbelief. He wasn't screaming. He was in shock. It was only when he saw a piece of his own flesh on the floor that he registered what had happened, and passed out.

Standing in front of the classroom Sapo smiled as only Sapo could; he slowly turned to the class, showing us his shining red teeth. He then calmly walked out of the room. Everyone was stunned. Blanca was the first one to shake herself and ran out of the room. "Help us, help us, Blessington's dying!" she kept yelling down the hall. A minute later the school nurse arrived. When she saw all that blood on the floor she took off her smock and put pressure on Blessington's neck. Meanwhile I went looking for Sapo. He had stopped by the bathroom to rinse his mouth and when he saw me he laughed.

"The nigga had that shit coming." He spat water.

"Sapo, bro, what you gonna do?"

"I could give two fucks," he said. "I never felt better. It's as if I let some fucken courier pigeon go free." At that minute Tapia walked into the bathroom, his face red with fury. It was the same anger he would show us when we let him down by not behaving, by not doing work or getting in trouble.

"Did he really have you in a headlock?" Tapia asked Sapo.

"Yeah, I saw it all, Ta—"

"Shut up! I'm asking Sapo!" I quieted down and backed away. Sapo nodded and Tapia paced the bathroom. He sighed loudly. He stopped in front of Sapo and placed both arms on top of Sapo's shoulders.

"Look at me," Tapia said. "Don't say that he had you in a head-lock—"

I jumped in. "But he did, Tapia—"

"Shut up, Chino! *Coño*, just shut up!" This time I did for good. Tapia breathed hard. His eyes were watery. "Sapo, look at me. If you say he had you in a headlock, when he recovers he will deny it. And it won't matter which of your friends backs you up, they will believe Blessington. Now, you listen to me and you listen good because I don't want you to go to Juvie. The police are on their way. When they ask you why you bit Blessington, you tell them you heard voices. You got that?" Sapo nodded. "You tell them the voices said to bite Blessington. You don't say Blessington said all this bullshit to you or that he had you in a headlock, you just say you heard voices. You got that?" Sapo under-stood and a slow smirk began to form on his big lips as he nodded. When he had completely registered what Tapia had told him, that smirk became a full-blown smile.

That whole year Sapo saw a shrink and thus avoided juvenile deten-tion. He must have lied, and I bet for a while he loved the opportunity to have an audience for those stories he was so good at making up. It was like getting away with biting Blessington's neck all over again. But then he got tired of it, started blowing off sessions, and ultimately he dropped out of school and moved out on his own. That year something happened to Sapo. He had always been Sapo but that year, after biting Blessington, he started turning into someone who wasn't afraid to die. It was the beginning of the adult Sapo. His was the sneaker you wouldn't want to step on because "sorry" wouldn't cut it. He became that person you wouldn't want to cut off in traffic because he'd pull a knife and slice you. He became that person you wanted on your side so you could unleash him on your enemies. Like the rest of us, Sapo was still a kid, but he was already turning into something else. He had reached that point in existence where he wasn't afraid to hurt anyone who threatened his only source of meaning, his love for himself.

I figure it was around the time he left school that he met up with someone who knew someone who knew Willie Bodega.

·

SEEING SOMEONE bite a chunk out of someone's neck and then spit it at their face isn't something you forget. That incident stayed with Blanca, as it did with all of us. And as *El Diario* kept publishing more facts about Salazar, Blanca couldn't help herself.

"Julio, you heard about that reporter, Salazar, Alberto Salazar?" I was cooking dinner and she was sitting at the table reading *El Diario*. Blanca would usually read the *Times* but *El Diario* was the only newspaper that bothered to cover the story about Salazar.

"Nah. What about him? You want more beans?" Blanca's religion didn't allow her to eat meat, so she had to get her protein elsewhere.

"That's enough," she said when I showed her the plate. "He was killed."

"That's terrible."

"Yeah, I know, Julio. They say that he was bitten before he was shot. They also say that he was—thanks," she said as I placed her plate on the table and sat down. I had served her real fast because I knew she had to pray and I was hoping that she would pray a long time and forget about Salazar. But Blanca prayed real quick, so I guess she just thanked God for the food and said Amen. "So they said that he was working on a story around here. He was investigating a possible drug lord and then they found him dead."

"Wow, that's too bad," I answered, and then Blanca told me something that somehow had escaped me.

"Have you noticed that this block doesn't have dealers on the corner? All four corners of this block are quiet. Have you noticed that, Julio?"

"No, I haven't," I answered honestly. Apparently, Bodega didn't litter in his own house.

"Julio, who owns these buildings? It's just amazing that somehow dealers steer clear from here. At times—"

"Blanca, count your blessings and eat up, all right?"

She smiled and felt a little embarrassed because she was talking with her mouth full. "Just tell me one thing, Julio." She swallowed and looked straight at me.

"Wha'?" I said with a mouth full of rice and beans.

"Tell me that you know for a fact that Sapo is not involved in that reporter's death. A piece of the man's shoulder was missing."

"So?"

"So we know who sells drugs and we both know who bites like that."

"Man, Blanca, you got some imagination. Sapo is this nickel-and-dime dealer. You knew him when we were kids. He wasn't the smartest of people. A good dealer at least could count what's coming in and what's going out. Sapo couldn't even do that." I was lying. Sapo was very smart. Blanca wasn't buying it. She stopped chewing and looked at me.

"Sapo is smart, Sapo was always smart. Those teachers never knew how to reach him. Well, maybe Tapia did. But he was always smart. He has to be, otherwise he wouldn't have that big car he drives."

"Maybe he got lucky."

"No, Julio, there is something else here. I don't know what. Sapo makes me nervous. And what really makes me nervous is that you are his friend." Blanca's voice was a bit desperate.

"All I know, Blanca," I said flatly, "is that you know he's my friend. A guy growing up in this neighborhood can get beat up. Sapo was always there for me. That's why I let him keep his stuff here. I know you hate it but I owe that much to him. Remember Mario DePuma? He broke my nose. If Sapo wouldn't have jumped in that Italian would have killed me, you know that." Blanca shrugged. She knew Mario DePuma. He'd always been making passes at her. That was the reason him and me had that fight. Then Blanca got up to get more water. She sat back down and continued to think about the possibilities.

"How is it, Julio, that as crazy as it seems you know nothing. I mean as crazy as it seems, you have no idea about this reporter getting killed."

"Why would I?"

"I don't know. Where's Enrique anyway? He hasn't shown his face in days."

"What a miracle, you of all people asking for Sapo." But that worried me: Where was Sapo?

"I hope that he stays lost, but it's too good to be true," she said.

"You know Sapo, he'll show up when he needs a favor."

"Fine, you're right. I shouldn't care." I was happy that was over with. But then she said something equally unnerving.

"Julio, I've invited Pastor Vasquez and Claudia over for dinner next week—"

"That's great," I said, dropping my spoon on the plate. "I hope the three of you have a good dinner. What did you do that for, Blanca? You know I don't like to be preached to—"

"They'll only be here for dinner. No one is going to preach to you, all right. You think that just because he's a pastor he has to always be preaching or something? I just want him around before the baby arrives. At least once."

"Well, when are they coming?" I grumbled.

"Next Friday. And you better be here."

"Blanca . . ."

"You better be here, Julio. I want you here when they visit," Blanca said firmly. I knew it was important to her so I just nodded, part in agreement and part in disgust.

"How's the husband-hunting for Claudia going?" I asked to shift the subject.

"Not too good." She pushed her food away, then rested her face in her palms, her elbows on the table. "But Roberto Vega—the seventeen-year-old anointed—is visiting our congregation and will give a speech." Just thinking about that, Blanca became animated again.

"You really believe he's anointed?" I was relieved to talk about anything, anything that didn't have to do with that reporter's death.

"Yes. I believe he is." She smiled and placed her hand on mine. "Come to church with me, Julio. You can see for yourself."

"Have you seen him?" I asked, turning my hand over to hold hers.

"No, but I've heard of him. They say he can lift an entire church. Please come. You can also meet Claudia."

Then the phone rang. I got up from the table and went over to answer it.

"You don't know me but I'm your brother." I got the Doobie Brothers' lyrics and knew it was Nene.

"How you been, I have the notes for you. Yeah, yeah, tell your cousin I have the notes for him." I hoped Blanca would think it was some guy from class and Nene would think it was from a song.

"Wait, don't tell me, the Grass Roots? Right? The Grass Roots?"

"Yeah, how you guess?" I couldn't care less. Why wasn't Sapo doing the calling?

"I knew it, I knew it. So, *mira*, Chino, my cousin wants ta see you tomorrow. Nazario will meet with you. He said he had to meet you. Some girl is comin'."

"Cool, tell him I will." And I hung up.

That was all I was going to do for Bodega. I had decided then and there that as soon as Bodega met Vera, I owed him nothing more.

When Blanca finished eating she asked me if I could go out and get her a Hershey bar with almonds, she had a craving. I was putting on my shoes to go out when Blanca switched on the TV to Spanish CNN. Like me, she studied with the TV on. She sat there with her nose already in a book, waiting for me to bring her chocolate. Then Alberto Salazar's death was mentioned. Her body stiffened and her head shot up as if she had been stabbed in the back.

ROUND 2

Everyone's a Thief

T H E day Vera was to arrive back in New York City I was walking out of our new building to go to work. As I stepped out I spotted a tall man in an Italian suit, standing in the bright spring sun glowing like an apparition. Some tenants were gathered around him as if he was manna from heaven sent by the Most High. Mothers kissed his cheek, fathers were bowing to him and introducing their kids to him and making them greet him. It was as if I'd woken up in a village on the mother island and on my way to get water I'd met fellow villagers acting with that modesty and politeness you only find in places so poor that all you can offer is your kindness.

"Julio, right?" Nazario walked over to me, extended his hand, and we shook. I knew I was to be the link between Bodega and Vera. I was determined to fulfill my part of the deal; once Bodega and Vera met I was completely free. I would sever all ties to Bodega. Now more than ever, I wanted nothing to do with Bodega because I was sure he was connected to Salazar's death. I hated to know that that would include Sapo too, but I had begun to wonder if Salazar was the first man Sapo had killed. If Sapo killed that reporter then he deserved to go to jail. I thought that, but I knew I didn't mean it. I felt bad for Sapo.

I also knew I would never rat out Sapo or Bodega. I wasn't going to say a word. It wasn't my job or my style. All I needed was to keep my part of the deal and get free of Bodega and free of my own conscience, which would nag me and call me names if I backed out.

"So Nene called you last night to tell you I was coming to meet you," he said smoothly, as if he and I had been friends for years.

"Nene called me," I said.

"Great." I could already see that Nazario was a chameleon. He had the uncanny ability to be stoically cold under pressure and extremely warm with the people. But from the day I'd met him at the Taino Towers I knew it was Nazario who went around carrying out the favors for Bodega. Like Bodega had told me, he needed people to represent him in his absence. Who better than Nazario to visit the people and give them help in the name of Bodega? It was Nazario who, by blending his education with politeness, had made himself be looked upon with love, respect, and a little fear throughout the neighborhood. His smile could be magically disarming but his head was crowded with practicality and genius. Unlike Bodega's eyes, which were pools of ghosts and sadness, Nazario's were black holes, nothing could escape them, not even light, as if he could read your mind. He inspired and at the same time intimidated me.

"I was thinking of telling Bodega to meet me in some restaurant and then taking my wife and her sister, Negra, and Vera to dinner. A family thing, you know, and Bodega could walk right in. With people around them that should diffuse some of the tension. That sound good?"

"That's brilliant, Julio," Nazario said, smiling. Then someone who had just stepped out of the building walked over to us. She gave Nazario a small packet of food wrapped in tinfoil. "For your lunch," she said. He refused to take it, gently suggesting she needed it more than he did. The single mother of two, who lived in 5E, told him it was last night's *pasteles*, which should still taste good, all he had to do was heat them up. He finally accepted, telling her in Spanish, "Who am I to take from you the gift of giving?" After that she kissed his cheek, then left to take her kids to school.

"Are you late for work?" he asked me when we resumed.

"I'm going to be."

"Then I'll walk with you."

"No, it's all right. It's just three blocks from here."

"Exactly, three blocks. What's three blocks? Some people have to take eight-hour flights in the company of uncomfortable people." He knew he made me nervous and he was smiling faintly. "You, Julio, just have to walk three uncomfortable blocks, with me."

Unlike Bodega, Nazario spoke cleanly and used his slang only when it suited him. Nazario's and Bodega's speeches were as different as a glass of tap water and a glass of wine. And unlike Bodega, who said exactly what was on his mind, Nazario would tell you only what he felt was necessary. Later on, as I sank deeper into all this mud, I would realize how much of his success Bodega owed to Nazario and his connections at City Hall. It was something about knowing who the important little people were, the forgotten ones who don't wear suits, the mailroom clerk, the secretaries, the custodial staffs. They would hide letters, delay them, too, steal files, copy disks, shred documents, all for Nazario. These workers who sympathized with Nazario knew that they had a union, so it would be difficult for them to lose their jobs. What Nazario offered them in return was something their union didn't cover, that if their sons and daughters needed legal help one day, he would be there. And so would Bodega's financial backing.

"That's a great idea, Chino. The restaurant. That way Willie can just walk in casually as if he didn't know anything. He'll see you, your wife, her sister, and Vera. Brilliant."

"Well, I hope it works," I shrugged.

"In theory, it works like a socialist peasant but in real life"—he stopped walking and placed his arm around my shoulder—"in real life we have to do what Willie says. He wants you to accompany him to the school this morning and see Vera."

"Wha'!" I was angry. "Hey, man, Bodega has waited more than twenty years. A few hours won't kill him. I gotta go to work. You know, it's bad enough I was going to miss a class tonight so he can see this woman. Now work, I can't miss work." Truth was I was angry because I was in the dark. I could tell something else was happening. Something big. Something that worried Nazario enough that he wanted to do anything he could to keep Bodega calm and happy. I didn't want to get more involved, but not knowing what was really happening might hurt me. With Salazar dead, I didn't want the cops coming to my house asking questions because Blanca would kill me, maybe even leave me. I couldn't chance that. Right then I wanted Nazario to level with me. But I decided to wait and ask Bodega himself, because if I asked Nazario anything, he would only do that lawyer thing on me, say a million things while telling me nothing.

"I understand." His voice was like small waves, like the swells at Coney Island. "I know exactly where you're coming from. You can't miss work." As Nazario said this an old man who was about to open his barbershop on 110th and Lexington crossed the street to greet him.

"Don Tunito, *bueno verlo.*"

"*Bueno verte a ti, mijo. ¿Y cómo va todo?*"

"*Bien. Este es Julio.*" The old man shook my hand and said I could get free haircuts at his shop. Their conversation was purely small talk. It was a silent agreement in which each party knew what proper respects to pay, a polite farce created to ease the strain of acknowledging who owed who and what.

Looking back, I figured Bodega must have taken a lot of pride in these favors he handed out through Nazario. It made Bodega feel like some kid with a lot of toys who is happy to share them with the kid next door who owns a broken tricycle. Bodega took pride in helping someone who had just arrived from Puerto Rico or Nicaragua or Mexico or any other Latin American country. He'd get them jobs, legal jobs that didn't pay a lot but got them started on their new life here in America. His buildings were run by good, hardworking men from Puerto Rico who just wanted to work. Bodega would make them supers or plumbers or *dishwasheros* at his pizzerias or anything. As long as they had some way of feeding their family and could hope to someday find something better they were happy. No wonder Bodega's name had spread like a good smell from a Latin woman's kitchen.

So, if someone wanted to set up a small business, be it a bodega or a fruit stand, but only had half the money and couldn't get a bank loan, that person would get in touch with someone who knew someone who knew this Willie Bodega. Bodega would then dispatch Nazario to talk with this person's neighbors and, depending on what he heard (whether this person was "good people" being honorable and trustworthy or some cheap-ass who would rip off the neighborhood),

Bodega would offer or deny him support. All Bodega asked in return was loyalty. For them never to forget that it was Bodega who got them on their way. Nothing dramatic would happen if they'd forget. Nothing would be broken. Nothing would be thrown. But usually they'd remember. Usually that small business Bodega had loaned money to, that just-graduated kid whose tuition had been taken care of, that person who'd just passed the bar and whose prep course fees had been paid for, or that family just arrived from Puerto Rico who had been set up in an apartment, never forgot who had helped them in their time of need. They were loyal to Bodega without ever having seen his face.

Sapo had told me one day, when he was drunk on his fifth forty-ouncer, that Bodega had met Nazario after the Young Lords broke up. Bodega was selling dope and Nazario was just getting out of Brooklyn Law School. Nazario had told Bodega to get himself a hot-dog vendor's license, place the dope inside a frankfurter cart with real franks in it and, before taking the money, to tell the customers that the heroin was free and that they were really paying for the hot dog. That way if an undercover cop bought from Bodega, he couldn't bust him for *selling* heroin. A year later Bodega did get busted. Nazario represented him and used the frankfurter cart as Bodega's defense. He told the judge that Bodega, as an American citizen in business for himself, could set any price he desired on hot dogs, since hot dogs were not controlled substances. That his client specifically let the undercover officer know, before taking his money and giving him the dope, that the officer was really buying the hot dog for five dollars and that the substance was free. The transaction did occur, which meant that the officer had agreed to the terms. It was brilliant.

The entire courtroom knew Bodega was guilty, but the officer had agreed that he was buying the hot dog and that the heroin was free. Nazario had found a loophole, though it was closed right after that case. But Nazario was always one step ahead. So instead of Bodega getting fifteen to twenty for selling drugs, he only got five for possession, then got paroled in three for good behavior. And now, years later, Bodega and Nazario were running an entire neighborhood.

"Where do you work?" Nazario asked me after the old man left.

"Right there, the supermarket. Only till I graduate and then I don't know. I have to find a real job; besides, I have no choice. I got a kid coming."

"The A & P? The one on the same block where the Aguilar public library is? No kidding?"

"Yeah, it's convenient. During lunchtime, I go there to read or study. It's the best library in the city."

"Hey, I should know," Nazario said, "I practically grew up inside that building. My adopted family were librarians and books."

We reached the supermarket. I told Nazario that I could meet Vera either later that day or some other time but I couldn't miss work. Nazario said that was okay and that he would like to talk "bookshop," as he called it, with me maybe even at the Aguilar branch, since he hadn't been inside that building in years.

A few minutes later I punched the clock and checked the schedule. I was penciled in at meat packing. I went to my locker and brought out my green apron along with a stained heavy sweater. I hated meat packing, it smells like what it is, a bunch of frozen dead animal corpses. Your hands get cold even if you wear gloves, and after your day is done you come out with a cold. But I had put on my gloves, sweater, and apron and was ready to get all bloody and smelly when I was called to the manager's office.

"Julio, you're sick, go home," he told me in front of the other employees.

"I'm not sick," I answered.

"Yes. Yes you are." He gave me this meaningful look that told me he didn't want the other employees to think I was getting special treatment. "You're sick. No shape to be in the freezer packing meat."

I got it. I coughed loudly and played it to the fullest.

"With pay, right? I get today off with pay?" I asked.

"No, you know we" — he looked at the other employees' faces — "we don't pay you for sick days."

"Well then, I can hack it. I mean, I'm sick but I can hack it, just put me shelving or something away from the freez—"

"Okay, but just this once," the manager said over the other employees' protests. "New policy. What do you want me to do? I can't have

Julio give everyone the flu. Knock this place right out of business," he said to save face.

I ditched my apron and punched out again.

Outside, when I crossed the street, there was Nazario. Standing straight, hands at his sides and stone cold, he told me, "The manager owes Bodega. We're going to your place. You have to change clothes."

On the way home Nazario asked me what I was studying. I told him. He nodded. Then he asked me, "You ever thought of going to law school when you graduate?"

"Nah, I hate lawyers. No offense."

"That's fine, but consider it. We'll take care of the expenses. We will need people like you in the near future. We will need as many as we can get." It was obvious by now who he meant by *we*. "A single lawyer," Nazario continued, "can steal more money than a hundred men with guns."

"I'm not a thief."

"Everyone's a thief. Crime is a matter of access. The only reason the mugger robs you is because he doesn't have access to the books. If he did, he'd be a lawyer. I'm not sure what you have access to"—he gave me a look as if I was guilty of something I myself was too afraid to say out loud—"but whatever it is that you have access to, that is what you will steal. What you are already stealing, Julio."

"If you see it that way it's cool," I said. "But like my father always said, '*El dinero robado tú te lo gastas con miedo.*' I'd rather make five bucks honestly and spend it knowing it's all mine than fifty and worry about my back."

"Then you don't understand, Julio. See, what Willie and I are trying to do is make sure that you, the future of the neighborhood, doesn't break its back. That this neighborhood isn't lost. Sure, some people are going to get hurt, but that's just the law of averages. Listen to me, Julio." He stopped walking.

"You guys," I said, laughing, continuing to walk, "are crazy, man."

He yelled at me and grabbed my arm, stopping me. "You, Julio, think small! You live small and you'll die small! Always paying rent because you never thought big. Like most of the people in this neighborhood you think that things are impossible!"

"So what? You puttin' down your own people now!" I shouted back and he calmed down and took a deep breath.

"Don't you see that it's always been only about our people," he said calmly. "All I ask is that you walk with me four more blocks north —"

"I thought you said Bodega was meeting me," I protested, preferring to be in Bodega's company than Nazario's. At least with Bodega you knew where you stood.

"Humor me. We don't even have to speak to each other," he said, laughing a bit. "I just want to show you something."

I nodded. The rest of the way neither of us said a word. Those four silent blocks with Nazario lasted an eternity, one of those moments in which you live a lifetime. I tried to think of other things, but all I could think about was why Nazario didn't just leave me alone. He must have something else to tell or show me; he was too practical to take pointless walks.

We stopped at 116th and Third Avenue, in front of what looked like a bodega. It wasn't. Inside that small space were framed gold records and instruments hanging from the walls and the ceiling. It was jam-packed with salsa memorabilia. There were the drumsticks Tito Puente used when he played Carnegie Hall in '72. There were album covers, Joe Cuba's congas, guitar picks, ticket stubs, all from salsa's golden days in the sixties and seventies.

"It's the salsa museum, Julio. The only one in the country," Nazario told me. I was in awe, because I didn't even know it existed. I had lived here all my life and didn't know we had this. I started to read labels of the gold records on the wall: Willie Colón, Hector Lavo, Cheo Feliciano, Celia Cruz, Rubén Blades, the Fania All Stars—all were represented. It was the history of salsa. Nazario pointed. "See that ticket stub? I went to that show. It was at Madison Square Garden, the old one. Great show. I danced salsa all the way home."

"This is awesome, man," I said, and for a moment I forgot about everything and wrapped myself in the glory days of salsa. Back then it was a different dance music than the one in my time. The salsa music was new and always evolving into something else, but it always returned to its *afro-jíbaro-antillano* roots. This place had a deep association with my parents' time, when the neighborhood was still young and full of people and not projects. It was a symbol of past glory, of early migration to the United States and the dreams that people brought over along with the music.

"That conga there belonged to Ray Barretto. Hearing Ray play was like watching Changó, the thunder god who suffered the consequences of playing with fire and became lightning itself—that was Barretto in his heyday. Night after night." Nazario went over to the drum and circled his finger over the skin. For the first time I thought I had seen in his eyes some sort of nostalgic sentiment, a weakness maybe.

"Hey, *no toque!*" the curator of the museum said, joking. Nazario quickly turned around. The two men embraced as if they had known each other for years. The owner was a kind man in his fifties. When Nazario introduced me, he proudly declared, "See, Chino, there's two museums in Spanish Harlem."

"Your daughter," Nazario asked him out of the blue, "did she get in?"

"*Sí, sí.*" They embraced again. They kept talking about the man's daughter, who would soon start med school. The man was thanking Nazario and telling him to thank Bodega for him. Nazario said he would do just that and then told the man he had to go. I shook the man's hand again and followed Nazario. The salsa museum was free, but upon exiting, Nazario put a twenty in the donation box. I had only three dollars and wished I could give more.

"I'll walk you home now," Nazario said, looking straight ahead.

"Sounds good," I said. Somehow that experience had made me like him. A little bit. I still wanted Nazario to go away but I knew he wouldn't, not just yet. I knew he hadn't taken me to the museum just because he'd wanted to show it to me. He'd wanted me to see something else. For me to understand something that escaped me. I tried to think, but I couldn't see what it was. The music of our people? No. Bygone times? Then it hit me. It was the man's daughter.

"The girl who got into med school," I asked Nazario, "she's in Bodega's program?"

"That's right. I was hoping she was around. I wanted her to talk to you."

"About what?" I asked, because I was just catching on that with

Nazario and Bodega you had to see the big picture. Their minds were not nineteen-inch screens but those of the big drive-in movies. They were so ahead in their visions and dreams that they left you behind, with your mouth open, trying to piece it all together.

"Don't you see what we're trying to do?" he said, and this time it was me who stopped walking. I wanted to hear it. "Willie likes financing Latinos who are going to college to study law, medicine, education, business, political science, anything useful. He plans on building a professional class, slated to become his movers and shakers of the future."

I wanted to tell him it was crazy. But then I thought, why not? Why not us? Others have dreams, why not us? It was from that moment on that I realized all these hopes were bigger than me, more important than any one person. If these dreams of theirs would take off, El Barrio would burn like a roman candle, bright and proud for decades. If Spanish Harlem moved up, we would all move up with it.

"Willie plans on building a professional class. One born and bred in Spanish Harlem." So now I knew why he was renovating all those buildings. He planned on housing his people there. "But it goes deeper than that, Julio. It's about upward mobility. It's about education and making yourself better. It's about sacrifice." We started to walk again. He would lecture like he always did, steely but committed. "If someone is a janitor, that's noble, it's a respectable job. But they should make sure their kids grow up to own a cleaning business." It was really an old idea, but never before had I thought that it was possible. With Nazario leading the fight for political, social, and economic power, anything was possible. It was going to be fought by intellect and cunning. Bodega and Nazario had seen what guns could do. They knew you could not attack the Anglo like that. You had to play by his rules and, like him, steal by signing the right papers. Nazario would lead, leaving Bodega to take all the hits, absorb the stigma, because of what he was. It would be Bodega and the likes of Sapo who would have the skeletons in the closet, all so Nazario could help create new hope for the neighborhood.

"This neighborhood will be lost unless we make it ours. Look at Loisaida, that's gone," Nazario said. "All those white yuppies want to live in Manhattan, and they think Spanish Harlem is next for the taking. When they start moving in, we won't be able to compete when it comes to rents, and we'll be left out in the cold. But if we build a strong professional class and accumulate property, we can counter that effect." We were two blocks away from my building. I could see what Nazario was really after. "This is not the sixties. The government isn't pouring any money in here anymore. It'll take some time. But one day we might be strong enough, with enough political clout"—and he pointed at the Johnson Houses—"to knock those projects down." Then he smiled at me as if he had just seen the sunrise for the first time in his life. "And we'll free our island, without bloodshed."

The Fish of Loisaida

I WAS happy when Nazario and I reached my building and even happier when he shook my hand, indicating he was ready to leave.

"Put on your best suit and wait for Willie, okay, Julio?" Nazario said as we stood in front of the entrance. "And I still want to talk. Maybe even meet you in the library." He shook my hand again and crossed the street. I stared at his back as he walked away. A tall gray suit, walking with pride and confidence all around El Barrio. A suit that could stand out and yet blend in with the neighborhood. He was like no one I had ever met. Even Bodega with his street smarts and cunning lacked what Nazario had. The presence that tells the people this man can lead. He was what we all wanted to be like, the Latin professional whom the Anglos feared because he was just as treacherous, just as devious, and he understood power. This was not some docile Latino you could push around. You knew he held aces up his sleeve. The neighborhood might not have trusted Nazario completely, maybe even been a bit afraid of him, but people were more than grateful that he was on their side.

I went inside the building and was a bit nervous about the whole Vera-meeting-Bodega thing, but then again I was also glad it would finally be over. Besides, it beat working, any day.

When the elevator reached my floor and I stepped out, there was Bodega in the hallway. He was dressed in a white suit, looking as immaculate and pure as if he had made an offering to Santa Clara to wear white for her, just for her. But his eyes were bloodshot and he was pacing like a man whose wife is in labor.

"Man, I'm glad yo'r here. Where you been?" He rushed toward me, his face a knot of worry. "You don't think I look too, you know, like I'm tryin' too hard to look fine?" he asked.

"Nah, you look good." We walked inside. Then he looked at me and began to curse.

"*Coño! Coño*, I should have brought a suit for you."

"Hey, I have suits, all right?" I said, a bit insulted. "I came here to change. Your lawyer hit man, Nazario, sprung me out of work and gave me no choice."

"But you do have a good suit? Man, I should've had Nazario get you one." He kept sucking his teeth and saying, *coño, coño.*

"I told you I have good suits, cotton ones," I said, but he began to complain.

"No, no, no, you'll throw her off. See, feel this, feel this." It felt like silk; it was silk.

"Nice." I shrugged.

"See, how's that gonna look, you in cotton and me in silk? She'll think I'm cheap. That I can't buy you, her niece's husband, a suit like mine or worse, that I don't have enough—"

"Relax! Look, you say Vera loves you, right? Not me, right? I can go in shorts and it won't matter." He calmed down a bit, and I went to the bedroom to change. He asked if he could get a drink of water.

"You own the building," I called out. But as I heard the water faucet I had an image, clear as day, of Sapo killing Salazar. I figured that now was a bad time to ask about it. I figured that if Bodega was right and Vera was still in love with him, nothing could ruin his day, so today would be a good time to ask him anything—but if he was wrong about Vera I was going to save the asking for another day. Then I smelled something.

"Wan' a toke?"

"I don't know if that's a good idea, bro. You're gonna go see someone you haven't seen in more than twenty years and you're gonna smoke a joint before you see her?"

"I'm nervous, what the fuck you want me to do?"

"Relax, all right? And you should put that out because the smell stays in your clothes." Bodega promptly threw the joint on the floor and killed it with his shiny shoe.

I went to the bathroom and combed my hair. When I came out Bodega was looking out the window. He was staring absently, as if he was seeing beyond what was there, as if he was back in some other place and time.

I shook him a little bit. He smiled, a bit embarrassed, as if he had been thinking about something sentimental, something weak. Something your friends might make fun of at your expense.

"Ready to go?" He cleared his throat and wiped his eye.

"Yeah, let's go," I said, making believe I had no idea what was in his head.

Outside it was a clear and warm day, one of those days that makes you happy you woke up early and hadn't wasted the morning with sleep and weren't going to kill the day with work. Walking with Bodega toward P.S. 72 on 104th and Lexington was like walking with a ghost that only I could see. Unlike walking with Nazario, when everyone came up and greeted you, saw you in a different light because of the company, with Bodega it was as casual as if you were walking with groceries. Only one man stopped us, and it wasn't because of Bodega.

"*Qué pasa.* My name is Ebarito, I saw you with Mr. Nazario this morning," he said to me. "*Si me haces el favor de decirle gracias por el seguro que me dió.* I want you to know that you are welcome at my social club anytime."

I thanked him.

"And tell Mr. Nazario I owe Willie Bodega." Bodega quickly motioned to me not to say a word. Not to introduce him as Willie Bodega. Ebarito shook my hand, then Bodega's. I gave Ebarito my name and introduced Bodega as Jose Tapia. Ebarito said that my friend Jose was also welcome to drop by his social club. Then he complimented us on our suits, told us we looked like *la aristocracia puertorriqueña.* Bodega found this funny and asked Ebarito for his name again. Bodega made a mental note of it. He was going to reward Ebarito in the near future, I could tell. We kept walking.

"I know what you're thinkin'," Bodega said, "but if you see God he won't seem that powerful anymore." He then licked his lips as he had been doing all morning, shoved his hands in his pockets, and then took them out again. He walked fast and I had to tell him again and again to calm down.

P.S. 72 loomed just ahead, the American flag on its roof wagging in the blue sky. A pompous pigeon, his arrogant chest stuck out like a banker's, sat on top of the flagpole. Then Bodega turned around and said "I'm going back." He said that this was all bullshit and that he had a neighborhood to run and had to create a new future. That he was sorry for putting me through all this bullshit.

"No way, man!" I went after him as he was practically running away from the school. "No, bro, stop!" I caught up to him and held him by the arm. He gave little resistance. He took out a cigarette.

"You've been waiting a long time for this, bro. If anything, at least let's go and meet Vera so you can show her what a mistake she made."

He lit his cigarette and took only one drag before he ground it out.

"Nah, bro, *eso no se queda así*. She made a mistake and she has to know it." He took out another cigarette.

"At least that way you'll get something out of this, bro, b'cause she married that guy for his money."

He lit up and took one drag. Then another. "Thass right. You're right, Chino." He looked at me with bravado, took a third drag, put out the cigarette. "You're right. Let's go see this bitch and show her what a fucken mistake she made. That bitch! That fucken, fucken bitch. Why'd she leave in the first place? She never wanted him, she always wanted me. And now she can't have me. Now she'll fly back to Miami and cry as if the plane was going down."

"Thass right, bro. You're goin' to walk right in there and show her that you had vision." He nodded rapidly.

We started walking toward the school again, like sour-grapes drunks. Bodega was ripping away at Vera, then at women in general, then at Vera's mother, then he was ripping Vera again.

I pretended to agree with everything as if this was new and enlightening.

"I hear you, I hear you."

"Cuz there ain't no difference between a whore who sleeps for money and one that marries for it! Shit!" He then went on about something else, something that only makes sense when you are afraid of death or desperately in love and will say anything to alleviate the terror.

"I hear you, bro."

We got to the school and the guard told us to go to the general office and get visitors' passes. We asked for directions to the auditorium, and when we got there the assembly had already started. The place was full of children and flowers. Kids whispered to one another, fidgeting in those uncomfortable auditorium chairs, kicking the chairs in front of them and rocking back and forth. Up on the small stage, the guests were sitting on yellow school chairs, waiting for their moment to speak. One was a tall woman in a blue dress who could easily have been Blanca twenty years older. I looked at Bodega. His gaze was fixed on her with an intensity that indicated nothing else mattered or existed. If I'd wanted to pick his wallet, I could have. He stared at her as if he was reeling back years, each year a ton of hate mixed with a love that never had had an opportunity to reenter the atmosphere and burn itself out. It was as if Bodega had hit rewind on an ugly romantic scene that should have been shot differently, a scene that, after all these years, after he had played it in his head every day, he was now going to shoot with the ending he had always wanted.

I elbowed him hard.

"Which one's Vera?" I knew but asked anyway. It had to be the woman he was staring at, the one waiting patiently, not showing any discomfort in the delay.

"The one with the blue dress. The one crossing her legs. Still has the legs, the legs never left her," he answered, continuing to gaze at her.

And then from behind the curtains came a figure looking like he wasn't just sorry he was late but also as if he hadn't done his homework. Nazario sat down and took his place among the guests.

That's when it hit me. All this time, I had been set up.

It had been Bodega who had donated the money to Vera's old school so they could call her up from Miami and invite her as their guest. I'm not sure he even knew they were going to name the auditorium after her but it didn't matter because it got him the results he wanted.

Nazario had probably handled all the paperwork and concealed where the money really came from. Nazario must have made some sort of dizzy razzmatazz nonsense about the donation being an anonymous gift but I'm sure he gave the school enough information to know it was Vera. Or maybe Nazario just skipped all that shit and went straight to the superintendent of District 4 with an offer he couldn't refuse. One thing was sure, I was there for one reason and one reason only, so Bodega could have one of Vera's relatives there next to him. Bodega probably had no clue how to reach Blanca or Negra and so he reached me. He reached me and he could now pass himself off as family.

The fact was that Bodega could have easily found Vera. He could have gotten Nazario to hire the best private investigator in the city and traced her all the way to Florida. But then what? Blood was thicker than water and that's what he wanted, blood. Family is family for Latinos: a cousin, no matter if it's third or fourth or seventh, is still a cousin, and nothing can cut that—regardless of how far away the family member is; he or she is part of that family. With me and Blanca he had an ace in the hole. He had helped himself and along the way had also helped Vera's family by giving her pregnant niece and her husband a nice apartment. And I had walked right into it.

At that moment I didn't like him. He used people and used his money to move them by remote control. He had used Blanca without Blanca even knowing it and I had been the one that had gotten us involved in all this. I was going to go home and tell her everything that I knew—except for the stuff about Sapo, because I knew Blanca would want me to go to the police.

Of course, once Blanca knew who owned the building, and how he got the money to buy and fix it up, she'd want to move out. I didn't want to move. It was the best living situation we had ever had and it was more than affordable, it was downright cheap. Besides, the baby was due to arrive by late summer and we needed that extra space, that extra room. Also, regardless of Bodega's activities, he was fixing up the neighborhood. For the first time in my life I had seen scaffolding all over Spanish Harlem. In almost every part of the neighborhood, some building was being renovated. And he was creating this professional class of his. Paying people's tuition in hopes of building a better future.

No, I thought, with Bodega all you could hope for is that the good would outweigh the bad. I decided not to tell Blanca and just leave Bodega stranded in a school auditorium.

So as Bodega and I were standing against the back of P.S. 72's auditorium, I pointed at Vera.

"Well, there she is. That's her, right? So I did my part. I'm out." I opened the large door of the auditorium and walked into the hallway. Bodega broke away from wherever he was at in his mind, peeled his eyes off Vera, and chased after me.

"Where you going?" He sounded surprised, as if I had agreed beforehand to stay. As if my staying was part of the deal.

"Hey, man, you said for me to find Vera, and I did. She's right there and now I'm gone and we're even, right? I'm your tenant, you'll have my rent on time, and thass it." I began to walk away. Bodega followed me.

"Chino, you can't leave. You have to be there with me, bro. Come on, don't be like that." I was taken back to the time when I first met Bodega. When he had talked all that tough stuff and I had turned him down, his face had collapsed. This was the same face. Just like that first time, Bodega needed something from me and didn't know how to ask.

"Nah, I got you what you wanted. If you want me to stay with you," I said, "you got to level with me."

He looked at my face carefully. He understood everything. Bodega gestured for us to go outside, and I silently followed him to the playground. The assembly was going to go on for at least another half hour. He picked an isolated but open space under a bent basketball rim, beside a broken water fountain. He faced the school doors.

"If those doors open we have to go back inside, all right?" he said.

"Where's Sapo?" I dodged the question because I wasn't planning on going back in.

"Sapito is hidin'." It wasn't a surprise.

"Why'd you have Salazar killed?"

"Because Salazar was crooked."

"But a few weeks ago I heard Nazario tell you he didn't take your money when you offered it to him."

"Thass right, he didn't, because he already belonged to someone else."

"Sapo is my *pana*. If he's in trouble—"

"Wha'? You think I'm gonna let Sapo fry? Let me tell you, Salazar was a worthless piece of shit who didn't even make a deal with his own people. He got what was co   in'."

"Shit, bro, just like that?"

"Yeah, just like that. J   t when I'm almost there, Chino, just when . . . this Salazar fuck   is to make static."

"You killed that guy, bro   I looked at the sun as if I wanted to punish my eyes. "I mean, when   u sell that stuff and someone buys it and dies, that's one thing. I m   in, it was his choice to go and buy it, but actually killing someone—"

"Yeah, I did." Bodega l   ked at the doors. "It wasn't the first. And let me tell you cuz I feel I   e it to you. Let me tell you why. B'cause Salazar belonged to Aaro   Fischman."

"Who?"

"He is this fucken guy   ney call the Fish of Loisaida. I been dealin' with that bastard for yea   now and I always do whass right. I've told him, 'This is my neigh   rhood and the Lower East Side is yours.' There's enough junkies   nd gamblers to go around, right? And the mutherfuckah agrees. I   y, 'No one wants a war.' With a war everyone loses money and things   t sloppy. So I back away and he backs away. Then out of the blue co   ies this reporter. This Alberto Salazar. I think I got problems becaus   he's a good man. Then Nazario finds out Salazar made a deal   ith Fischman. He's gonna get all this shit together on me, ignore Fischman. Salazar was almost there, too. He only needed a few more pieces, and he would have called all this atten-tion to me."

"No way. You think the cops don't already know what you're doing?"

"They might be sniffin', they ain't that stupid. They got a little piece of it too. But everything is still layin' low. No noise, and as long as there's no noise, cops don't care. But if the media makes a big deal out of it then the cops look bad. They'll have ta come after me. That's what Salazar was planning on, exposing me for buying buildings with so-called dirty money. I couldn't let that happen." He kicked the ground as if it were dirt and not concrete. "Thass the way it works, Chino. Then I have to deal with the police and that would weaken me. And with me out of the way Fischman would move in on my neighborhood. I got tired of that bastard. Salazar wanted to be the hero around here. Well, I sent Sapito to make calcium of him and I'll deal with Fischman later."

"Shit, you gonna kill that other guy too?" Most practical people would have cut the cord right there, would have broken away from Bodega like a rancher shoots a horse with a broken leg. But I didn't. I didn't want Sapo in jail, that was part of it. And though I didn't want to admit it, secretly I was rooting for Bodega. I had been all along.

"I don't know yet," Bodega said. "I don't wanna to do anythin' hasty. Maybe Nazario can still talk. Find another solution. That fuck Fischman did some work with this big Italian in Queens, can't just get rid of him like that. But I'm not going to worry about that right now," he said, glancing at the school doors.

"Right now, Chino, all I'm askin' is for you to help me find some sort of happiness. Remember when I told you at the museum that when Vera arrived I was going to ask somethin' else from you?"

I nodded.

"Well, I'm askin', all right. I don't like people to think I'm weak, because I'm not. Never been. But you, Chino, if yo'r as smart as I think you are, if you've studied your history, you would know that the most powerful men have turned to garbage, *basura*, when they have fallen in love. All of them." He got defensive. And because his everyday speech didn't have any diplomacy, he defended his case the way he always did.

"Chino, bro, last week I saw a special on channel thirteen about Napoleon. And when that nigga was about to lose Egypt, you know what he was really afraid of? Losing Josephine." He looked at my face, hoping I wasn't going to make fun of him. "See, Chino, he was far away and Josephine was rumored to be two-timing him with some other guy. While he was fighting to expand her empire she was like . . . like . . . you know what I'm sayin'?"

"What're you gonna do about Sapo?" I hadn't seen the special and didn't care much about Napoleon.

The school doors opened. Bodega shot me a desperate look.

"You gonna get Sapo off somehow, right?"

"I'll help Sapo. Nazario is workin' on it. Wha'? You think this Vera situation has clouded my mind? Nah, you wrong. I love that woman but it was me who sent Sapo. It will be me who will bring him out."

"So, you gonna get Sapo off?"

"Of course. I don't know how, but you have my word."

"I have your word, then?"

"My word is bond."

"All right. So tell me what it is you want me to do." Now Bodega smiled as if he had swallowed the canary, but there was still something childlike in his look.

"I owe you, Chino, I owe you."

"Yeah, yeah. Just tell me what you want me to say to Vera."

"See that limo parked over there?" He pointed. I didn't turn my head but could see it out of the corner of my eye. "I want you to go over and tell—" He caught himself. If he and I were now family, he shouldn't give me orders anymore. "Could you please, my main-mellow-man." He laughed and put out his hand for me to give him five. I skinned it but I didn't feel like laughing. "Just go tell Vera you are married to her niece Nancy, and that your landlord, William Irizarry, Izzy to her, is waiting for her inside that big, black, very expensive car ovah there."

A Diamond as
Big as the Palladium

BLANCA'S aunt Vera seemed born to money. Her gestures, her voice, her social graces had been so well studied and cultivated that she could have fooled anyone who wasn't familiar with her past. With her light skin, semiblond hair, pale seagull blue eyes, she could easily pass herself off as something other than a woman born and raised in East Harlem. She spoke as if she had spent her formative years in some boarding school, walking around with a big-lettered sweater tied around her shoulders.

Actually, Vera had barely graduated from Norman Thomas High School and hadn't set foot in a building of higher education since. Yet she had successfully sold the notion to her circle in Miami that she was a Barnard girl. Although she had told her Florida friends she was coming to New York City because she had done the "trendy" thing of donating money to an inner-city school, she really didn't know how the donation had been made. She assumed that her accountant must have done it to get her a tax break. What did she care? But she had to come alone, otherwise her friends would discover her true origins.

She was returning to her old neighborhood to gloat, to show her family what she had made of herself. Yes, Vera had reinvented herself. But unlike William Carlos Irizarry, now Willie Bodega, Veronica

Linda Saldivia didn't want to be considered Puerto Rican. Hence the name Vera.

The rich Cuban family Vera had married into still kept the pink slips of their nationalized lands in Cuba, along with high hopes of reclaiming them once Castro was ousted or finally, finally died. Vera was no longer a Saldivia but a Vidal, and with that misleading last name she could fool anyone into thinking she was some middle-aged Anglo woman who had a taste for shopping on Fifth Avenue, threw dinner parties, and loved expensive jewelry.

I'm not a person who likes to judge why people fall madly in love with some types of people because I don't believe such things can be explained. It's like chemistry, some elements are attracted to each other and it doesn't matter that they can explode. It's just the way it works.

·

SO THAT day, I did as Bodega pleaded. I walked over to Vera, who was outside talking with some teacher. Her posture was ramrod straight; her back at a perfect right angle with the ground. When she talked, it was in the prim and proper voice of someone who understands flower shows and country homes. And when she'd say something she thought clever, she would laugh this phony laugh like she was doing you a favor.

"Julio?" Nazario said, surprised to see me. He appeared out of nowhere and stopped me just as I was about to introduce myself to Vera. He saved me the bother.

"This is Julio Mercado. He's in college now and I'm hoping he will continue on to law school," Nazario informed Vera. Closer, I could see that Vera's face had the resonance of a former highly prized beauty. Years ago the entire neighborhood must have gone mad for her. I thought of Blanca; I had always believed she'd become even more beautiful when she got older, that her features—eyes, hair, cheekbones, her entire body—having traveled for years would settle down like some quiet, transparent stream. I would still be there with her and, no matter what pictures of her when young would remind me of, I'd still love her and never trade the history we had together.

"It's a pleasure," I said. "Actually, we're related." She responded like someone who instead of saying thanks when being served by a waiter only lowers her eyes.

"Are we?" Her delicate voice sounded like crystal.

"Yes, I'm married to Marisol's daughter Nancy."

"Isn't that wonderful!" she exclaimed. "Marisol's daughter all grown up and married." She drew near me and gave me a weak hug.

"Actually, there is someone—" but I was interrupted by a teacher who wanted to shake Vera's hand. It was recess, and the children had started pouring out to go play in the schoolyard. I saw Nazario leave to speak with a heavyset woman who looked like the principal. Then Nazario broke off his conversation and walked back to join us. After excusing himself, he asked Vera if she needed a cab back to her hotel. I knew this was my cue to usher Vera to the limo where Bodega waited.

"Actually, there is someone here that will drive you," I said.

"Oh no, no, I'll just find a cab. Don't bother yourself on—" and then her face went white and I turned around to see what had scared her.

"William?" she whispered. Bodega had gotten out of the car and was walking straight toward us.

"Veronica." He looked miserable. His hands were in his pockets, his shirt collar soaked with sweat. His face looked as if he were dying. Vera swallowed hard then drew herself up to her full height and regained her composure.

"Well, it's absolutely wonderful to see you, William. How . . . how . . . how . . . are the Lords?" I was happy to see her stumble. Nazario had vanished and the three of us were left there, standing among the schoolchildren.

"The wha'?" Bodega got closer to her, cupping his ear.

"Your friends, the Lords," she said artificially as if she had gone back to the data banks of her memory and could only come up with that reference. Bodega jerked his head back.

"Oh, yeah, the Lords, yes, yes," he said without really answering her. For a few seconds no one said anything.

"Let's take a ride," I said to break the horrible tension.

"Yes, yes, let's go around the city," Bodega quickly agreed, and to my surprise, Vera just followed him. When she saw the car her eyebrows shot up.

"It's not rented," Bodega blurted out. "I . . . I don't use it much, you know. I still walk almost everywhere."

"Is this really your automobile, William?" Vera seemed impressed and Bodega took this as a triumph. His chest was a peacock's. Vera turned her face toward me. "We haven't seen each other for over twenty years."

"Twenty-one years, three months, fourteen days," Bodega said. And then Vera laughed. And with that laugh, Bodega was happy. The driver ushered us all into the car. When the doors were shut, the coolness of the air-conditioned limo was a relief but the stillness and silence made it possible for me to imagine I could hear Bodega's heartbeat.

"I have something to show you." His voice shook.

"I'm more than happy to see it," she said.

"It's not Miami, Veronica, but—"

She laughed that laugh again. "I really hate Miami, William. Despise it with a passion. Everything is so pink and blue."

Bodega smiled as if he had won another small battle. He must have believed that if he kept winning these tiny skirmishes, victory would eventually be his. After that there was a long silence, so I thought I'd fill it in.

"I didn't like Miami either," I said. "I went to visit friends of mine, Ariel and Naomi, and man, that place was a mall wasteland. There was nothing to do." That wasn't true. I had actually had a good time in Miami.

The car pulled up in front of my apartment building on 111th between Lexington and Park. Bodega pressed a button and the tinted window slid robotically down to frame the five newly renovated tenements.

"I own those and others like those, all around the neighborhood." Her eyes told him she didn't understand what he meant. "I'm in real estate."

"Are those really yours?" She leaned her body toward the window to take in the entire view. Her face glowed. "And you have others, you say?" She drew her body back and looked at me for confirmation.

"He's my landlord." I began. "He owns—"

"No, they are not mine," Bodega interrupted. "Veronica, they are for you. They've always been for you. I knew you'd come back some day and I wanted you to come back to something different." She stared at him blankly as the chauffeur opened the door. He extended his hand to Vera, who had to take her eyes off Bodega's eyes long enough to get out of the car. She stepped out and we followed. Bodega looked around and took a deep breath as if he were smelling a rose rather than Spanish Harlem air.

"I have something else to show you." Bodega led us to a newly reno-vated brownstone. There was an art gallery on the first floor, and the three of us stepped inside.

"You like art, right, Veronica?"

"Yes."

"I saw a special on channel thirteen about that big museum in Moscow."

"You still watch public television, William?" She laughed and reached her hand to Bodega, who clasped it like a drowning man would a life raft.

"Well, I remember you watched some of those shows too," he said, smiling and pointing a finger at her as if he knew something she had forgotten.

"Yes, I'm afraid I did," she confessed, nodding.

"Anyway, I saw a special on that big museum in Moscow."

"Which one?" Vera asked.

"The big one," he said.

"You mean the Hermitage?"

"Yeah, that one," he said, and snapped his fingers because he was embarrassed about his pronunciation and didn't want to repeat the name. "Yeah, the same exact one. Anyway, I learned that during the Russian Revolution, Lenin sent soldiers to look after the museum so that looters wouldn't rob the place. That was something. He didn't care about the czar's palace. Looters were like all over the palace stealing sil-verware and stuff but he didn't want the Russian people to lose their art. Wasn't that something?" he asked her. She just nodded her head and looked dutifully impressed.

"The second, third, and fourth floors are where the artists live," he said.

"William, you, a patron? That's . . . That's . . ." She couldn't find the words to describe her disbelief.

"That's right," he said, liking the sound of it. "I'm a patron. This gallery is for painters from the neighborhood. It's the neighborhood's art. I got the idea from Taller Boricua," he said proudly.

"You're still the same, William. Still the idealist, eh?" Holding hands, they began to swing them together, slowly, not saying anything.

"Well, it was nice meeting you," I said, thinking it was better to leave them alone. "I'll tell Nancy that you're in town. Maybe the two of you could see each other before you leave."

"Yes, I would like that very much. I held her once when she was a child." She extended her free hand toward me and gave me a limp handshake. Her blue eyes held mine for a second. Then I extended my hand to Bodega, who all of a sudden looked worried. I knew he wanted to tell me something, but when he didn't utter a sound, I walked out.

"Wait, I have to speak with you!" He let go of Vera's hand with no apologies and followed me outside. For the first time since encountering Vera, Bodega acknowledged my existence. All this time he hadn't taken his eyes off her and had treated me like I was a dust particle. I hadn't really cared much about that, though it was bad manners.

"Where you going?" he whispered as if he didn't want Vera to hear him, which was impossible because she was still inside.

"I live right there," I said, pointing.

"You can't just leave me, that's not cool." He was sweating again, like a guilty suspect in a lineup.

"What's not cool is you leaving Vera all alone in the art gallery. That's what's not cool, and you know wha'—"

"Don't talk so loud," he interrupted.

"Look, man, Vera is as nervous as you. I could hear her heart beat inside the car," I lied.

"Her heartbeat? You heard her heartbeat? You sure?"

"Yeah, *pana*, she's just as nervous as you. So go back inside there and tell her exactly what you always wanted to."

He didn't say anything to me, just looked down at the pavement, nodded, and walked back to the gallery, back to Vera.

I went inside my building and took the elevator up. When I got to my apartment, I took off my suit and fell asleep. I don't know when it happened, how long I was out, but a loud knock interrupted my sleep. At first I thought I was dreaming. But when my eyes opened and I saw the ceiling, I knew for sure I was awake. I went to open the door.

"Happy New Year, Julio!" Vera yelled, all silly and sloppy. There was a champagne bottle in her hand.

"You're being drafted. Here." Bodega pushed another Dom Pérignon to my chest. "It's a new year. It's a new life."

"Oh, let's go to Central Park, Izzy. I miss Central Park. You will join us, won't you, Julio?"

"Well, I have a class later tonight and was hoping to get some sleep—"

"Nah, you coming with us," Bodega interrupted. "You'll get enough sleep when yo'r dead."

"I guess things went well," I muttered to myself.

"Is my niece home? I would like to see her. Besides, there's enough champagne for all the Saldivias, isn't there, Izzy?" She gulped it down so fast that some came streaming out of the side of her mouth. I wanted to tell her that I wasn't a Saldivia, I was a Mercado, and that Blanca was now a Mercado too, but then I thought that was just stupid pride, so I stayed quiet.

"Champagne for all the Saldivias, right, Izzy?" she repeated, laughing. Bodega laughed with her.

"A warehouseful, Veronica." Then to me, "*Pana*, when you going to open that bottle?"

"I don't know," I said, tilting the bottle a bit, pretending to study the label. Not that I would know what I was reading, all bottles of champagne are the same to me.

"Um, Nancy is at work and she's pregnant so I—"

"Pregnant! My niece is pregnant! Now that calls for more champagne. You tell her I must see her. I'm dying to see her." She leaned against the hallway and rocked her head back, lifted her bottle, and served herself a few streams. "Dying to see her," she gasped, like an actor who doesn't know a subtle emotion.

"Come on, Chino," Bodega urged. His tie was loose and his shirt was wrinkled. Vera's dress was in worse shape. And her mascara had smeared completely, as if she had been crying.

"Chino?" She laughed that laugh again. "They call you Chino? My niece is married to a Chino? *Que bonito y pronto van a tener un chinito.*" She laughed, a little hysterically. "*Un chinito, qué lindo,* get it?" It was the first time I heard her speak Spanish. It sounded as natural as her English. Like she was two people.

"Come with us, bro!" Bodega wrapped an arm around my shoulder.

"Yes, do come," Vera interjected.

"Where you guys going again, Central Park?" I didn't want to go but had no way of getting rid of them. I wanted to ask them how old they were, just out of spite. But then I thought that people in love should act however they want. Especially Bodega and Vera, who I realized just then were from a different time.

I pictured Bodega back in those days so young, flying with invisible wings. Thinking that freeing an island from U.S. control could be done with passion and intellect. I pictured Bodega gazing into the eyes of the teenaged Veronica and telling her that nothing could be better than the two of them just lying in the Central Park grass, holding each other and merely existing. I pictured Veronica going home to meet her friends on the stoop to talk about her liberator, this Izzy. Her liberator who was first going to free her from her mother, then free Puerto Rico, and later they would both sail back to America like conquistadors in reverse. They would arrive in New York Harbor and Latinos from all five boroughs would be there to greet them. I pictured her telling all this to her friends until they were so sick and tired of it that Veronica herself began to question her liberator until finally the day arrived when she gave Bodega the ultimatum, the Young Lords or her.

"Yes, Central Park sounds good, and then maybe to the Palladium later tonight, Izzy?" She whispered the last part.

"Wherever you want to go," Bodega told her, and then took a swig. "Just imagine it and I will take you there."

Vera was right. Bodega was still the same, believing he could recapture what had been lost, stolen, or denied to him and his people. As if the past was recyclable and all he had to do was collect enough cans to make a fortune and make another start. When they arrived at my place plastered, I felt happy for them. Especially for Bodega. His cellular phone, which must have been tucked somewhere in his blazer, kept ringing but he never heard it. He was living in a universe of two, feeling invulnerable.

"I hope you guys know that the Palladium doesn't exist anymore. They tore it down." I had no idea why I said that to them. It was the stupidest thing to have said, and considering I was the only sober one I should have been the one with insight.

"Oh, pooh," Vera pouted, and then got happy again. "Let's just go, go, go anywhere and do silly things and drink a little more and I want you to teach me how to smoke a joint. You never taught me how to smoke a joint, Izzy. You said you were going to teach me how to roll and smoke but you always put it off."

"I'm sorry, I was stupid back then, I thought that women shouldn't smoke joints." When he said this her eyes lit up.

"Do you have guns, Izzy?" A spark of mischievousness appeared in her eyes.

"Guns?" Bodega was lost. "What about guns?"

"I want to learn how to fire a gun," she said.

"Why?"

"I always wanted to. Like wanting to roll a joint."

Bodega smiled as if this was a part of Vera's street education that had been denied her. A piece of her being that had been dormant all these years and it would be he who would revive it.

"I always wanted to," she repeated. "And now I'm back."

"Yes, now you're back," he said, and for the first time they stopped talking and just stared at each other.

"Yes, now I'm back," she said softly, and then took off her engagement ring. A big beautiful rock that you needed to wear shades to look at. A glare that blinded you and brought visions of sunsets and golden sands. "Keep it," she said, handing it to me. My heart jumped.

"I can't take this," I said to her, knowing full well I could. The ring was still warm from the heat of her hand. All I knew was I had never held anything that expensive in my life.

"I don't want it. I never did," she said, her eyes still on Bodega.

"Take it!" Bodega said to me. "I'll buy her one bigger than that. One with a diamond as big as the Palladium."

They stood there facing each other and for a second I thought they had reached that stage of intoxication where silliness gives way to melancholy and self-pity. When everything and nothing brings you sadness. They embraced and I thought the weeping would start. But then they broke apart and started to walk away from me as if I had never been there. They walked down the stairs holding hands, taking gulps of champagne, and singing, *"En mi casa toman Bustelo! En mi casa toman Bustelo!"* They sang, drank, laughed, and sang some more.

The War Was in Full Bloom

AFTER Bodega and Vera left I went back to bed. All I can remember of the rest of the afternoon was waking with Blanca next to me. She had arrived home tired, hadn't even bothered to take her clothes off, and flopped down on the bed. Blanca is not a light sleeper, so I got up thinking I didn't have to be very quiet.

"What's that bottle of champagne doing in the kitchen?" she mumbled.

"Wha'?"

"The champagne. What's it doing in the kitchen?" I told her. "When did she arrive?" I told her that, too. "Who's this Izzy?" With my help she remembered. "Oh, that's the guy she was going to marry but didn't." Her voice conveyed complete exhaustion. She shifted her body into a more comfortable position. I was happy that she didn't really care and happier still that I had not used Bodega's name but rather his old one, Izzy, keeping her from making a connection.

I went to the living room, opened the window, and took the ring that Vera had given me out of my pocket. It was as I remembered it when she'd placed it on my palm; just as radiant, golden, and heavy. The inside was engraved *For My Wife, Veronica.* Not anymore, I whispered to myself. This is my wife's now.

Then I thought, no woman wants another woman's ring. But the diamond was huge, so that took care of that. But then Blanca would read the engraving and know whose it was, so that was a problem. What about sending it to an engraver to scrape the inside, get rid of the dedication? But Blanca would still ask me how I'd got it. I found it? Nah. So that left me with the truth. The truth was all I had and Blanca believed in the truth. To her the truth would set me free. I hoped that it would at least let us keep the ring. So I waited for Blanca to really wake up. When she opened her eyes, I showed her the ring.

"We have to give it back!" she said without hesitating.

"She doesn't want it."

"They were drunk, Julio. It's the right thing to do."

"Look, your aunt never wanted to marry this guy," I said as Blanca held the ring up to the light.

"She loves this Izzy guy. Always has. You should have seen them, they were like kids." Blanca stared at the ring. She liked it, but her conscience was a strong judge. I wanted her to have it, so I lobbied as hard as I could.

"No one will know."

"God will know," she said, taking her eyes off the ring to glare at me as if I had personally ripped the ring off God's finger.

"Yes, but He knows everything, so why even bother? No disrespect, but since He knows everything, even the outcome of our lives, why even have Him be an ingredient in this discussion? Look, she gave it to me. It's like throwing it away and me finding it. Can that be bad?"

"Yes, you're right, let's leave God out of this because you know nothing about God. And we didn't find it," she said, clamping her lips together firmly. "If my aunt doesn't want the ring, the right thing to do is to give it back to the man who bought it for her."

"Why!"

"Because it's his ring."

"Not if he gave it to her. If he gave it to her, that makes it her ring and if it's her ring she has the right to give it to whoever she wants."

"This is wrong, Julio." Blanca gave me back the ring. "Return it."

"NO! I'm keeping it. If you don't want it then I'm pawning it. We have at least four or five months' rent here."

"Give it back. He gave it to her as part of a promise. She broke that promise so she has to give it back!"

"Blanca, come on—"

"I'm not going to be a part of this, Julio. Pastor Miguel Vasquez and Claudia come on Friday . . ." That did it. That day I said things I shouldn't have ever said, or at least not the way I did.

"You know, Blanca, you really light me up when you get this way. You constantly knock me about being sexist and whine that all Latin men have some sort of sexism in them and that you feel as if your intelligence is being ignored when I do certain things, even though they are for the good of the family, may I add—"

"Julio—"

"No, let me finish. Then you come up with this shit about sin and your church. And see, Blanca, you can't fully believe in that book"—I pointed to the bookshelf where Blanca kept her Bibles—"because it's the most sexist book ever written. Yet you get on my ass and say I disrespect you when I sin, when I do things that I shouldn't do, like when I smoke a joint here and there, when I want to keep a ring that was given to me, but"—I was on a roll—"when you go to church you get disrespected all the time. The women are treated as if they were just there to glorify their husbands, their children, and their pastor." And with that remark, I saw Negra in Blanca's eyes. I looked around for things she might throw at me.

"You know nothing!" she erupted. "Let me tell you, Julio, just because I believe in God doesn't make me a weak woman! My mother was strong. She paid the bills, she made the decisions, she fixed up the house, and she still went to church."

"Oh please, Blanca, your mother never had your education. Even her sister Veronica only got lucky and married well, in terms of money, that is. But if they'd had your education maybe they'd have done other things with their lives. You are going to be your family's first college graduate and you know things they don't. You were influenced by ideas your mother never knew existed. When you complain that you're gonna feel awkward graduating with a big belly, I know what you really mean. You mean people are gonna think, 'She may be smart, but she was stupid enough to get herself knocked up.' But when you go to church it all changes. They like you pregnant and you like them to like you pregnant." Blanca just smirked, crossed her arms, and looked at me with the confidence of someone who had plenty of ammunition for a counterattack.

"*Qué bonito,* eh. *Qué bonito.* You are lecturing me about what it is to be a woman balancing her intellect and her faith. When all you really want is to keep some stupid ring for the cash."

"It's not just about a ring, Blanca. You get mad at me for, as you put it, leaving you in the dark. But you know I read that entire Bible and rarely did any of the men tell their wives what they were going to do, they just went and did it. *That's* the book you live by. Me, I know that's wrong. I know I should tell you things because I know you can help me. I know that you're good for me. And I know you're smarter than me." She raised an eyebrow. "I mean it, Blanca. You're smarter. But at times I think that the things I'm going to tell you will clash with that book and so it's better not to tell you. Either way, I lose." I wanted to go for broke and tell her other things. Like, I knew who killed that reporter. But I just couldn't. She would send Sapo to jail and maybe leave anyway.

"Blanca, why does me becoming Pentecostal have any bearing on you getting your privileges back? On you playing the tambourine in front of the congregation? Why do they look at me and my faults and not you and your merits?"

"Because it was my decision to marry you. Therefore I am responsible. It makes sense. Listen, if I'd cared more about playing the tambourine in front of the congregation than for you I would've never married you. I would have married a believer. But I didn't, right? I married you. I know that the pastor can be wrong at times. The pastor makes mistakes. But God doesn't. And He knows that I care for you, and if it was wrong to have married you then I just hope His mercy is truly bottomless. There is no sin that can't be forgiven."

"Never mind, I don't want to talk to you when you start preaching." I started getting my books ready for that night's class. There was a small silence. After I packed my knapsack, Blanca stepped in front of me. She crossed her arms again.

"I saw Negra today."

"So what? Look, don't you have class tonight?"

"She was beat up pretty bad."

"Victor?"

"Yes."

I wasn't surprised. "Hey, Blanca, I got my own marital problems—"

"Stop it! Just listen! She's in the hospital and she told me to tell you to get in touch with someone named Bodega." My heart jumped. I stopped what I was doing and looked Blanca in the eyes. I wondered what Negra had told her. "She said that you would know this Bodega. And that this Bodega would take care of Victor, because he owes you. And you owe Negra."

Have you ever had that feeling, like when you were a kid and had played hooky all last week and thought you had gotten away with it, and then at the most pedestrian of times, let's say when you are making a peanut butter and jelly sandwich or just watching TV, your father comes with a letter from school in one hand and his belt in the other. And your head feels like it's on fire and your mouth feels as dry as a saltine.

"I know something is wrong, Julio." Blanca was calm. Blanca was always calm, especially when she had the upper hand. Her eyes would be steady and her face expressionless. Only her lips would move when she needed to talk. "Is there something you want to tell me, Julio?"

"You know those two, Blanca. They're schizo. One day they're like Punch and Judy and the next they're Romeo and—"

"Bodega," she said. "That was the man Enrique took you to see that night. And don't you lie to me. I've heard his name too many times since then. They say he owns these buildings. They also say other things about him. Some good, some bad."

"Yeah, I heard them too, so what?" I brushed past Blanca to make believe I was going to get something from the fridge.

She followed me. "What do you have to do with him?"

"Nothing." I opened the fridge but there was nothing in it I wanted. I closed it and there was Blanca in front of me. "I've got nothing to do with him."

"You sure?" Arms folded, she moved in closer and pinned me

against the fridge. Her face was right there and she must have seen my pupils grow small.

"Nothing. Other than we have to pay him rent," I said, and moved my body away from her. Blanca cocked her head slightly, making a mental note of this.

"Julio, tell me whatever it is that you are doing."

"Negra is crazy! Victor is crazy too!" I lost it and began to shout at Blanca. "And you're crazy for even listening to her!"

"This isn't about Negra, it's about you," Blanca said, raising her voice and poking a finger at my chest after every syllable. "It's about you and what you're not telling me."

"Aren't you pregnant? God, that kid must have a headache."

Blanca trailed me around the apartment. "This has nothing to do with Negra. I don't want us to get involved in Negra's marital affairs. This has nothing to do with them. It has to do with you hiding things from me about this guy, Bodega, whoever he is. This is what it's all about, you hiding things. It's not about church or God or sexism or whatever it is you want to bring up in this fight. It's about you"—she poked my chest again—"hiding things from me."

"All right, you win! You want to know everything," I said, holding up the ring. "You win! You win, Blanca. When I give this back to your aunt you just come with me, cuz he'll be there."

"Who'll be there?"

"Bodega. Thass who. He is this Izzy, the same guy your aunt really wanted to marry. And if you want to ask him anything, anything, any damned thing, then you go ahead." Blanca fell silent.

That was the day I knew Blanca would leave if she found out all that had been happening. So I had no choice but to throw Bodega at her, knowing he wouldn't tell her everything and it was just as well. Stupidly, I was hoping for the best. As if things left alone can fix themselves. I hoped things would bury themselves, like reverse evolution, creation going backward. I hoped that everything would just take care of itself, that the hurtful things Blanca and I had said would be forgotten when the baby came along. The baby would make us allies again because the baby was more important than either of us and we had to be together to fight all those horrible things the world had in store for our kid.

Afterward, after the yelling, the apartment took on a sinister hue. Blanca did everything in her power not to speak to me and I did the same. When we both needed the bathroom we had to say a few words to each other. Small, polite words that meant no more than when you brushed a stranger in the street and apologized.

I walked out of the apartment fed up with all of them: Blanca, Negra, Victor, Bodega, Vera. All of them.

AFTER CLASS I decided to wander around the neighborhood and look for Sapo's car. I didn't see it and asked around. No one seemed to know anything. I had to leave it alone because it was obvious something was being covered up and I didn't want to look like some idiot who didn't get the picture. So that night, I kept walking amid sounds of fire engines and the smell of smoke. But the night sky looked calm and the concrete beneath me was no different than before, covered with gum wrappers, tinfoil, plastic bags, and other garbage. It was a good night to walk and think. What worried me was Negra. I needed to talk to her about Bodega. I needed to find out what Negra knew about Salazar. Because if Negra knew everything, I didn't want her telling Blanca. Unlike Negra, Blanca would go to the police and then they'd be closer to Sapo.

I really didn't want to ask Negra why Victor had beaten her up; I wasn't their marriage counselor. And there was no way I was going to ask Bodega to beat Victor up. I had my problems, Negra had hers, Bodega had his.

But it was too late for visiting hours at Metropolitan Hospital, so my talk with Negra would have to wait for another day.

I didn't want to go home with Blanca still angry at me. I decided that just this once, I would go and meet her at her church. Maybe that would lighten her up, get me back on her good side.

So I ate a slice and killed some time reading until it was time for church.

LA CASA Bethel Pentecostal, Blanca's church, was filled to capacity that night. Many Pentecostals from neighboring temples had come to see and hear for themselves the seventeen-year-old anointed, Roberto Vega. He who was supposedly anointed by God and would rule with Christ for a thousand years. I couldn't have picked a better night to show up and make up with Blanca. I arrived a bit late, but when I went inside the temple, anyone that caught my eye smiled knowingly at me, as if they were saving me. They were always looking out for new converts. Knowing I was Blanca's husband, one brother ushered me to the row where she was sitting. Blanca was really into the sermon, and only when she saw it was me sitting next to her did she smile and squeeze my hand. She quietly introduced me to the stocky, short woman with beautiful black hair sitting on the other side of her. It was Claudia, the girl from Colombia that Blanca was trying to help. After that, Blanca just held my hand and her eyes returned to the figure standing alone behind a lectern on the platform.

"There was once a slave girl," the tall, handsome, and very young Roberto Vega said calmly in Spanish. "And she was bought at a huge price by a king who transformed her into a princess, *me oyen*? And she was given laws and riches, *me oyen*? And out of all the princesses she was the most beautiful because her king blessed her, *me oyen*? And he treated her with respect, kindness, and love." Someone yelled "Alleluia!" "He treated her like she was his flesh. Like she was gold, silver, and jewels. *Me oyen? Ustedes me oyen?*" Yes, we hear you, the congregation murmured in unison. Blanca and Claudia were hanging on this kid's every word, like he was telling them a love story.

"And he loved her. And she, and she—don't tell me you don't know what she did. Don't tell me you don't know that she later left to fornicate with other kings. Don't tell me you don't know that she left her king and went with others, and don't tell me you don't know this princess was called Israel. And she went with other gods and slept with many idols. You still don't know what she did?" *Alleluia!* Tell us, tell us, *sí dinos*, the congregation begged him. Roberto's speech was picking up speed. He talked faster and faster but he knew exactly when to apply the brakes and give the people time to contemplate what he was saying. "I'll tell you what she became. You all know what she became, don't tell me you all don't know what she became. She became a harlot!"

Alleluia!

"A whore!"

Alleluia!

"A prostitute!"

Alleluia!

"A slave girl to the nations again!" Roberto's words rushed one after another, like a Catholic reciting the rosary. "And you know who her king was. Don't tell me you don't know who her king was. He was the Lord Jehovah who bought her, paid highly for her! She was a slave in Egypt. And He broke her chains, sending her to Moses to free her. And the Lord treated her like a queen. Treated her like gold, silver, jewels."

Now Roberto Vega was bouncing his head as if jazz were being played somewhere not far away and the congregation was coiling slowly like a snake, waiting for the Holy Spirit to strike. Roberto's arms waved in the air like windmills and his face was no longer that of a boy but of a prophet baptized by fire.

"But she forgot who saved her! Who took care of her! Who brought her out of bondage. And to punish her, to punish her, to punish her, you know what happened? Don't tell me you don't know what happened. I know you know what happened." Although they know, they beg for the answer. They can feel the Lord in their midst. Their souls are swollen with excitement, just waiting to erupt. They will soon fly with angel wings and He will wipe every tear from their eyes, and death will be no more, nor will mourning or strife or pain. "To punish her He made her walk in sand for forty years. And she returned to her king, the Lord, and He loved her and sent her David!"

Alleluia!

"But when David died, she returned to her immoral ways!"

Alleluia! Cristo salva!

"And He sent her Isaiah!"

Alleluia!

"Sent her Jeremiah, to make her quit being a whore!"

Gloria a Dios!

"A prostitute!"

Alleluia!

"Sent her Ezekiel! And she didn't repent!"

Cristo salva!

"Sent Daniel! And she didn't repent!"

Bendito sea el Señor!

"Sent her Zechariah, Malachi, but she didn't repent!" The congregation was growing angry because Roberto had imbued them with outrage. When was the Holy Spirit going to strike? How could the nation of Israel have done this to their Lord, who treated her so kindly? "And then He sent them the ultimate prophet! Don't tell me you don't know who that is. Don't tell me you forgot who delivered you. Don't tell me you forgot who took you out of slavery. Who is your savior? *Cristo!* *Cristo* is your savior and He carried your sins! And He healed you! And He—! And He—! And He—!"

"*He saved me!*" someone cried, leaping from her seat. "He saved me, He saved me."

On the platform Roberto Vega wiped his forehead, pointed at the sister in tears. "Yes, yes, He saved you! And He paid a price for you. He gave His life for you. He was nailed for you. He became a man for you."

"*He delivered me!*" another person confessed, joyfully bouncing up and down.

"Yes, for you too! He died for you! For who else, for who else?"

"*Gloria a Dios!*" someone from the back shouted.

"For who! For who!" It had started. The Holy Spirit had invaded. I was thinking, Please, Blanca, don't freak on me. Please, I've never seen you like this ever, I know you do this but please, not in front of me.

"*He saved me!*" Claudia shouted. Her thick torso and hips were shaking, her eyes watering, her small hands pounding at her heart.

Roberto pointed at Claudia. "Yes, He saved you. Before, you were a slave. A prostitute! A whore! A harlot to the ways of the world. But now He has delivered you!" Claudia began to wail as if someone close to her had died.

"*He saved me! Cristo salva!*" some brother cried, poking at his eyes as if he was in torment; as if he was Oedipus about to rip his eyes out. Blanca smiled an enlightened smile as tears poured down her face.

Her eyes glowed as if she could see the kingdom of God. It was a strange glow, lighting eyes all over the room. Blanca's face didn't look hysterical, just a little transfigured. She had been there, in paradise. Had seen it for herself and it was all true.

"And He carried your sicknesses! Your sins! Forgave your transgressions! Your imperfections!"

Alleluia!
Alleluia!
Alleluia!

It was infecting every corner, spreading in all directions, resonating from wall to wall. A palace of vibrations praising Jehovah.

In a church full of Latinos with tear-stained cheeks, young and old had gathered together to hold hands, rough hands, soft hands, and pray and reach out to the Lord. They had waited for the Holy Spirit to arrive and take over their bodies. And now, that joyous moment was at hand. I felt strange and wished I could believe like they did. But I couldn't. Blanca's hand was sweaty and hot in mine. Her heart beat just as fast. The congregation was about to sing, to make a joyful noise to the Lord. Roberto Vega was leading them, making them see the promised land. Even though they lived here, in this concrete desert, tonight they would go home, walking the streets of Spanish Harlem fearing no evil, for the Lord was with them.

Now Roberto was telling them love stories. About God in love with mankind. Of Jehovah being the personification of love. It was a love song he was yelling, although only I could hear him yell, to the rest he was whispering.

"Owing to the fact that I have found you precious in my eyes," Roberto read quietly from the book of Isaiah, "you have been considered honorable and I myself have grown to love you. And I shall give men in place of you! And nations in place for your soul!" The Holy Spirit was calmed, like an ocean after a storm. Many people had returned to their seats. Roberto had calmed them, calmed the Spirit of God. He now spoke softly; I could feel the young girls start to swoon. The older women shut their eyes and returned to their past; the older men envied Roberto. Blanca for a moment was in love with the figure standing alone on a bare platform with only the American and Puerto Rican flags keeping him company.

It was a humble place, made up of rows of folding chairs and walls of Sheetrock covered by cheap wood paneling. A dirty red carpet, with huge gum-stained circles as big as cherries covered the floor. The ceiling had two fiberboard panels missing, exposing the electrical wires. The room provided no distractions. Perfect for those like Roberto Vega who wished to have all eyes, ears, and hearts tuned to their words.

"My brothers and sisters, never leave the truth," Roberto pleaded. "Never turn from the light. The darkness will enslave you, like before, before the Lord saved you. Our Lord Christ will never turn His back on us. Even if we leave Him, He will never leave us."

Then what's the point, I was thinking. If He would stay with me anyway, why should I pay Him all this attention?

"He suffered for us. He was crucified, nailed for us."

I agreed. They nailed his left hand to Spanish Harlem, his right to Watts, his feet to Overtown, Miami. The slums were full of his followers. His words were all over the neighborhood, murals screaming at you in the street, that He was your Lord and Savior. His spirit was all over El Barrio, but I didn't see Him living among us. You wouldn't catch Christ, in the flesh, living in the projects.

"Please, now," Roberto said, his voice lifting again, "join me in song." The congregation rose. Blanca reached for her tambourine. Some brother put a record on an old player and music began booming from the loudspeaker. Four sisters joined Roberto at the head of the platform to clap their hands and pound their tambourines. It was a privilege to praise the Lord on the platform, to lead the congregation in song. Once, before she married me, it was Blanca up there, and it still pained her to have lost such a privilege. But that night I knew she was happy. Like the rest, she was high on Roberto Vega's words. They had seen the coming of the Lord. He was coming soon, maybe even that very night. Roberto Vega had told them so. The kingdom of God would arrive, and they would all go to heaven, to the penthouse in the sky. Until then, they would go back home to the rats and roaches.

"*Arrepiéntete, arrepiéntete, Cristo salva! Arrepiéntete, arrepiéntete,*

Cristo salva," they sang. Blanca, her heavy body, baby and all, joined in the song. The sounds of feet stomping, hands clapping, tambourines shaking, and the sobbing of both men and women filled the room. Whole families were worshiping: aisles full of husbands; wives near the broken piano, babies asleep in their arms, as if angels were covering their tiny ears so they wouldn't wake up as everyone praised the Lord at full volume. *"Hoy se ven todas las señales! El fin está cerca, arrepiéntete, arrepiéntete, Cristo salva!"*

Afterward, Roberto said a prayer, and when he had finished everyone murmured Amen. The church now had its feet back on the ground. Everyone was back on planet Earth, the Holy Spirit had left the building, and casual conversations started up.

Blanca hugged me. "I'm so happy you came," she said.

"I'm happy you're happy," I replied. From the corner of my eye I saw Roberto Vega join his parents and hug them. Others came up to shake his hand, congratulating him on such a great sermon.

"So you're Claudia. I've heard all these good things about you," I said in Spanish to Blanca's sister in faith, but she didn't acknowledge my presence. Her eyes were still on Roberto Vega.

"She's in love with him," Blanca whispered as Claudia left to go to Roberto's side. He was the Lord's stud, swarmed by sisters in Christ who all hoped to be his chosen.

"Let's go meet him." Blanca took my hand and led me toward him. I was just happy that the fight we'd had earlier seemed to be forgotten.

"That was beautiful. As if Paradise was there in front of me," a teenager gushed to Roberto.

"All praise be to my Lord, Jesus Christ. We are all but vessels for Him to use," Roberto said modestly. Sweat streamed down his face and his shirt was drenched. His mother was holding his hand, his father standing tall because his family had been touched by God.

"When he was just nine years old," his mother told the brothers and sisters that surrounded them, me and Blanca among them, "I remember I was cooking. I was making *pasteles* and Robertito walked into the kitchen. He had the most beautiful expression you can imagine. His face was always handsome but that day his face was so beautiful that I knew something had happened. So I asked him—"

"Mami, please, not again—" Roberto protested, half joking.

"Just one more time, Robertito. . . . He walked into my kitchen," she continued, "and his face was like a fire. And he said, 'Mami, I want to get baptized.' I said, 'You are too young to get baptized. You have to study more about the Bible before you can make a commitment like that.' But his face was still aflame, and that's when he told me, 'Mami, last night, He came and spoke to me, Christ spoke to me.' And it was his face that made me believe him."

"So he took his Bible studies," his father interrupted, to his wife's annoyance, "and got baptized at nine years old."

"And later," his mother jumped back in, "later he told us that the Holy Spirit had told his soul he had been anointed." No one questioned them. No one doubted for a second. Who would after that speech? I wouldn't. If that kid was going to heaven to rule with Christ, then I just hoped he wouldn't forget the little people and would put in a good word for me and Blanca.

Claudia extended a nervous hand toward him and introduced herself. He smiled and asked her where she was from. Blanca butted in and invited Roberto, his family, and Claudia over for dinner. I knew what she was up to. Fortunately, they politely declined her offer. That's when Pastor Miguel Vasquez joined us.

Pastor Vasquez was in his late fifties. He always wore polyester suits, even during the summer. He was from Ponce but had grown up in the neighborhood, and when he gave his sermons he'd stress how Christ had saved him from a life of petty street crime. I had seen him in action a couple of times, when his church picked a corner and, using the electricity from a lamppost, plugged in a mike and some electric guitars and preached the hell out of the neighborhood. You could hear them blocks away. "*Cristo salva! Alleluia! Ven regresa al Señor!*" They'd hand out leaflets and later jam their church salsa, with the guitars and tambourines and a drum set. All that church music bounced off project walls, circling its way around the neighborhood. I had seen Blanca join in those sessions, but I had always avoided the chosen corners.

"*Julio, qué bueno verte, muchacho!*" Pastor Vasquez called out. He always spoke in Spanish, though he understood and could speak English when he needed or wanted to. My parents are the same way.

"*Estoy tan ansioso de cenar con ustedes este viernes.*" As soon as Roberto's mother heard that Pastor Vasquez was coming for dinner on Friday, she had a change of heart.

"Of course we'll have dinner with you, Hermana Mercado," Roberto's mother told Blanca. Claudia's face lit up.

Afterward, Blanca stocked up on the religious cards, booklets, and leaflets she hands out every Saturday morning. Then she kissed half the women in the congregation goodbye, making small talk along the way. I waited patiently because it meant a lot to her. Finally, after more goodbyes and gushing about how great a speaker God's anointed was, Blanca and I were out the door and walking home.

"So that's Roberto Vega. Impressive. I thought he was very convincing."

"You should see, sometimes brothers come from as far away as New Jersey to hear him talk."

"Blanca," I said, "if you know Claudia is in love with Roberto, why did you invite him to dinner? He's only seventeen and Claudia looks at least thirty."

"She's twenty-seven."

"For a Latina that's not married, twenty-seven is ancient. Nobody is going to want to marry her." Okay, I could have phrased that better. I waited for Blanca's wrath. I had just patched things up with her and now here I was, starting something new. But Blanca didn't get mad, in fact she agreed.

"Yes, isn't that terrible, Julio?" I was surprised at her reaction. "That's not one of our finest qualities." I wasn't sure if Blanca meant Latinos or her church. "It's a terrible thing that we feel a single woman at twenty-five is over the hill. You should listen to some of the sisters in the congregation bug her. 'So when are you getting married, Claudia? So when are you going to have children, Claudia? You're not that young anymore, Claudia, *te vas a quedar jamona.*' So much pressure on that poor girl. Meanwhile all the single brothers, young or old, want nineteen-year-old virgins. It's amazing."

I started laughing; I liked it when she trashed them.

"Don't laugh, Julio. Roberto Vega is different. True, he is still young, but he is as mature as a man in his thirties. And Claudia is the most spiritual girl in the congregation. Once he sees that, he might marry her."

I laughed even harder. "So you think, Blanca, that Roberto Vega is going to give up his celebrity status in your religion to help this girl from Colombia? Blanca, you can be so dumb." She knew I was half kidding.

"So? It could happen. It could happen. If it's God's will it will happen," she insisted, laughing in spite of herself.

"Of course it's God's will. I know God. We go way back," I said.

Blanca just rolled her eyes at me, punched me softly in the stomach, and said, "Stupid."

Then she said, firmly, "Well, if Christ wants it to happen, then it will happen." She knew that part of Roberto's appeal was not just that he was young and anointed, but single, too. If he got married at eighteen he'd be ruining all that. But she had hopes.

I gave her a quick kiss on the forehead. I was glad I had gone to church, because it had made her happy. That night, walking home with Blanca near me, the streets seemed cleaner, the neighborhood quieter and gentler. We saw a little kid kicking a garbage can bigger than him, yelling that he was the Master of the Universe. What was he doing out so late? If he had been a little girl, I bet his parents would've been more concerned. When he kicked the can over and all the garbage spilled on the street, his mother yelled at him from a window above. "*Mira*, Junito, get your ass up here, *o te meto una pela.*" We burst out laughing, then began talking about the baby. About names again and about education. We talked in a cute and silly private language of our own. But all that was broken when we reached 109th and Third, three blocks from our home.

"Chino! Chino! Blanca!" A man we knew came running over toward us. It was Georgie Vato. We called him that because his name was George and he was Mexican. When we were kids the play *Zoot Suit* was very popular, and the characters in it kept calling one another *vato*. The name stuck. Plus, he was a fat little kid and we would tease him, jeering, "Georgie Vato ate all his tacos and then his *gato.*" He would protest, "Yo, I ain't got a cat!" which was the dumbest thing to say because then we could answer, "Thass right, cuz you ate him."

But that night, his face was serious.

"Chino! Blanca! Your house is on fire!" he called out urgently. "The trucks are still there."

Blanca and I looked at each other. In El Barrio you always think that the fire engines are headed to someone else's house. You never think it will be your own home that's on fire, but when it is, all the toughness, the calloused nonchalance of watching fires and hearing sirens falls away. It takes away your immunity, makes you knock on wood and count your blessings the next time you hear a siren at night.

We ran home. From a block away, it looked as if they were filming a movie. Red lights were flashing. The red-orange blaze engulfing the building looked surreal. The people looked like extras on a set, watching in a tight group from across the street. Every time the fire consumed a new window, the wind creating fireballs that would fly out into the air and dissolve in mid flight, the people who didn't live in the building would yell, "Olé! Olé!" I saw a woman run down the fire escape with a bucket of water. When she reached the floor where the fire was she threw the contents through the window. Everyone laughed. "Oh, that'll help." Someone said the fireman that was escorting her down the fire escape let her do it, because she wouldn't go with him otherwise. When we reached our side of the street, Blanca drew herself toward me and, shaking, buried her face in my arms. When she pulled away from me a bit, she saw one of our neighbors.

"Are you all right?" Blanca asked.

"I'm fine, everyone got out. And we didn't have much," she answered, half in tears as her kids clung to her legs. It might not have been much, I thought, but it was hers. Blanca nervously placed her hand on her stomach. I knew she was thanking the Lord that the fire had happened while she, the baby, and I were at church.

"*Cristo salva, gracias al Señor.* It's not the end of the world."

As we watched the fire grow more stubborn, fighting the firemen and their hoses, our faces were blank. I knew Blanca felt what all of us who lived in that building were feeling. Displaced. Disoriented. No insurance, no new place, everything lost.

Then something happened.

Someone appeared. Someone who looked like he came out of the fire itself. Slowly, like a mirage from a desert sandstorm, a figure emerged walking toward the people. A tall, elegant man came into focus with his arms outstretched and a face of pure empathy. It was Nazario. When the people saw him, they rushed him. They all wanted to touch him as if his touch could make the blind see, the deaf hear, and the mute speak. Blanca and I just stayed where we were.

"Who's that?" Blanca asked.

"I don't know," I said automatically, because when our eyes locked, even from a few feet away, Nazario's eyes told me all I needed to know.

Fischman had done it. The fire was in retaliation for Salazar. The war was in full bloom.

After the Fire

AFTER the fire was put out, we tenants were let back inside to retrieve what remained of our belongings. The building had been completely drenched with water and the stairs had become little waterfalls. Glass, pieces of Sheetrock, broken furniture, cups, nail polish, pans, hair brushes, mirrors, bottles, plates, rugs, clothes—almost everything imaginable floated in streams of water from apartments that looked like flooded basements. The elevator didn't work and all the windows were broken. The firemen had axed their way through what seemed to be every wall and every door, leaving the place looking like a bomb had gone off. The fire had left the ugly smell of smoke stamped and sealed on every piece of clothing that had survived the flames.

Soon word spread around the building that someone had spilled gasoline down the trash chute. A match had been dropped in and the fire had shot straight up to the roof. Between the fire and the water damage, no apartment was habitable. No one in their right mind could have spent the night in that building.

Blanca and I tried to salvage what we could. We needed Vera's ring more than ever. And I also needed to find the Apple Jacks box containing Sapo's stuff.

Meanwhile Nazario played his part beautifully. His face led you to believe his place was among the ruins. Nazario was moving from apartment to apartment, reassuring the tenants that they'd have a place to stay within a month. I believed him; I knew Bodega had three buildings on 119th and Lexington that were almost ready to house people.

I always knock the people in Blanca's church, but a lot of them were right there that night helping us move our things, everyone splashing around ankle-deep in water. If we hadn't had Blanca's spiritual brothers and sisters we would have been moving things out all night.

I had left the ring on top of the bureau, but it wasn't there. No doubt it had been knocked down like everything else. I bent down low, looking for a reflection of light in the water, and then I saw it glittering like a goldfish. I reached through the water, snatched it up, and put it in my pocket. The Apple Jacks box was a problem, and I started to get a bit scared when at first I couldn't find it, but then I saw it floating, the paper box dissolving like a wafer. I took Sapo's stuff out and hid it under my shirt.

A little later, downstairs in the lobby, which looked like some purgatorial setting, Nazario had assembled most of the tenants. He spoke eloquently about Latin pride, about a sense of community and trust. He compared the fire to a tragedy like the ones that occurred in the Mother Island or our other Latin countries, where the most important form of help you got was from your neighbor, not the government.

"You have to tough it out. Help each other. We're Boricuas, we're Latinos! Where are you from?" he asked, pointing to one of the residents.

"Mayaguez," the woman answered.

"I have an aunt in Mayaguez. She raised me," Nazario continued. "We were *pobre, pobre*. All I had to play with was a cat named Guayo. A tough cat named Guayo, who would dive into a lake like a bear and emerge with a fish in his mouth." The people laughed a little. "He hated to go in that lake but he had to eat." The people understood. "You have to tough it out! We are one people, one island, one Latin continent." Then he raised his index finger in the air. "One people! One month! Tough it out for one month!" The tenants all began to murmur in agreement. "Remember it was Willie Bodega who sheltered you."

At this, Blanca glanced my way, with the look of a student who wants to ask a professor a question but knows the class is almost over and her question won't be appreciated by her peers, who are dying to go home.

Nazario continued, "And it will be Willie Bodega who will shelter you again. Any man or woman who believes in community and pride will be included in his love for this neighborhood. Stay with your mother, your brother, your sister, your friend, your priest, anybody for a month. Give Willie Bodega a month and he will shelter you." Then Nazario looked at Blanca, telling the tenants in Spanish that this woman was pregnant and couldn't wait a month. He asked Blanca if I, standing behind her, was her husband. Blanca said yes, almost in a whisper. I played along and held her shoulders. Blanca knew this was a farce. She already knew, I could see, that anything connected with Bodega was trouble. She was still not completely sold on my claims of ignorance about that reporter's death, and as soon as she heard Nazario mention Bodega I sensed she was sure he was one of Bodega's pawns. But right now was no time to ask questions. Now there were more important things at hand. The questions would come later, and I knew I would have to have some fucking great answers.

Right then there was the whole tragedy of the fire staring us in the face. Nazario announced that Bodega would take care of pregnant women and one-parent families first, and that Blanca and I would be rehoused the very next day. No one seemed to have a problem with this. The other tenants even said Blanca and I deserved it because we were good kids. But I knew Bodega couldn't have Vera's niece home-less, even temporarily.

Nazario then continued to circulate, moving like a panther from one place to another, making sure all the tenants had seen him, while he looked for an opportunity to speak to me alone. The moment came when most of the tenants, Pentecostal, Catholic, or whatever, got together to pray in the lobby. No one noticed me not joining in. Maybe Blanca did, but she knew where I stood on that.

"Fischman?" I asked Nazario as we stood in the flooded apartment of someone who was probably out praying with the rest of the tenants.

"I have something to ask of you," Nazario said.

"Name it." I wanted a piece of Fischman myself. This fuck could have killed my wife, who had nothing to do with him or Bodega. He had pushed me to the point where I could either break completely away from the situation or dive in completely. I was in.

"I want you to come with me tomorrow to Queens."

"What's in Queens?"

"We have to speak with someone. And should something happen to me, I want this person we are going to see to be familiar with your face for future reference. Understand?" I didn't, but I nodded anyway.

All I understood was that Bodega was in trouble. Not with the fire department, which would know right away it was arson and dismiss it as another case of pyromania in a neighborhood crawling with fire-bugs. Nor with the media, who needed sensation and since no deaths had occurred would give it only passing mention, like a footnote in a thousand-page book. The Harry Goldstein Management Agency would receive little attention, making it the only good thing, besides no one dying, that Bodega had on his side. What Bodega had to worry about was this Fish of Loisaida making tidal waves.

"Where's Bodega?" I asked Nazario.

"Vera" was all he said.

I was about to ask something else when we heard the tenants say Amen in a chorus of hope and then begin to disperse.

"I'll send for you tomorrow, after you've moved," Nazario said, and left.

That night Blanca and I slept at Blanca's mother's. Blanca was too tired to ask questions and went straight to sleep, knowing we would need rest because tomorrow we would be moving again.

Watering His Peach Tree

BLANCA and I missed work so we could move. Bodega sent someone over with a lease. Maybe it was the immediacy of the situation or maybe she was just too tired, but Blanca asked no questions. We signed the lease, then got friends and family to help us pack up and move into a two-bedroom apartment, two buildings down on the same block as the burned-out building. Bodega had had a beautiful row of five newly renovated tenements and now the middle one looked like a missing tooth in a pretty woman's smile.

As I made a trip to the U-Haul van to remove a rug and take it upstairs, I heard a familiar voice.

"Yo, homeless guy! I hope you ran into the flames and rescued my shit." It was Sapo in his familiar black BMW, going around and collecting money from Bodega's crack houses and numbers joints.

"Where you been, bro? With all the peace around here I thought you was dead." I was happy to see him. No matter what, Sapo had never done anything to hurt me. If anything, Sapo had always been around when I needed someone to watch my back.

"Get in." He opened the door for me, smiling his Sapo smile.

"Can't. I'm in the middle of moving, bro."

"Too bad, Nazario sent fo' yah."

"I can't just leave. I got stuff ta move, bro," I said. Sapo reached for the car phone. I waited. Sapo dialed, and after a few uh-huhs and yeahs he hung up the phone.

"You have two minutes to give an excuse to your alleluia wife and her alleluia friends cuz you comin' with me," he said.

"I can't go wi'choo, bro. I got things to finish."

"You's comin, Chino. Now, I've done a lot of things in my days but I ain't never kidnapped nobody. But I will if I have to cuz that was Nazario on the phone."

I had to go. So I told one of Blanca's church friends, Wilfredo Reyes, that I had forgotten something important uptown and had to retrieve it. He just smiled and said not to worry, but I felt really bad because I wasn't lending a hand when it was my stuff they were breaking their backs carrying. Still, I had to go, so I jumped in with Sapo and we took off.

"Where we going?"

"Pa' viejo."

"Yo, that ain't original. You should never repeat yourself."

"I hear that. So this's the deal. You and Nazario are goin' to talk with some wops in Queens."

"'Bout what?"

"Wha', I look like Walter Mercado to you? I don't fucken know 'bout wha'." We drove.

"Yo, Sapo," I said in a low tone. "Did you kill Salazar? Did you kill that reporter?"

"Nope."

"Get the fuck. Why you lie to me, bro?"

"All right, I'll tell you. I ain't kill the sonofabitch."

"Yeah, so how come he had a chunk missing from his shoulder?"

"I didn't say I ain't bit the nigga. I bite 'em but ain't kill 'em."

"Yeah, then who did?"

"You see whiskers on me? You see a tail? You see me likin' cheese or somethin'?"

"All right. But you were there, bro, that's guilt by association. They can get you for that."

"They ain't gettin' no one," he said, slamming the brakes suddenly, and my body jerked forward. I knew Sapo didn't like me asking him about any of this. He was telling me to back off. I didn't.

"Yo, I asked Bodega himself. He said you killed Salazar."

"Bodega wasn't there, how he'd know?" He shifted really hard and gritted his teeth.

"But he sent you, right?"

"Nazario did. But Bodega okayed it. Still, I didn't kill the fuck."

"Then where you been, bro?"

"You know, Chino, I never thought of it but like you sittin' on a bunch of info. Thass not a good chair to be sittin' on, know what I'm sayin', *papi*? If I was you I'd move my ass and sit somewhere else." Now I knew he was really serious, and I backed off.

We had reached 116th and First. Sapo double-parked.

"Come with me, bro. This will only take a minute." Sapo and I got out of the car and entered a city-owned abandoned building. Such buildings made perfect places for crack houses and numbers joints. The electricity was easily siphoned from a lamppost socket or the nearest building (via the roof). The windows facing the street were covered with plywood and only the first floor was renovated so it looked as if the fire that emptied the building hadn't affected that floor. A phony business was set up, be it a candy store, a comic-book shop, or a florist. By the time the cops busted the place Bodega had made a killing and couldn't be traced because he never owned the building, the City of New York did. Anybody arrested who worked for Bodega had Nazario and his suits taking care of their backs in court.

This numbers joint fronted as a candy store. It had a few comic books, some lollipops, gum, jars filled with hard candy, and a Pac-Man machine. When Sapo walked in the guy sitting behind the counter quickly rose to attention, like he was in the army or something. Then he relaxed when Sapo slapped him five and they laughed at each other. They went to the back and left me there with two other guys who were playing Pac-Man and talking about some guy from the old days.

One of them hit the machine as if it was its fault he had lost his turn. "That fucken red ghost got me! Frankie, it's your go." He made way so Frankie could have a try at the joystick. The music of little dots being eaten up and ghosts following the smiling yellow cartoon was the only sound in the candy store. No children went there to buy candy, they knew better. And the numbers for the day had come out already, so betting time was over. It was an ugly, desolate store, with posters of Marvel superheroes taped to the wall, where all you heard were stories of things that might have happened.

"So, Angel, what happened to the nigga?" Frankie asked as he played.

"Dead," Angel said.

"How he die?"

"That shit was a shame."

But before I could learn the details of Angel's fate, Sapo returned with a paper bag in his hand and we left. Inside his car, he drew out a knapsack he had hidden under the seat. He stuffed the bag inside the knapsack, which was filled with other wrinkled-looking brown bags. We took off.

"I thought you was takin' me to Nazario, whass this about collectin'?"

"That was the last one, don't freak on me." He turned on First Avenue and we headed uptown.

"So like you know I was with this white girl las' night and they like good in bed but like they say stupid shit. You know, like, Spanish girls, they moan to you, 'Ayy *papi*, ayy *papi*.' See, I like that. But white girls, white girls say shit like, 'Oh, God, oh God' or shit like 'Oh yes, oh yes.' I'd rather be called *papi* in bed than God."

"Spoken like a true existentialist," I said.

"All right, nigga, use them big-ass college words on me, call me a fucken extraterrestrial, but I know you understand. I mean, I know you like white girls. You always liked white girls. You hate to admit it, but I always knew you did."

"Blanca's Latin, bro."

"Yeah, thass right, but they call her Blanca. Why? Cuz even though she might be Spanish, she's a white Spanish—"

"So what you tryin' to say, Sapo, that I don't like our girls?"

"Nah, I'm telling you, you don't like our girls. If the shoe fits, wear it, mothafucka."

"Why you want to go on and say that to me for, bee? You got somethin' against my skin preference?"

"All I'm sayin' is, if Blanca weren't white you woulda nevah married her."

"Yo, you been stayin' up all night figurin' this out? Or like Bodega, you've been watching fucken psychology shows on TV. What the fuck."

"Face it, Chino, you got plexes. You got plexes with your kind in bed."

"Please. I ain't got no complex about Latin girls."

"Hey, man, I ain't like tryin' to get you angry or somethin'. You know whass your problem, Chino, you're like a Schick razor, you're ultrasensitive. But you my *pana*, I mean we go way back." Sapo stopped talking when we reached 125th. He pulled over opposite a black Mercedes.

"See that car?" Sapo pointed. "Nazario's in it. I'll see you when I see you. And I want my shit. You still have my shit, right?"

"Yeah, I got it." I stepped out of Sapo's car. "I'm happy to see you, bro."

"Yeah, yeah, you just better have my shit," he said, and sped out.

I walked toward the Mercedes and the driver opened the door for me. I climbed inside. The air conditioner was on full blast and the car was freezing. It was only spring and the day was cool. There was no reason for the air-conditioning. Nazario had some notes on his lap and a suit hanging beside him.

"Good to see you." He shook my hand. His was warm, how I didn't know. He handed me the suit. "Go inside that building," he said, pointing. "Knock on 1B. An old woman named Doña Flores will open the door. She will let you take a bath and change into these clothes. And don't forget to shave. Please, Julio, don't take too long," he said nicely.

"Five minutes," I said, and did as I was told.

·

CROSSING THE Triborough Bridge to Queens, Nazario kept silent and just studied a ledger, at times making little notes in it. I didn't speak and didn't let him know that I was cold. I just looked out of the window.

When we reached Queens I felt taller. Manhattan humbles you. Many times when I walk around Manhattan I feel as if I'm walking among giant sequoia trees in the California Redwoods. Everything is so above you, so intimidating and grand. But in Queens the buildings are small, mostly private homes, and those that aren't are only a few stories high. In Queens you're Gulliver among the Lilliputians.

When we arrived in Rego Park, the driver pulled over and parked in front of a two-story house. Nazario put his ledger down and finally spoke to me. "Just be cool and let me do all the talking. There isn't much for you to do here except make me look more important than I am." We stepped out. It was good to feel some heat.

A heavyset Italian man opened the door and led us inside. After seating us, he said a Mr. Cavalleri would be with us in a minute, that Mr. Cavalleri was out in the garden. The house was ugly, full of cheap furniture and cheaper paintings of horses and saints. We waited and waited. Nazario said nothing to me and I said nothing back. We waited for one hour and most of another. I didn't say or ask anything. Nazario just looked straight ahead like he was in the fifth hour of a twelve-hour drive. The house was silent, as if the only ones inside were Nazario and myself. Finally the same man returned and apologized for the wait.

"Sorry, fellas. Has it been long?"

"Not long at all," Nazario said, calmly.

The man led us through the house and out to the garden. There he sat on a chair in the shade, his eyes on an old man wearing a sweater who was watering a peach tree. Nazario didn't move until the old man motioned for him, and then he walked the two steps toward him.

"Mr. Cavalleri, it was kind of you, a busy man, to make time on such short notice to see us. I won't insult you by recapping what you already know. My associate William Irizarry asked us to see you." Nazario stopped himself as if he had said too much. He waited. The old man kept watering the tree. Then he turned the water off and lifted his hand to caress the wet leaves. He moved his eyes and head slightly toward Nazario, who began to speak again.

"We know that you have worked well with Aaron Fischman in the past. We know that he has made a lot of money for you. For my associate and I to act without consulting you would be foolish." He stopped. Cavalleri moved his head slightly, this time with a little more energy, a nod of agreement. Nazario then started talking again.

"What has happened between William Irizarry and Aaron Fischman should have no bearing on you or your well-respected name. This is strictly between my associate and Aaron Fischman. I am here to make sure that you, Mr. Cavalleri, and Aaron Fischman have no future ventures planned that would harm you and your name should something happen to Aaron Fischman." Nazario stopped and waited for the nod before resuming.

"But should you have ventures planned with Aaron Fischman, my associate will compensate you for any loss." Nazario and I waited for the old Italian.

"Tell this . . ." Cavalleri finally said, in a low and gravelly voice.

"Mr. William Irizarry," Nazario answered.

"What does he have in case I have something planned with Aaron Fischman in the near future?"

"Mr. Irizarry knows you are the last of the great old-timers. He knows that you believe in the rules and that you remember fondly your youthful days in the old neighborhood."

Cavalleri made a slight movement with his fingers, gesturing for Nazario to come closer. I stayed put. Nazario began talking again.

"When you were young, East Harlem belonged to you. In fact, there were two little Italys, one downtown and one in East Harlem. When your bones had plenty of calcium, Mr. Cavalleri, remember that 116th and First was called Lucky Corner because all the politicians would make that street their last stop on the eve of elections. They knew who had the power in the city and who had financed them. The likes of Vito Marcantonio and Fiorello La Guardia all came to pay respect to the men who had placed them in office before the votes had even been counted. Men like you, Mr. Cavalleri."

The old man looked at the soil that fed his peach tree. He looked at the puddles he had made and contemplated what Nazario was saying.

"And through the years all that has been lost. The only hold you still have is around Pleasant Avenue. What William Irizarry can offer you is his friendship and his promise that nothing will ever happen to that last remnant of Italian East Harlem. It would remain sacred. You have his word that no one will ever hurt it."

At that Cavalleri turned his face away. Nazario had made a mistake.

"Tell your . . ."

"William Irizarry."

"Tell him that we don't need his protection on Pleasant Avenue. Tell him it was presumptuous of him to think so."

Nazario waited a few seconds, and just when he was about to apologize the old man lifted his hand to indicate he wasn't finished yet.

"The old days are gone. That's fine. We don't own what we used to own. So many groups out there. It's like the U.N. now." He paused, then looked at Nazario once again. "I've heard what's going on in my old neighborhood. I've heard only good things about this, this . . . ?"

"William Irizarry."

"I heard he doesn't sell it to children and I heard he's rebuilding the place. I have heard about some crazy idea to pay for people's schooling. He's a character. He runs detox programs in the basements of his buildings and at the same time deals in the street."

"My associate believes anyone who takes it should have a chance to rid himself of it. But anyone is free to decide—" Cavalleri raised his hand again. He'd heard enough. Nazario quieted down.

"I'm an old man, I know what it's all about. I don't need speeches." His face was in a tight knot of irritation. "I personally hate drugs. It's too much risk, but the more the money the higher the risk. Tell this . . . ?"

"William Irizarry."

"Tell him I've severed all my ties with that Jew. Tell him I'm old and couldn't care less who comes out on top." The old man then turned back to his peach tree. Nazario bowed slightly, and just when we were about to turn around and leave, Cavalleri spoke again.

"But tell this . . ."

"William Irizarry," Nazario repeated without a note of irritation.

"Tell him should he come out on top, I could work with a spic like him. One that believes in the old days and plays by the rules. It was smart of him to see me before reacting. It shows the man can think. Tell this . . ." Just as Nazario was about to repeat Bodega's name, the old man lifted his hand to stop him. "Tell this William Irizarry that should he come out on top, from this day forth I will remember his name."

As Long As Latino Kills Latino
We'll Always Be a Little People

WHILE riding back to Manhattan Nazario made a call. "Make sure you get all the logos," he said. "It doesn't matter. Just get them and then get back at me. Get the corners too." He paused and frowned, as if the person he was talking to was in front of him. "Any news on the building? No? All right." He dialed another number. "Find Nene and get back to me." Then he told the driver to turn off the air conditioner. I guess after the meeting he didn't need to be so cool, he could sweat if he wanted to. He dialed again. "He's coming the day after tomorrow, in the afternoon. Do you have the flight number? Good. I'll send someone to pick him up."

It was a victory for Nazario and Bodega that this big Italian guy had told them he was staying out of their way, but to Nazario it was just one of many hurdles he and Bodega had to overcome.

The last number he dialed received no answer. I knew he was calling Bodega. He must've been too busy with Vera to answer. But Nazario didn't mutter a curse under his breath, he just closed his eyes and sighed.

"Good news," I said cheerfully to Nazario, "can wait."

"You think this is good news, Julio?" he said, eyes still shut. I stayed quiet. "Did you see how we were fucking humiliated?" I had yet to see Nazario really angry. His emotions were always in check. Seeing him mad now made me realize things were in bad shape. "Did you see how he kept us waiting? Did you see how he controlled everything?"

"You needed a favor from him, right?" I said after a few seconds of silence. Nazario was looking out the window.

"Getting rid of anyone is bad. Especially one of your own." I guessed he meant Salazar.

"Salazar was dirty, though."

"Yes, but"—his eyes left the window and looked straight at me—"as long as Latino kills Latino," he sighed, "we'll always be a little people." Silence fell again. Nazario's eyes returned to the window.

"Nazario, I got a question to ask you," I said, breaking the silence. "Do you promise not to be a lawyer and tell it to me straight?"

"I don't promise you anything," he smiled faintly, "but don't be afraid to ask."

"Why am I here? I mean here with you, today. I don't bring you any advantage over anything or anyone—" He cut me off.

"Who said? That's the mentality I'm trying to change, Julio. I spotted you a mile away. I know what you can be. What you might bring to us."

"Us? Who the fuck is us?"

"Us, man," he said, a little annoyed. "Us, Latinos, the neighborhood, who else? We want you to join the program, quit that job of yours at the supermarket and concentrate on school." I knew that I could never do that. If I was going to finish school it would be on my own. "We're trying to do things here."

"Through crime?"

"Through whatever means are at our disposal." He straightened himself in his seat. When he spoke, his voice was cold. "Behind every great wealth, Julio, there's a great crime. You know who said that?"

I didn't.

"Balzac."

"Balzac? The writer?"

"Look around, Julio. Every time someone makes a million dollars, he kills some part of the world. That part has been us for so long, and it will continue to be us unless we fight back. The day will come when, just like the white guy, we will also steal by signing the right papers."

"And it'll all be legal?"

"That's right. But in the beginning, you have to do certain things. What do you think, it comes from nothing? America is a great nation, I have no doubts about that, but in its early days it had to take some shady steps to get there. Manifest Destiny, that was just another word for genocide. But now, when you go out west, Julio . . ." Nazario looked my way and paused but focused his eyes on nothing. "You ever been out west, Julio?"

"No, I never been out west." He had to know that.

"It's beautiful, Julio. The red and orange desert, the hills, all that space, the Rockies, the wildlife. When you see that, then you will understand why the Americans wanted it and called it Manifest Destiny and not what it really was, theft."

He looked out the window again. What he said was nothing new to me, but I felt like a stagestruck actor who forgets his lines because he's worried about the audience. That was always my problem; I wanted to be onstage, close to the action, but without having to say any lines. Unlike Bodega and the rest, I never had the balls to hold my own in a big scene, much less an entire show.

But I had started to wonder if Nazario and Bodega were right all along. I mean, on good days, what I was learning in college excited me in ways the street and its erratic and petty rules never could. I wanted to think it was my family that had kept me away from the street scene Sapo had built his life around, but it wasn't. I had enrolled at school thinking about other ways to come out on top, ways that didn't hurt anybody and weren't as dangerous. Graduate, get a good job, save, buy a house—but those ways were slow. And like Nazario's and Bodega's ways, they held no guarantees of success just because they were legal. They, too, were gambles, rolls of the dice.

Nazario and Bodega, they were talking something else. How life is born from chaos and explosions. Big Bang. They were talking about starting out as a piece of trash from the gutter and transforming yourself into gold. Nazario and Bodega saw it as all or nothing. You couldn't have change without evolution and some people would get hurt and become extinct in the process because they couldn't adapt. Nazario's and Bodega's ways made sense to me. But so did mine and Blanca's, and in tense moments, I didn't know who made more sense or where my loyalties should be placed.

"Tomorrow." Nazario swallowed. "Tomorrow it will be all over *El Diario* that Salazar was a bought reporter." He took a deep breath and loosened his tie. "Once it's out about Salazar being dirty, we're hoping nobody will care." That had already started—*El Diario* was about the only newspaper still covering the murder investigation.

Nazario brought out his ledger and started jotting down some numbers. He seemed to be good at adding and subtracting quickly and without a calculator. Only his lips moved, like he was praying. I left him alone. It was getting dark and the Fifty-ninth Street Bridge loomed ahead. Manhattan at night seen from its surrounding bridges is Oz, it's Camelot or Eldorado, full of color and magic. What those skyscrapers and lights don't let on is that hidden away lies Spanish Harlem, a slum that has been handed down from immigrant to immigrant, like used clothing worn and reworn, stitched and restitched by different ethnic groups who continue to pass it on. A paradox of crime and kindness. It had evolved spontaneously on the island, accessible to everyone. East Harlem had no business being in this rich city but there it was, filled with broken promises of a better life, dating decades back to the day when many Puerto Ricans and Latinos gathered their bags and carried their dreams on their backs and arrived in America, God's country. But they would never see God's face. Like all slumlords, God lived in the suburbs.

As the car sped over the bridge, I looked down on the East River. I pictured explorers in their ships arriving at the shore and making deals with the true native New Yorkers, the Indians. A twenty-four-dollar rip-off, I said to myself. Bodega and Nazario were just reversing the roles. They were buying the island back at the same bargain rate. They were getting it while it was still cheap. El Barrio, run-down and abandoned, was just waiting for them to take it. East Harlem was ugly real estate that no one wanted. No one but Bodega and Nazario, who loved that tired piece of land just off the East River. They would rebuild it, repaint it, and watch as others stepped back, looked at it, and pulled their hair in dismay. "This was always a beautiful place. Why couldn't we see that before?"

•

WHEN WE were back home in the neighborhood, Nazario said he
would speak with me some other time and to keep the suit, and my
eyes, ears, and mind open. I was happy, but I was worried about
Blanca. She must be fuming, I thought. Blanca would ask a million
questions, and I went upstairs braced for another confrontation.

When I reached our floor and went inside our new place, our second in about a month, it got me down to see it full of boxes. All our
things were so out of order, out of place, though the phone was hooked
up. I walked toward the bedroom. I could hear laughter and small cries
of *Gloria a Dios*. When I entered Blanca was sitting on the bed.
Roberto Vega and Claudia were standing, holding hands. Near them
were suitcases and tote bags. When they saw me, the room fell silent.
Blanca smiled and carefully stood up, and I hugged her, not knowing
why Roberto and Claudia were there. In a way I was glad they were,
because I knew Blanca would never argue or grill me in front of them.

"Did you eat, Julio?" she asked.

"No, I'm just tired," I said.

"Where did you go?" she asked. "We still had a couple of things to
move."

"Like I told Wilfredo Reyes, I had to get something I left behind."

"Oh," she said frowning. "*El Hermano* Reyes must have forgotten to
tell me." Blanca then faced Roberto and Claudia. "Can you believe
this, Julio, they've been seeing each other in secret all this time and
now they want to elope!" I congratulated them, shaking their hands
and telling them that was great. Roberto and Claudia seemed happy
but also a little dazed.

"Thank you," Roberto said. "*La Hermana* Mercado has always been
a good friend to Claudia and we wanted to know if you can lend us
some money."

"Sure." I had Vera's diamond ring in mind. They could go far with
that.

"Well, I'm happy for them," Blanca interrupted, "but they shouldn't
just get married."

"Blanca, let them do what they want," I said. I looked at Roberto and
as casually as possible asked him, "You've finished high school, right?"

"Yes, when I was sixteen." He must have skipped a grade.

"Good, and you have a place to live, right?"

"Yes, I have a brother in Chicago. We'll get married and stay with him until I can get a job and Claudia can get her papers so she can look for work also."

"See, Blanca, let's just give them what money we can"—diamond ring included—"and let them go to Chicago." I thought Robert was a smart guy. Besides, if he was really anointed by God then God was looking after him, and if he wasn't, well, his plans were still pretty sound. He wasn't talking about love conquering all. About love being all you need. Roberto was talking about paying the rent. This let me know he was, as Blanca had told me, an adult. Roberto and Claudia probably had a bit of money saved up and now they were doing the right thing, trying to get more. I had no problem with it.

Blanca was thrilled: The girl least likely to be chosen had been. It was like the story of Esther all over again. What bothered Blanca was the disruption this would bring to the spiritual peace of the congregation. The gossip and turmoil they would create by doing this in secret.

"Claudia," Blanca said, "you know your sisters will hate you. They will accuse you of corruption. Roberto's mother will hate you."

"She hates me already. But I did nothing wrong, Roberto is in love with me and I love him." Claudia was not in tears. She was worried but happy.

"Claudia did nothing wrong," Roberto interjected.

"Roberto, you're supposed to be an example. More than an example, what about your mother?" Blanca said to him. "You eloping will kill her. Just go and tell her you fell in love with Claudia and that you want to marry her. Let everyone know the truth. If they hear it out of someone else's mouth then you will be ridiculed." That made me uneasy. Without her knowing it Blanca was talking to me about Bodega. About things that I had yet to tell her. Things that I hoped she would never hear from anyone's lips, Negra's or anybody's. "Roberto, you have to tell your mother. This elope stuff is wrong."

"My mother won't understand," Roberto said. Claudia held his arm now, and nodded in agreement.

"Blanca," I said, a little annoyed, "let them go. We can lend them at least three hundr—"

"No, Julio, this is a mistake," she snapped at me. Then she looked at Roberto. "This is a mistake, Roberto, just go to your mother and tell her. Please."

"Blanca, let them go." I sighed. I was ready to hit an ATM. I thought it was all great. And I was actually happy that somewhere in this neighborhood young people were still falling in love. Of course they were. People are always falling in love, but at times it was easy for me to forget because even though I still loved Blanca, it wasn't the same as before we were married, when nothing seemed impossible and even her religion wasn't an obstacle.

"Thank you, *Hermano* Mercado."

"All right, all right," Blanca said. "Please tell your mother that you're going to marry Claudia. If she disapproves, then you leave."

"Blanca, let them go," I said. "You have a place to stay in Chicago, right Roberto?" I asked him again. Blanca jumped right in.

"Do you know who this older brother in Chicago is, Julio?"

I shrugged. "A brother is a brother, right?"

"Well, that's what you think. Remember Googie Vega?" Blanca puckered her lips and shook her head from side to side. "Roberto is his younger brother."

Everyone had known Googie Vega. He had once been a good Pentecostal. He was seen all over the neighborhood preaching and playing handball. Those were his passions, Christ and a pink rubber Spalding. He was a tall, good-looking guy and, like his little brother, he was very popular. Googie was a bit older than us. He had gone to school with Negra, and she was always talking about laying him and all that stuff. Lots of girls liked him. It was common to hear girls say when they saw Googie preaching with his brothers on a street corner, "Thass a waste of a church boy." And they would accept the leaflets he'd hand out, and agree to go to his Bible studies.

No one knew what had happened to him. Not even Negra. The Pentecostals said that the Devil must have gotten inside him. That demons invaded his thoughts. That he made the mistake of entertaining an evil desire and that desire gave birth to sin. It didn't just turn into a sin, it destroyed him. When it was obvious what he was doing the church kicked him out and guys from the neighborhood started calling him the Junkie Christ. He would hock anything and his eyes were like ashes. The same women who once harbored crushes would whisper as he passed by, "That guy was a church boy once and now he steals from his mother."

"Why didn't you tell me before, Blanca?" I turned toward Roberto. "You know, Roberto, Blanca is right. Go tell your mother."

"You will kill her, Roberto. First Googie, now you," Blanca implored.

Roberto stayed silent.

"Claudia." Blanca held her by the shoulders and looked directly in her eyes. "You have to make Roberto tell his mother." Then she turned to Roberto and said, "You know you will lose all your privileges."

"We've talked about that," Roberto said. "I don't care if they take away my privileges, I can serve Christ as a regular brother. I don't have to have all this status." I liked him. His modesty and humility made me want to believe he might be anointed after all.

"Is there something you're not telling me?" Claudia asked Roberto. "Because I feel Blanca doesn't want to be the one to tell me. That leaves it to you."

"My brother in Chicago, *Dios lo bendiga*, had a really bad drug problem. This was a few years ago. I was a little kid, the Lord hadn't spoken to me yet. But when He did, my mother sent my brother away to Chicago to live with an aunt of ours, so that he wouldn't embarrass me." Silence fell in the bedroom.

Claudia understood everything. Roberto had been sheltered all his life. His mother was determined not to make the same mistake twice. She was going to protect her youngest from everything. Especially since he was one of the chosen, the 144,000 Revelation speaks about. The ones that will rule with Christ for a thousand years. Roberto's mother had sent the eldest into exile and put all her hopes in the youngest. He was a great orator. That was a fact. But in the religious order to which Blanca and her Church subscribed, Roberto was something much more. He was a heavenly prince Christ himself had handpicked to sit with Him at His table.

"Let's go tell your mother," Claudia softly said to Roberto, whose eyes began to water. They said goodbye to Blanca and me and walked out the door.

Blanca and I stayed silent for a moment. She was sad. Her friend had landed the biggest prize of her religion, an anointed one, but somehow she felt as if she was ruining someone's life.

Blanca smiled faintly and then sighed. "I need to study and this place is a mess. I'll be at my mother's." Blanca was spent. She picked up her schoolwork, kissed me goodbye, and before heading out the door asked me again if I'd eaten. I was happy because I knew that as soon as Blanca finished studying, she would talk with her mother a little, maybe have some coffee, and then return home too tired to talk. That suited me fine. She kissed me goodbye again and said I should study too. Finals were coming. I said I would.

I didn't study. Even with the apartment empty except for boxes, it felt good to be all by myself. The wooden floors were all shiny. The place seemed huge. I went to the bedroom and got a pillow. I stretched out on the living room floor and it felt like I was swimming. All this space and freedom.

Then the phone rang.

"Got my stuff, bro?"

"Hello to you, too."

"Fuck that shit, you know it's me. Listen, I need that stuff. I've got work to do."

"Yeah, I got it."

"I'm comin' ovah and, Chino, Bodega wants ta see you like now."

I waited for Sapo downstairs with his envelope. I saw his car turn the corner and I walked over to the curb. He opened the door for me. He was halfway through an entire large Domino's pizza. I handed over the envelope and he nodded, placed it in the glove compartment, and resumed eating his slice.

"Yo, Sapo," I said, "you know that Domino's gives money to those people who fuck up abortion clinics? You helping that shit."

"Nah, get the fuck? You lying, Chino." He seemed amused. He finished the slice, with his right hand reached into the backseat, uncovered the pizza box, and brought out another slice.

"Ho, shit, you still gonna go eating that shit?"

"I don't care who they finance. Their pizza's good."

"Where's your social conscience?"

"My wha'?"

"Something you stand for."

"Tell you what, Chino, since you have plexes with the pizza, I promise to throw the box in the ga'bage. And as for what I stand for? I stand for myself. One man. Above God. With liberty and just enough patience with your fucken social conscience shit to kick yo' ass out of my car. I'm like gettin' tired of drivin' you around. Bodega must think my car is yellow with a big fucken checkered flag on tha side."

That night Sapo dropped me off at one of the new-old buildings Bodega had renovated on 119th and Lexington. Those buildings had been condemned for years. The City of New York takes so much time to either renovate or bulldoze a condemned building it's like those guys on Death Row who die of old age rather than execution. Bodega had bought the entire row from the city and had slowly renovated three of them. He had improved the block. Improved the neighborhood. Given people a place to live.

After dropping me off, Sapo left in a hurry as if he had a lot of work to do. Nene was waiting for me downstairs.

"Whass up, Chino?"

"Whass up, Nene?" But I didn't have the energy to meet his eager expression that night.

Going up, the stairs didn't creak and the walls were freshly painted. The doors were new and the air smelled clean and moist as if it had just rained inside the building. Bodega had chosen a neatly furnished three-bedroom for himself. When I walked in he quickly placed an index finger on his lips.

"Shhh," he whispered, "Vera's sleeping."

"You got problems," I whispered back.

"It's all going to be taken care of tomorrow." He accompanied me to the kitchen, the room farthest from the bedroom where Vera must have been sleeping. Nene was in the living room watching VH1 at low volume, almost mute, as if it was the images that he cared for. I didn't want to ask Bodega how he was going to take care of things. But he told me anyway.

"I'm meeting her husband tomorrow in the afternoon."

"What are you talking about, bro?"

"Vera's husband is coming tomorrow."

"Wait, wait." I couldn't believe it. "Nazario just met this Italian about Fisch—"

"Hey, look, thass my problem. You here for something else?"

"Your problem? So why you had me go with Nazario in the first place?" I was upset. We weren't on the same page.

"Cuz he handpicked you ta go. It wasn't my doin'." I remembered what Sapo had told me, that I was sitting on a lot of information and that wasn't a good place to be.

"So, Chino, he arrives the day after tamorrow."

"Who?" I was lost in thought about Nazario handpicking me, dragging me out to Queens. Why me? Why not someone else? He had tons of better-suited candidates, no pun intended. Bodega wanted me around because Vera was family; no matter how far apart they had been, she was still Blanca's aunt. But what did Nazario need? He was the type who needs very little from anybody and if he ever did need something, he could get it from you without you knowing you had given it to him.

"Vera's husband. That's who."

"Yeah, that's right, you told me."

"You all right, Chino?"

"Yeah, I'm cool." I was still thinking about Nazario, but I had to let it go. I would ask Sapo or maybe Bodega at another time. I could never ask Nazario.

So I tried to shift gears.

"Bodega, you happy about this guy comin'?"

"Yeah, and I want you to be there, with your wife, you know. For support, you know." His face was that of a kid on Christmas Eve who can't wait till midnight to open his presents.

"Who the fuck invited him to New York?"

"I did." He sounded as if that was obvious.

"Why?" I thought it was a stupid idea, but couldn't tell him that.

"B'cause Vera needs to tell him"—he lit a cigarette—"that she never loved him."

"Wait, wait, how does Vera feel about this?"

He turned away from me. He looked at the floor and then, taking a drag, looked to his left and right before exhaling. "She's confused," he said sadly. "See, Chino, she's a little shaken cuz she's spent the last twenty years with that guy. You know she got to feel something for him, but she still loves me and always has." His eyes looked watery, his face drawn. They must have been discussing this all day long.

"I know what yo'r thinking, Chino. But Vera is not like that. It's just that she didn't want to talk about it any longer, she was really tired, thass all." He seemed to desperately need to hear Vera say that she had never loved her husband. He needed to hear it and wanted others to be there as witnesses. It was as if he had forgotten where he stood in the universe and only those words coming from Vera could reorient him to his place in the cosmos. He needed to hear it and he wanted it to be said in his backyard, in East Harlem and not in Miami or anyplace else.

"Look, Willie, you got Fischman, who wants to kill you. You have cops looking around the neighborhood for leads on who killed Salazar. You have this neighborhood thinking you're some sort of goodies bag. Man, why make things worse by inviting this guy?"

My question went right past him. "I think having you and your wife maybe, her sister, too, near Veronica would help." He began pacing and then realized that one of the parquet panels on the floor creaked. He walked over it again to make sure which one was the culprit and told me to avoid it so Vera wouldn't wake up. Then he continued.

"Vera needs support and the more family there the better."

"If Vera needs family there to support her, then I'm sorry, bee, but you just have to accept that she can't say it—"

"She's been with this guy for years!" he loudly hissed at me. "You think thass easy to forget? Wha' you want, her to just say the magic—"

"If she really loved you, Willie, she wouldn't need any help from you or anyone else," I hissed back.

"*Come on people now, smile on your brother.*" Nene glided into the kitchen with a huge grin.

"*'Tá todo bien,*" Bodega assured Nene.

"It's cool, then?" he asked Bodega, not me. "Because I like Chino and I would be like sad if I had to hurt him."

"Don't worry about it. No one is hurting no one," Bodega said, and Nene patted me on the back. "I found out your real name is Julio," he said as he headed back to the living room and the TV. "Thass a dope name, Julio. *Meet me and Julio down by the schoolyard.*"

"Why don't you just get out?" I said to Bodega. "You have Vera, you have money. Just go away. Buy some beach property in San Juan and you and Vera can lie on the sand and watch the world go to hell." I didn't think he'd heard me. His face was blank. His eyes were focused on the closed bedroom door down the hall.

"Did you see that TV special on the Jewish immigrants?" Bodega's eyes were still locked on the bedroom door.

"Nah, missed it." This was hopeless.

"Yeah, well, I was thinkin' that after this is all over, I should open up a school. You know, like the Jews did cuz their kids were like always bein' discriminated and so they gave a lot of money to private schools that had no ties with any religious groups or anyone and so their kids went to these schools without bein' scared. You know what I'm sayin'?"

"I know what you're sayin'."

"So, like, you in college and you hate law, so when you graduate you want to be in this?"

"In what?"

"My school, for our kids. Be a teacher since you hate lawyers."

"Maybe," I said, but I knew I didn't mean it.

"Have you seen that old burnt-down school building on 100th and First? That shit has been abandoned for years. But Nazario got it for us from the city. I'm renovating it."

"Sounds good," I said. I took the ring out of my pocket.

"Look, if Vera wants this back," I said, "you'll know the truth." His gaze fell on the ring in my palm. He nervously took it from me and read the inscription. He didn't say anything. I was about to walk away.

"Need anything, Chino, you see me. Ask Sapo and see me." He put the ring in his pocket. He smiled and then stared back at the bedroom where Vera was sleeping.

As I was heading out, I heard Nene singing, *"Mama, I just killed a man."* His voice was strange, tense and tight. I turned toward him, saw the image on the television, saw it had nothing to do with the song. What was on was a shoe commercial. I stared at Nene for a little while, lost. I thought of Sapo. No, Sapo hadn't killed Salazar. It wasn't Sapo.

Nene saw me looking at him and smiled. I nodded and left. I took a shortcut through a huge vacant lot. I stopped for a minute and even though it was dark I studied the rubble of a building that once stood there. Scorched bricks with wild grass growing all around the lot. A toilet seat lay on its side, a sink and a bathtub too. Fireflies were flashing, lighting up the lot. Once people lived there, I thought. And some fire displaced them. The city did nothing, as if the problem would go away all by itself. In time the buildings eroded. Later, the city wrecking ball knocked them to the ground.

Bodega, I thought, was at least doing the opposite. He was renovating. And when Alberto Salazar discovered who—and what—was behind all the renovation, Bodega sent Nene to kill Salazar. It was hard to believe Nene was a killer. But Nene could be as imposing as a block of granite. It didn't matter that he was slow, it doesn't take much to kill. Nene must have gone with Sapo to do in Salazar together. With Nene and Sapo, you have a lot of brute strength on your side. Bodega did it to protect what was his. He did it to stop the vacant lots from multiplying. Didn't he? True, Vera was his reason for dreaming all this up, but whatever evil deed had been committed, something good was coming out of it. I looked around the rubble-strewn lot and knew someone had to do something about it. Someone had to step forward and do something. Bodega had, because no one but one of its own residents was going to improve Spanish Harlem. No one.

I Liked the Way You
Stood Up for Us

THE next day when I got home from work, our apartment was still a mess. We'd be living out of boxes for at least another week or two. Somehow, though, a sofa had been installed in a corner and there, drinking coffee, were Blanca and Pastor Miguel Vasquez. After greeting me in Spanish, Pastor Vasquez suggested I join Blanca to hear Roberto's sermon later that week. I politely declined, saying I had other things going on.

Blanca jumped on that. "With your friends? He has bad associations, *Hermano* Vasquez. He won't tell me what he does with them but I know it's things that Christians don't do." I was relieved when the pastor politely explained that since I wasn't baptized in the Truth he wasn't going to impose the ethics of a Christian on me. Of course, if I wanted some Bible guidance that was another matter entirely.

"He needs it, *Hermano* Vasquez," Blanca implored. "He associates with that man Bodega." Pastor Vasquez's eyes grew big and he laughed nervously. He tried to change the subject, told me how the Lord had saved him at a time when he was one of the biggest junkies in the neighborhood, injecting anything and everything, even *gasolina*, he joked. I was enjoying hearing his saga of being thrown out of his home, living on the streets, and doing short stints in jail for petty theft. But then the Lord appeared to him and I lost interest. Yes, he informed me, he was a lost sheep and the Lord had saved him, *gracias a Dios*, and who knew, I was probably a lost sheep too. Blanca hung on his every word, nodding her head and taking sneak peeks at me as if to say, "Listen to this, this is for you."

He was reaching into his fat briefcase, to retrieve his Bible so he could read me a text, when the doorbell rang. I excused myself to answer it, breathing a sigh of relief.

"Who is it?"

"Police."

When I opened the door two detectives were standing with their badges out.

"Does a Julio Mercado live here?" one asked.

"Julio?" Blanca stood up and walked over to the door. "What do these gentlemen need to see you for?" she asked with artificial formality. Pastor Vasquez was right behind her.

"I'm Detective DeJesus and this is Detective Ortiz. We would like to ask you a few questions." Both were tall and heavy, so heavy that if either were two inches shorter he'd have been considered fat.

"Concerning?" I said, as my stomach knotted.

"May we come in?"

Now, I know that cops love to get you to invite them in because then they won't need a warrant and anything you have that's illegal and in plain view they can arrest you for. It's a trick they like to pull when they suspect someone but don't have enough evidence. They invite themselves in and then look around. If you have so much as a half-smoked joint in an ashtray, they'll haul your ass down for booking. Never let cops inside your house unless they got a warrant, that's my philosophy.

"Of course!" Blanca said, because she didn't know any better. To her, authority figures were always good. But I knew that it didn't matter that these two cops were Hispanic, cops are a race unto themselves. It's blue first, brown second.

"Would you like some coffee?" Blanca asked them.

They declined, and then looked at me. "Are you Julio Mercado?" It was more a statement than a question.

"That's me," I said.

"It looks as if you just moved in," DeJesus said, stepping over a small box.

"We did," I said.

"Do you know an Enrique Guzman, goes by the name of Sapo?" That right there told me that although they were Hispanic they weren't homegrown. They knew as much about East Harlem as Oscar Lewis. Only Blanca referred to Sapo as Enrique. Sapo was always Sapo. Just Sapo. Nothing else.

"We went to junior high together."

The detective that wasn't asking the questions started looking around. His head rotated like an owl's. Blanca and Pastor Vasquez were whispering nervously to each other. At that moment all I wished was for Blanca not to be there. If I could only send her to buy groceries or something, because I intended to say as little as possible to avoid digging myself a hole.

"Do you still keep company?"

"It's a small neighborhood," I said. My distrust was palpable.

"Mr. Mercado, we are just here to ask you some questions about the murder of Alberto Salazar. Heard about it?" Another question disguised as a statement. Like welfare caseworkers, the ones that stare at you and your children and know full well what the answers to the questions are but still ask, "What is your sex? Do you have any children?"

"It was all over *El Diario*," I answered, stealing a peek at Blanca, whose nostrils were flaring.

"Anything you can tell us would be beneficial."

"Other than what I've read, I don't know anything."

"The woman at the botanica, Doña Ramonita, said you were Enrique Guzman's best friend."

Even when you're bleeding you should cover up your wounds. Detectives are good at getting things from you. Like a friendly machete they clear a path through the grasslands for you and then lead you into a pit.

"Exactly, I *was*. Back in junior high." I saw angry tears form in Blanca's eyes.

"We have reports that you've been seen riding in Enrique Guzman's car."

"He gave me a lift to school once or twice."

"Where do you go to school?"

"Hunter College."

"Is that your girlfriend?" He motioned with his head toward Blanca.

"No," I said, lifting my hand in a fist and showing him my wedding ring. "That's my wife." I could see that this upset DeJesus a bit, so in my most respectful voice I said, "Look, detective, that's my wife and that's Pastor Miguel Vasquez. We were having Bible study. So unless you need something else from me, could you excuse us?" They looked at each other for a second.

"Would you mind coming with us? We have a few pictures and documents we'd like to show you at the station. Take your time. We'll wait in the car until your meeting with the pastor is over. You're not under arrest or anything."

Of course they wanted me to come down to the station; they could have brought those documents and pictures with them. But I couldn't point that out to them.

Instead I said, "Sure, anything to help."

"Pleasure." They both nodded to Blanca and the pastor as they made their way out the door. I now had to look Blanca in the face and explain myself. I wasn't ready, I had no idea what to say to her. In fact I was shaking with nerves. I had promised to let her know the truth but I had kept things from her.

"I'll be at my mother's," she said, standing. "I need to study. I have an exam tomorrow and I think I'll stay at my mother's. Please excuse me, Pastor." She was crying, and moving around the room with a heavy grace, collecting her books.

I followed her around the living room as she started putting her things in her bag. "It's nothing. You heard them, no one is arresting anyone."

"That's good, because when I see you tomorrow, we'll need to talk."

"Blanca, it's nothing."

"Nothing! It might be nothing to you, but do you know what just happened? The police were in my house! What do you think you're doing?" She turned and headed into the bedroom.

I heard her ripping open boxes. She gathered her vitamins, her schoolbooks, and a few items of clothing. She returned to the living room with a duffel bag. Pastor Vasquez obviously felt uncomfortable. He didn't say anything, just looked down at the floor as if he had mistakenly opened a women's bathroom door while someone was in the stall.

Blanca was embarrassed too. She knew the congregation would hear about this. "*Bueno. Que Cristo te proteja,*" Pastor Vasquez said to me as he took Blanca's bag. Blanca didn't say anything. They just walked out. I knew they'd talk about me as they walked to Blanca's mother's house.

I didn't know which I dreaded more, dealing with Blanca later or with the police now. I waited a minute before going down to meet the detectives.

They weren't waiting for me inside the car like they had said. DeJesus was in the lobby, but the other one was missing.

"Where's your partner?"

"He went to get some coffee," DeJesus said. We headed out to the car.

A minute later, Ortiz walked out of the building and joined us. He must have been on the roof, looking down. They had made sure I wasn't going to escape by going out the window and down the fire escape.

The last thing I wanted to do was let on that I had caught them in a lie, so I didn't ask Ortiz what happened to his coffee.

"This won't take long, Mr. Mercado." Ortiz drove.

"Where you from?" I asked them but neither answered. I didn't bother to ask again, and we rode the rest of the way in silence.

At the 23rd Precinct on 102nd between Lexington and Third, they ushered me inside. It was hot and dimly lit. Hanging from the ceiling were those yellow energy-saving lights from the seventies. It also smelled musty, like old papers, old books, old newspapers with pale brown edges and little bugs crawling everywhere.

They sat me down on a bench and told me to wait. DeJesus and Ortiz went over to a desk across the hall and started to joke around with the cop that sat there. It was busy, cops typing reports, taking complaints, talking on the phone, and I sat there totally unnoticed until DeJesus and Ortiz came back and waited with me.

"The captain has a few things to run by you."

"What's the captain's name?" I asked. They didn't answer me.

After about ten minutes being sandwiched by the two, I asked, "Will he be long?" Again they didn't answer me.

"Look," I said, standing up. "I am here on my own time. If you want me to cooperate with you, then answer my question. Out of common courtesy, one Latino to another."

DeJesus, the shorter and therefore fatter of the two, showed his nails.

"You and me have nothing in common," he sneered. "I'm Cuban, you're Puerto Rican." I decided not to point out that I was only half Puerto Rican.

"Take it easy," Ortiz told his partner.

"Well, this ain't Miami," I said. "You're in my backyard, so don't disrespect me."

"You better watch your back, Mercado," DeJesus muttered, sneering.

"Take it easy, DeJesus," Ortiz repeated.

"You're so into it you smell like Boricua!" DeJesus didn't seem to have heard his partner. "If it was up to me I'd send you all back to that monkey island of yours." That did it, I had to say something.

"You're from a monkey island yourself. At least Puerto Ricans leave of their own free will. Castro kicked your ass out!"

"What did you say!" DeJesus rose and got up in my face.

Ortiz stepped between us and sat me down. He didn't say anything to his partner. Just then a door a few feet in front of the bench opened and DeJesus shut his trap.

The detectives led me into the office, where the captain sat behind a desk. I was seated in front of him and the two detectives sat on a little couch by the window. I thought about the first time I had met Bodega. It had been a similar set-up, Bodega sitting behind a desk and me sitting in front on some cheap-ass chair. Somehow even then I knew that meeting would lead me here, to the precinct. But the damage was already done. I was here and all I could do now was try never to come back. The hard part was doing that without ratting on anyone.

"Mr. Mercaydo, I'm Captain Leary," he said, mispronouncing my name. He was a tall man with white hair and a ruddy complexion. He looked like he had been around a long time just getting ready to retire.

"You need something from me, Captain?"

"Funny, isn't it?" he said, sliding a crime-scene picture across the desk. "A piece of his shoulder was just chewed right out."

"Well, I'm sure you've seen funnier things," I said calmly. But inside I was on fire. At that minute I was mad as hell. I was mad at myself for getting into this and I was mad at that Cuban detective for being a pig. And I was mostly mad at the fact that I could do nothing about it.

"Oh yes, I've seen much funnier." The captain talked as if he were bored; it was all a formality, something he had done too many times and could do in his sleep. He then opened an envelope and handed me some documents.

The Harry Goldstein Real Estate Agency. There were copies of all the building's leases, showing ownership by that company.

"Do you recognize that agency?"

"Sure. My wife and I write them a rent check every month." Out of the corner of my eye I saw DeJesus squirm in his chair. Ortiz just sat on the couch quietly.

"Does the name William Irizarry mean anything to you?"

"No."

"What about the name Willie Bodega. Mean anything?"

"No." I was in America and in America you can say that rain falls dry and you let the jury decide if it's true or not.

"Look, son." He folded his hands and said in a paternal tone, "I know you're a good kid. You go to school and work hard. Your wife is expecting, you're going to be a father. That's great. We checked you out, you're clean. You hopped a few turnstiles when you were fifteen, but that's about it." He leaned back in his chair. "You have nothing to worry about. But at times good people are led astray. They don't know any better because they think that these people are their friends. If Bodega has got something on you, you can tell us." Right then I knew they may have known a lot about Bodega but they had very little on him. They needed evidence, testimony, something concrete.

"I've no idea about this Bodega, sir. And I'm not your son." And then, with a more respectful tone, "Sir."

The captain leaned forward, smiling slightly. "Let me give you a scenario. You have a reporter that gets in over his head. He gets killed and then you find out that reporter was dirty. He belonged to another drug lord. He was killed by that drug lord's rival. It's only a matter of time before the other guy fights back, and then what do you have?" He wanted me to say a war.

"Sounds like trouble."

"He's jerking us around," DeJesus said. "He's been seen with Enrique Guzman. If you know Enrique Guzman you know Willie Bodega."

"Hey." I faced DeJesus. "When Frank Sinatra was alive he'd be dining with a bunch of mafiosos every night, but you guys never brought him in for questioning."

"Sit down, please sit down," Leary said to me calmly. Ortiz patted the air near his friend, telling him to calm down.

"Look," I said, "I've got things to do. Now, I told you what I know and, like you, I have a job to do. So if you are going to arrest me for something, you tell me what it is and let me call a lawyer. Otherwise don't waste my time and yours." I bluffed, because if they were to detain me, Nazario was the only lawyer I knew and that might lead right to Bodega.

"Bullshit." DeJesus spat. Leary sighed. Ortiz just shook his head.

"You're free to go," Leary said. Sounded like salsa to me.

"What! Leary, come on!" DeJesus said, getting up from the couch.

"I'll walk you out, Mr. Mercado," Ortiz said to me. I thanked both him and the captain. I had nothing to say to DeJesus.

"Just one thing, *son*." This time Leary emphasized the word, patronizingly. "If I see you as much as jaywalking, I'll have you right back here, and next time I won't be as understanding." As if he had been. But it was all right. He had nothing and was just trying to scare me.

Ortiz was silent as we walked out of the precinct and onto the street. I was ready to walk away, but Ortiz wasn't through.

"*Mira*, Mercado, I was raised in Jersey, but I'm originally from San Juan. I hope you understand," he said, "that DeJesus is my partner. I didn't like what he said about us. But, right or wrong, I have to back my partner."

"Sure." I understood.

"Good. Now, I really hope you told the truth. I really hope you're clean, Mercado," Ortiz said. "Cuz I liked the way you stood up for us."

The Saddest Part Is
Turning Off the Lights

was still shaking when I got home at about eight-thirty. I wondered if I really was clean, or if I was somehow involved in all of this more than I wanted to think. But what worried me more was that Blanca might not come back. I should have bought a machine so I could check messages, but I had never gotten around to it. So I called her mother's right away.

"Nancy?"

"Yes, it's me." She knew I'd call.

"Everything's all right, see? I'm home."

"I wish I was one of those people that stays mad, Julio. I wish I was one of those people who hates forever; you deserve it. You've been lying to me all this time—"

"I'm sorry, Nancy."

"You could've told me the truth from the beginning and still counted on me."

"Nancy, from now on, I swear I'll never hide anything from you. I'll tell you the complete truth—"

"I don't want to know the truth," she said. "It's too late for it and I don't want to hear it. Let's not say anything right now, okay? I'm going to be staying at Mami's for a while. At least until the baby is born. I think that's best. Best for both of us."

"All right," I said sadly. "Just promise you'll come back."

"I'll be back," she whispered. Then, after a pause, "Just not, not right now."

"All right. But you know I love you."

"Please!" Her voice sailed a notch. "Just let me stay at my mother's for a while, all right?"

"All right. Whatever you want."

"I'll be there tomorrow with *la Hermana* Santiago to pick up some things. And Julio . . ." She paused. "I don't know how to say this, but I hope you aren't home when we get there."

"Okay." I was in no position to bargain. When your wife says she's leaving you, whether it's for a few days or months or forever, you don't object. You just let her go. You might want to ask her if she needs money, but in our case Blanca always had more money than me.

"Do you need money?" I asked anyway.

"Do *you* need money?" she quickly replied.

"No . . . I'm okay," I said, knowing I was broke. "Call me when you can."

"Take care of yourself." She hung up. I looked around the apartment. It was a mess, so many things out of place. All of a sudden the place seemed empty and dark. The boxes that were stacked up against the wall would remain unopened. There was no need to make this place feel like home.

The phone rang. I jumped at it.

"Nancy!"

"Nah, it's Negra."

"Negra, I've no time for you, okay?"

"Well, you better make some time, Chino—"

"Blanca just left me." I wanted anyone's sympathy all of a sudden.

"You serious? Don't play with me, play lotto. You serious?"

"Walked out."

"That's fucked up."

"So listen, she might call back. Can you leave the line free, please?"

"All right. I'm sorry to hear that, but you do owe me, Chino. Just remember that."

"Negra! Get off the line!" I yelled.

"Dag, it's not my fault my sister left you—" I hung up on her and went to wash my face. The phone rang again.

"Nancy!"

"Chino, you owe me big." It was Negra again. I sighed and let her talk. "You owe me big." I sort of knew what she wanted. Blanca had told me.

"Negra, what makes you think I can have your husband beat up?"

"Don't insult me. I know who your friends are."

"Even if I could, Negra, I ain't having Victor beat up, all right? That's all."

"Come on, Chino. He won't even know you had something to do with it."

"You solve your own marital problems, Negra."

"Chino, just a little bit. Get Nene to knock him around some or Sapo to bite him. Like the way they tag-teamed that reporter." I was silent after that. How did she know?

"What are you talking—"

"Come on, Julio, don't take me for a fool."

"All right, all right. The cops were here, that's why Blanca left."

"No shit. They've been talking to a lot of people. But no one's saying anything."

"Have they talked to you?"

"Not me. But you ain't getting out of this one. Victor. What are you going to do about Victor? I want him hurt. You owe me."

"All right. I'll see what I can do," I said, even though I didn't mean it. I just wanted her off the phone.

"You serious, Chino?"

"Yeah," I sighed.

"Now, I don't want him dead," she said carefully. "Or broken, you know, because I want him back. I just want to teach him a lesson, thass all."

"Of course."

"I like his nose. Don't let anyone break his nose."

"Is that all?"

"Actually, leave his face the way it is, I always thought he was cute. Go for the body."

"Of course. Look, I have to go."

"Leave his balls alone. Like I said, I'm planning on taking him back."

"Negra, I have to go!" I shouted.

"All right, all right." And then, Negra allowed herself to become a bit human again. "Chino, I'm sorry about Blanca, okay. You two will patch it up."

"Thanks," I whispered, and Negra hung up.

I had gone to bed hoping that Blanca would call, but after two hours of tossing and turning I gave up hope. The hardest thing was falling asleep. It was as if I had snorted all the coke in the world and my eyes hurt but my brain couldn't shut itself off. Thoughts of Blanca, the pastor, the cops, Bodega raced through my mind like the Wonder Wheel at Coney Island. I began to think at what point in time I could have done things differently. Where were those interesting lines that I could have avoided?

I tried to empty my mind, but I still couldn't sleep. The refrigerator hummed loudly, like a Buddhist on crack. I could hear every noise in the building. A pot fell in 4F, a baby was crying in 3B, they were watching television in 2A. Every sound was magnified. I realized I hadn't made love to Blanca in over a month.

So I got up. I turned on the television but the reception was bad. I made myself a sandwich. I opened a box where some of my books were and found *The Stranger*. Maybe I could get lost in someone else's misfortunes for a change. I fixed up my pillow and began to read. It was a book I had once loved and carried around with me, but I knew the real reason I was reading *The Stranger* wasn't because I wanted to drift back into the past. It was simpler than that. I was afraid and missed Blanca. And when you've been with someone for a long time and they leave you, the saddest part is turning off the lights.

Worth All the Souls in Hell

THE next day I went to work. It felt good to go, because it took my mind off things. It felt good to be busy and not have to think about my own troubles. I wanted to see Bodega like I wanted to see a leper, so I avoided the places I knew Sapo might be driving around collecting. Besides, I had Detectives DeJesus and Ortiz to worry about. As for Blanca, I didn't want to think too much about her, for I might have broken down and started crying in public, embarrassing the hell out of myself. I kept telling myself that she was safe and that she would return to me once she'd had the baby, maybe sooner. I kept telling myself that Blanca believed strongly that all kids should have a father and a mother. With that in mind, I tried to let it go.

After work, I had class, so I went home to pick up my books. As soon as I entered I knew that Blanca had been there. I saw that some of the boxes in which she had packed her clothes had been emptied and some were even missing. It made me feel sad. I gathered up the books I needed and got out of the apartment as quickly as I could.

After a few blocks, I bought a *piragua* from the old man dressed like a sailor who walked around the neighborhood pushing his *piragua* cart, which had fake sails. On the side of his cart read, *"Aquí me quedo"*—here I stay. He made the best *piraguas* in the neighborhood. I was asking for a *tamarindo piragua* when someone called my name.

"Chino. So, like, I hear you were asked to dinnah?" It was Sapo. His car was right next to the curb.

"Look, man," I said, checking for DeJesus and Ortiz, just in case, "they want your boss. Now I told them nothin', but from now on he's on his own."

"Thass cool. I heard you were a fucken rock. Like they brought in the nuns and even them bitches couldn't make you talk."

"I have a class," I said, tired of Sapo and all the rest.

"I hear that. So, *mira*, Chino, I know your alleluia wife booked—"

"What the fuck—? Who the fuck told you that?"

"Negra, thass who. Somethin' about gettin' Victor beat up? Anyway, don't sweat Negra, cuz—"

"Look, I have to go. Wan' a *piragua*, tell me now," I said to him.

"You. I wan' you, bro. I was sent to get you, homey."

"I ain't going nowhere with you."

"Yes you are, cuz Vera's husband is waiting for you at Ponce de Leon Restaurant, you know that restaurant, doncha? That place by 116th and Lex?"

"I ain't goin'."

"You told Bodega you was gonna go."

"Not anymore."

"Well, this might change your mind. Afterward Bodega and Vera are gonna pay a visit to her sistah. Thass right, your alleluia wife's mother." I perked up. "Thought that'd get you horny." Sapo smiled his Sapo smile and the old man finished scraping his big block of ice and packed the tiny icicles in a paper cup.

"See, Chino, this will make you mad happy. Bodega and Vera plan to stick up for you. Vera plans on convincing her sistah to convince her daughter to return to you. I mean, it's not like you been dickin' other women. Thass all the *bochinche* I have for you now. Still goin' ta class?"

The old man colored the tiny icicles a light orange-brown by dripping a homemade *tamarindo* syrup all over my *piragua*. He wrapped a napkin around the paper cup and offered it to me. I paid, thanked him, and got in Sapo's car.

"You know those two detectives, Ortiz and DeJesus?" I asked Sapo.

"Yeah, they sorry niggas."

"This is serious, bro."

"I know. They been sniffin' at Bodega fo' evah. They been like askin' Bodega's tenants questions and shit. Thass how they got to you, some fucken person in da buildin' pointed your way. We'll find out who and make the nigga homeless."

"Sapo," I said, "I know you didn't exactly kill Salazar." He didn't answer me and I left it at that. Sapo then made a left turn and we were on 116th and Third.

"'Memba the Cosmo useta be here?" Sapo pointed at a department store that was once a theater.

"Yeah, they showed the worst movies in all the nine planets."

"You got good weed, though, and the movies were mad cheap."

We reached the restaurant, which was down the block, just opposite where the Cosmo used to be. I got out of the car. I finished off my *piragua* and threw the paper cup in the trash.

"Inside, go to the back, Chino. All the way to the back. Behind the kitchen. You'll see him back there. Can't miss 'im. Nigga is old. I don't know where the fuck Bodega dug up that fossil." And then Sapo took off.

I walked inside to great smells. *Arroz asopado, pasteles, lechón asado, empanadas, camarones fritos.* A waiter saw me and seemed to recognize immediately that I was not there to eat. He ushered me all the way to the back of the restaurant and into a small room behind the kitchen. I could hear the sounds of dishes hitting against one another as they were washed by hand.

In the room was a small table with a candle and an old man sitting with a suitcase at his feet. He was well dressed. His suit looked expensive and he wore cufflinks. He smelled of good aftershave and his shoes were polished to a high shine. His watch was expensive too. But his face was a wasteland, as if his best years had been spent working in a coal mine. It made me want to trade in the watch and the suit in return for him not having worked as hard as he obviously had to get those things. I went over to him and introduced myself.

"Hi, I'm Julio Mercado." I extended my hand and he got up from his chair to shake it.

"John Vidal," he said in a tired, old voice. "Could you please tell me what this is all about?" I didn't say anything. "My wife called me a day ago hysterically crying, and told me to come up to New York." He sounded worried. "I asked her why. Why she didn't just return. She continued to cry, so I agreed to come. On the phone she gave me this address. I thought this was a hotel." He sat down. I felt a little bad for him; he was lost and Miami was far away.

"I met your wife, she's my wife's aunt." I couldn't think of anything else to say. He jumped to his feet again.

"Then you must know where my wife is. Vera is not like this at all. She wanders . . . but always comes back to me."

"She'll be here," I said.

"The waiter said the same thing. But I've been waiting for hours."

"Have you eaten?" I was desperate for something to say.

"No, I'm not hungry. I just want my wife." He sat back down defiantly. "I've got things, important things to do back in Miami. Vera, you better have a good reason for doing this," he said even though she wasn't there. When the waiter walked through the door and brought us coffee, placing the cups carefully on the table as if they were live grenades, Vidal didn't even bother to look up.

"Who are you really?" he asked.

"I'm Vera's niece's husband. My wife, Nancy, is her—"

"Yes, yes, yes," he said, and waved away the rest of my response. "Yes, yes, you've told me. Now, look here, young man." I would never have guessed he was Latin. He was more American than Mickey Mouse and just as old. "I'm going to go to the police. I get the feeling my wife is being held against her will."

"Your wife will be here." Bodega was punishing him. I was too tired to feel bad for Vidal or anybody; I had my own problems. I started to get hungry. The good smells were overpowering. I asked him if he was hungry again but he didn't answer me. It felt uncomfortable to be in that room with him, but I had to stay. If what Sapo had told me was true, I knew that Vera's talk with her sister would influence Blanca. I needed allies to get Blanca to return. What better ally than Blanca's mother?

The time dragged. So I thought about Blanca and the early days. All the places we went to and the things we had done. Like the day she told me she was pregnant. How she had wrapped a present for me and, smiling, said happy birthday. I told her it wasn't my birthday and she punched my shoulder and said she knew. When I unwrapped it, there was a baby rattle. She hugged me, telling me that unplanned babies are the most loved. I got nervous because we were still in school and didn't have real jobs, but I was happy. God, that was only a couple months ago. When did things start going bad? I needed to get this all fixed up. I wanted my wife back.

Finally Bodega and Vera walked in. Bodega was wearing a new suit. It wasn't all white like the one I had last seen him wear. This was a very fine dark blue suit, probably Italian, with a satin red handkerchief poking out of the breast pocket. His shirt, tie, and shoes were color-coordinated, evidence that Vera had dressed him for the occasion.

When Vidal saw Vera, he shot up from his seat and headed over to her, but Bodega stopped him. I could see he didn't want the old man to touch her. Vera was silent. Her head hung low. She looked like she had been crying.

"Vera, is everything all right?" Vidal asked.

"Everything is fine," Bodega answered him.

"And may I ask who you are?" he inquired politely.

"William Irizarry," Bodega barked. Vidal looked at Bodega for only a second. He was trying to figure it all out but couldn't. He didn't have a clue. He then looked back at his wife.

"Do you owe this gentleman something?" he asked her kindly. "Money? Anything? Vera, please, speak to me." He was going to touch her hair, to comfort her, but Bodega knocked his hand aside. Vera was silent.

"Listen, Mr. Irizarry. I'm not sure what this is all about—"

"Stop it! Stop it!" Vera cried. "John, I'm . . . I'm . . . I'm leaving you." She forced it out of herself.

"What are you talking about?"

"Your wife, she never loved you," Bodega blurted as Vera buried her face in Bodega's shoulder. "She always loved me." His chest swelled up. Vidal stayed silent for a few seconds. Bodega stared at him like a cobra waiting to bite. Vidal looked at Bodega for a moment before his eyes returned to his wife.

"Vera, please, let me help you. Tell me what is this all about." Like Vera, he was almost in tears. He looked tired and hurt. Bodega then cradled her face in his hands.

"Tell him," Bodega almost whispered. "Tell him you never loved him. Tell him you're staying with me."

Vera looked at Bodega as if the suggestion was inappropriate. As if affairs were all right just as long as they were kept in the dark.

"William," she cried. "I'm leaving him, isn't that enough?"

"Yes, but tell him you never loved him," he said gently, letting go of her face. She then looked at her husband, whose head shook in disbelief.

"John." She sniffled. "John, I cared for you once because—"

"It's okay, Vera," he said tenderly. "Just come back with me."

"Don't you see?"—Bodega got closer to the old man—"She's leaving you." Vera's husband seemed intimidated. Bodega was the block bully. Bodega took a step back and stood behind Vera, placing his hands on her shoulders. She looked at the floor. Her tears dropped onto the wood, leaving little clear dots on the floor.

"I'm sorry, John. But I still feel young," she said, lifting her head and wiping her tears away.

"When I met you I was just a teenager and you were this, this man, from a world that was foreign to me." She swallowed hard and Bodega squeezed her shoulders, urging her on. "I liked your life. My parents knew, I knew, I needed to get out of this place."

"It's all right, Vera. It's all in the past," Vidal said. "From now on, we'll do things—"

"Don't you see, John? I don't need you anymore. You are an old man!" He staggered back. Her words were like daggers. "You are useless. You can't even make love anymore."

"I see," he said calmly. But Vera wouldn't stop.

"You are just an old man who can only find comfort in how much money he makes." Bodega seemed proud of her. He watched with the assurance of a parent who is in the audience watching his daughter perform. I could tell by Vera's hesitation in telling her husband those horrible things that it was Bodega who was really talking, through her. Maybe it was something that he had practiced with her, had her recite until she got it right. Vera might have been in love with Bodega all along but somehow I didn't think she meant to say all those cruel things to her husband.

"I see," Vidal repeated. He then gathered himself up, adjusted his tie, and brushed his blazer. He cleared his throat. "And may I ask," he said to her, "may I ask who was there when you needed money? For your salons? Your new clothes that remain untouched in your closets? Your health foods and yoga classes?" He paused when Bodega let go of Vera's shoulders and clenched his fists. "The day I took you to the Met. Remember? You had been living in this city all your life and had never been there. Remember that day—"

"Stop it! Stop it!"

"You wanted to see everything and know everything."

Bodega dug in his pockets. He took the ring and held it up to the old man's face. He then let it fall slowly from his hand, like a drop of water. Vidal recognized the ring. He knelt down and silently picked it up, then held it in front of him for a moment before putting it in his pocket. His face was serene.

His eyes left Vera and looked at Bodega. "You want her? Then I must tell you things about my wife."

"I don't need to hear anything from you. I know everything about Veronica—"

"Veronica?" Vidal laughed, his eyes mocking Vera. "Veronica. I haven't heard you called that since our wedding day."

"Shut up, John." She seemed desperate for him to be quiet.

The old man's eyes returned to Bodega. "But you see, I must warn you about my wife. About her affairs. There have been so many. I personally never cared. She always came back to me. You see, her body is an international hotel, it has taken in men from all over the world."

"Say one more fucken word and I break your face."

"Ah," the old man said, looking at Bodega more closely, "now I know who you are, you are that old boyfriend." He started to laugh. "Now I know what this is about." His eyes left Bodega and went back to Vera. "How long has this one been going on, Vera?"

"Just shut up! Shut up!"

"Did you get tired of the ones in Miami? Did you come here for this ex-thug who—"

Bodega lost it. He grabbed the old man by the blazer and shoved him against the wall. I tried to pull Bodega off. Bodega let go of the blazer. Vidal laughed even harder.

"What are you going to do, kill me? Pah!"

Bodega gritted his teeth. "I'm not a nobody."

"I spotted your kind as soon as you walked in the door with my wife. You're one of those nickel-and-dime drug people. It figures, that's all you people in this neighborhood can do. You couldn't make an honest buck if the work was given to you. My wife isn't going anywhere with you and this nonsense is over." He grabbed Vera by the hand and pulled her over. Bodega slapped him and pulled Vera back. After the old man regained his balance he reached inside his blazer and took out a cellular phone.

But before he could finish dialing, Vera shot him.

She shot him only once but it was enough. The sound of the bullet didn't disturb anyone. It was a dull pop, a sound drowned out by the dishes being washed next door. For a second Vidal stared blankly at Vera, lost in a fog of shock and disbelief. He spat, coughed, and then fell flat on the floor, his hand still clutching the phone. Bodega quickly went over to Vidal, propped his head up, and looked for a pulse. Bodega looked hard into the old man's eyes as if he wanted them to look back at him and share his strength, come back to life. But the old man's blood was running backward in his veins and God wouldn't reconsider.

I looked at Vera, who had let the gun drop and was backing up against the wall. She slid all the way down to the floor until her legs bent and her knees pressed against her chest. She hid her face with her hands.

I had done nothing but watch in a sweat.

"Jam the door, Chino!" Bodega said to me, as he pulled the table-cloth off the table. Everything that was on top fell to the floor, like the old magic trick done wrong.

"Don't let anyone come in." He laid the cloth on the floor and rolled the old man in it. I didn't know what else to do so I did as I was told. Then Bodega began to curse.

"*Coño!* Fuck! *Carajo,* what the fuck was that shit for?" He stormed over to Vera. "Shit, Vera, who the fuck told you to shoot him!" he yelled.

"I'm sorry!" she yelled back, still hiding her face with her hands.

"*Ave Maria, coño, me cago en la madre.*"

"I'm sorry, William," she said, still crouching on the floor. "I'm sorry."

Bodega then knelt down beside her. "Vera?"

"Oh my God, I've killed him. Oh my God, I'm sorry, William. You can't let me go to prison, please, William."

Bodega moved her hands away, uncovering her face. "It's all right, *mami,* you won't go to prison," he said softly.

"I'm sorry."

"Chino, help me get her up."

Vera's legs were weak; like a calf that is learning to walk, she was wobbly and disoriented. We sat her down and she placed her head on the table, hiding her face in her hands again. Bodega knelt down beside the old man's body, now wrapped in the tablecloth. Bodega took the phone out of Vidal's clutch. He made a quick call. He spoke very quietly, making sure I didn't hear. Not that it mattered. I knew that Nazario was on the other end of the line. Then he hung up.

"Listen." He placed his hand on my shoulder. "You were the only one here." He looked straight in my eyes and whispered, "You were the only one who saw me shoot."

I froze. "What?"

"I shot him," Bodega said, making sure Vera didn't hear anything. "You understand me, Chino?"

I nodded, but right then I knew Bodega was lost. His dreams about the neighborhood had been too close to his love for Vera, incestuous cousins that had no right getting involved. When he looked at me that night, his face still had that radiant look, that well-focused beam that couldn't miss its target. But miss it, it would.

"It was my gun."

"What was she doing with it?"

"We'd gone shooting by the East River," he said.

To this day, I think that in a weird way Bodega was actually happy that Vera's husband was dead. His bloodstained suit didn't put out that spark in his conscience that told him Vera was all his. Her vows had been severed for sure. Now, as in the past, he and Nazario would clean up the mess and he could continue dreaming. Only this time, Vera would be by his side.

"Do you understand?"

"I hear you." I didn't understand and had nothing else to add.

"I'm sorry about your wife," he said sadly, and then looked back at Vera, who had lit up a cigarette and was nervously smoking it.

"I'll deal with it," I said, looking at Vera.

"I'll help you," Bodega said, as if I was the one that needed help. As if a dead man was not lying on the floor.

"No *te apure*, we'll get her back." He smiled. "I'll see you tomorrow. We'll see what we can do about it."

"Sure."

What else was I supposed to say? Bodega went back to Vera, sat next to her, placed his arms around her. Her face looked absent, as if she were slowly going mad.

"Hey, Willie," I said as I was about to walk out the door, "I think you're worth all the souls in hell. Thass thousands of more souls than there are in heaven. So you're worth a lot, *pana*." He laughed a short laugh; his eyes met mine very deeply, then shifted away. And he just sat there next to Vera as he waited for Nazario.

I left them alone with that dead guy on the floor, who meant nothing to me. Wasn't family or anything. I left them there in that room sitting next to each other like two birds on a branch.

•

WHEN I got home, I realized that telling Bodega that he was worth all the souls in hell was the only compliment, if it was a compliment, I had ever given him or would ever give him. The next day, Bodega was dead.

"The Way a Hero Sandwich Dies in the Garment District at Twelve O'Clock in the Afternoon"

THE following day El Barrio resembled a country under martial law. It was a battleground full of squad cars, reporters, and camera crews.

Earlier that morning I had been awakened by loud pounding on the door.

"Who is it?"

"Mr. Mercado? Open up, we need you to come with us." It was Ortiz and DeJesus. I opened the door.

"Am I under arrest?" I asked.

"No. Not at all." Ortiz made it a point to be straight with me.

"Then I can't go. I have to go to—"

"William Irizarry is dead," Ortiz said. My empty stomach began making dying-animal sounds.

"When?"

"Last night. He was shot."

"Who shot him?" I asked.

"Come with us," DeJesus growled. I didn't really care. It was too early to worry about his dirty looks.

I got dressed and went with them.

Outside, the streets were dark blue in the early morning light. There was a lot of brass commanding teams of policemen; sending them by fours and at times by sixes, all combing the neighborhood for something or maybe as a show of force. It was cruel arithmetic. Four men with guns to a single corner. Other than cops, the streets were pretty much empty of people. Only cops roamed the streets, if not on foot, then patrolling in squad cars, slowly driving up and down the avenues, from First to Fifth, from 125th to 96th, circling Spanish Harlem like sharks. Instead of salsa music, police walkie-talkies were on full blast, bombarding the streets with what sounded like a nest of hissing snakes.

But I wasn't thinking of anything but Bodega. Bodega was dead. The last time I'd seen him, he was going to take the rap for his love. I kept picturing him reassuring Vera that everything was going to be all right. Reassuring her so often and in such a heartfelt way that she probably believed him. I wondered if Vera was dead too.

As soon as I entered the 23rd, with Ortiz and DeJesus, I saw Nazario. At first I thought he was under arrest, but when I saw Vera sitting next to him on the wooden bench, I knew he had been waiting for me.

"This man is also my client," he said to DeJesus and Ortiz. Vera was very much alive and seemed more composed than when I'd last seen her. But she also seemed exhausted. Her makeup was smudged and her clothes rumpled. It reminded me of the day when she and Bodega had arrived at my place all drunk and happy.

"He is not under arrest," Ortiz said.

"Then let him go home."

"The captain wants to ask him—"

"But it's all already there," Nazario said calmly. "All the reports have been signed. All accounts taken, all eyewitnesses questioned. It's all there." Nazario must have been at the 23rd a lot longer than I thought. I knew he knew everything: who had killed Bodega and why. I was wondering how much of the whole truth, if any, Nazario had told the police. And how much of the truth would he tell me?

"No! It's not all there," DeJesus barked. "We have reports that Mercado was a witness." I stayed quiet. Nazario coldly gazed at DeJesus, like a snake studying a mouse.

"Can I have a minute alone with my client?"

"Sure. He's not under arrest," Ortiz said. They backed away a few steps and Nazario and I turned our backs to them. Vera stayed seated.

"Just say you weren't there when John Vidal was shot," was all he said.

"What happened to Willie?" I whispered back, but he ignored the question.

"Don't worry." Nazario rubbed his eyes as if he needed sleep. "Just say you weren't at the restaurant, and we'll all go home." He released a deep, tired sigh.

We faced Ortiz and DeJesus. Nazario went over to where Vera was sitting, and told her that he'd be coming back. She nodded and dug in her purse for her compact. She had cried a lot and needed to check the damage. DeJesus and Ortiz led us to Leary's crowded office. Leary was being mobbed by people who didn't look like cops, but I couldn't have cared less. When he spotted DeJesus, Ortiz, Nazario, and me, Leary excused himself and met us outside his office. Leary looked at me. He pursed his lips and shook his head. Leary's eyes were as tired as Nazario's.

"So, let's keep it simple. Mr. Mercaydo, were you at Ponce de Leon Restaurant at any time yesterday?"

"No."

"Fine." He gestured for Ortiz and DeJesus to take us away. To him, this was all a formality, as if he knew what I was going to say beforehand, as if he was happy that I'd said this because it would cut his paperwork in half and he could wrap things up.

"Shouldn't he sign a statement, Captain?" DeJesus protested.

"My client doesn't have to sign anything," Nazario interjected.

Leary agreed. He had all he wanted. It didn't matter that he might have a few loose ends here or there. The most important part, two of three homicides—Alberto Salazar, John Vidal, and William Irizarry—had been solved in one day. William Irizarry was being held responsible for the murders of both Alberto Salazar and John Vidal. I didn't yet know for sure who had killed Bodega, but like Leary I had an idea.

Without saying anything to Leary, Nazario and I walked out. Leary went back into his office, braced for the mob inside. Nazario and I went over to get Vera, who sat silently at the bench. The three of us exited the precinct, Vera's heels clacking in the early morning.

Outside a car was waiting for Nazario. He opened the door for Vera. She hadn't spoken a word to me and I didn't really care. I had nothing to say to her. Nothing.

Vera got in the car. Nazario told the driver to wait for a moment.

"Willie is dead." He looked at the concrete. "It was Fischman."

"How?"

"He shot him. Listen," he said coldly, "we had to lay all the blame on Willie, because Willie was already dead. Understand?"

"I understand. When was he shot?"

"On his way to give himself up."

"For Vera?"

"Yes."

"Then you know it was Vera who shot John Vidal," I said.

He didn't answer me.

"Why didn't Nene or you go with him when he went to turn himself in?"

"He wanted to go alone."

"And you let him?"

"It's late." That's all he said. His eyes pressed shut as tight as a lizard's. I didn't bother to press him because Nazario would never tell me everything. I would have to ask Sapo. Nazario just got in the car.

I understood Nazario. Bodega was already dead. Why have other people locked up? Nazario was cutting everything loose, even if it meant letting the cops deal with Fischman. Too many people were dead already, and why have others die by going after Fischman? Without Bodega, there was no point in continuing. Nazario was too practical for vengeance. He had cut everyone's losses and just wanted to get home with whatever it was he could salvage. It was all he could do because it was all over. Bodega's dreams were dead. They died quickly, "the way a hero sandwich dies in the garment district at twelve o'clock in the afternoon," as the poet Piñero put it. All he could do now was protect Bodega's friends, Sapo, me, Nene, and of course Vera. It was what Bodega would have wanted Nazario to do.

That's how I thought the pieces fell. It was all over.

Then, later that day, Negra paid me a visit.

•

SHE KEPT banging on the door, harder and harder, saying, "I know you're in there, Chino, open up!" I was lying on the sofa with those unopened boxes all around me, staring at the ceiling. I was in no mood to see her. My life seemed too sad for me to talk to anyone. "Chino! I know you're in there!" Blanca was gone and Bodega was dead. The neighborhood was all in blue. Cops were all over the place and I didn't want to go to work because I didn't want to go back out and see the streets that way.

Negra kept pounding at the door, but there was no way I could get up. I was defeated and wallowing in self-pity. Then the pounding stopped. I thought Negra had gone home. Maybe now I could get some sleep. Maybe I'd wake up and feel a bit better. Maybe even visit Blanca after she got out of work. If she'd see me. Would she see me? Yeah, she might.

I kept thinking all these useless things and by the time I realized that the window to the fire escape was open, it was too late. I leaped off the sofa and headed toward the bedroom, where the fire escape was, but when I got there Negra was already climbing through the window and into my house.

"I knew you were in here!" she yelled at me.

"Aw, Negra, what do you want?" I said, and returned to the living room and lay down on the sofa.

She stood over me. "Chino, Victor's still okay."

"Amazing," I said, "the streets are crawling with cops and you break into my house. Amazing. New York's Finest." I sighed, thinking that my fire escape faced the street and yet no one spotted her. Or maybe nobody cared.

"I don't give a fuck about what's happened. I want Victor hurt."

"I thought you took him back. Why you still want him hurt? Besides," I said, lifting my head a bit to look at her, "how do you s'pose I'm going to do that now, when Bodega is dead?" Just saying his name out loud made me feel sad. It was somehow tied in with Blanca leaving as well. There was too much absence in my life all at once. The events were compound words that could never be ripped apart.

"You know Sapo."

"Yeah, but Sapo won't do anything for you, Negra."

"Yeah, but he'd do it for you. He must owe you. Ask him for a solid."

"Negra, I've no time for this, all right? Do you know what just happened? Do you know?"

"Yeah, I know, so what. Bodega was killed by some guy from Loisaida." She took out a cigarette. "He never did anything for me. The neighborhood talked about him like he was God, but he ain't never did shit for me."

The doorbell rang. I didn't bother to get up.

"Go away!" I yelled, but nosy Negra went over to open the door.

It was Blanca.

I got up, whispered "Hi," surprised and happy to see her.

"Don't you kiss your wife, Chino? Dag," Negra said, but I felt so useless and stupid that I didn't want to disturb the universe or Blanca anymore. Maybe she would pull back and I would be very hurt. But Blanca walked over to me and placed her hands on my face.

"Are you all right?" she asked.

"Yeah, I'm fine," I said nonchalantly, as if I was Mr. Cool, because I didn't want Blanca to feel bad for me.

"Your friend is dead," she said, her voice sad. Sad for me because she hadn't really known him. "I came by to see if you were all right."

"He was never my friend," I said to her, but quickly realized that I shouldn't lie to Blanca anymore. "No," I said, "he was a good friend. I think he would have built up the neighborhood. I don't know if you can understand."

"I do understand," Blanca said. "For me, it was always about you thinking I wouldn't understand."

"Are you fine, the baby fine?"

"Yes, we're both fine—"

"How long will you two torture me!" Negra pretended to gag. "Blanca, tell him what you came here to tell him." Blanca let go of me. She sat on the couch and I sat next to her. She began.

"You told me that my aunt Veronica was in love with your friend." She looked me in the eye.

"*Tía* Veronica? *Tía* Veronica?" Negra laughed and lit another cigarette. "*Tía* Veronica was in love with half of El Barrio. She was the biggest *puta*, my mother told us. They should have a plaque for her in the Boys Club at 112th and Second."

That's when it hit me. My blood ran cold just thinking about what had really happened. And as Negra kept talking, not letting Blanca say anything, it was all falling into place. Could it really be? It seemed too sad and cruel. So cruel you'd never think that people could do such a thing.

"*Esa mujer es como un carro rentao. Si tú tienes el dinero te da las llaves.* My God, Mami says that, growing up Veronica gave head to anyone with a credit card."

"Shut up, Negra!" Blanca snapped, and Negra wrapped her lips tight around her cigarette. "My mother tells me that years ago her sister went out with a lot of guys, but that the guy she supposedly was in love with, Julio . . . his name wasn't William Irizarry." The worst had been confirmed. I closed my eyes in disbelief, leaning back against the couch. I didn't want to hear it but Blanca told me anyway. "The guy she really loved, his name was Edwin Nazario. You, Julio," she said, talking like her sister, "have been played."

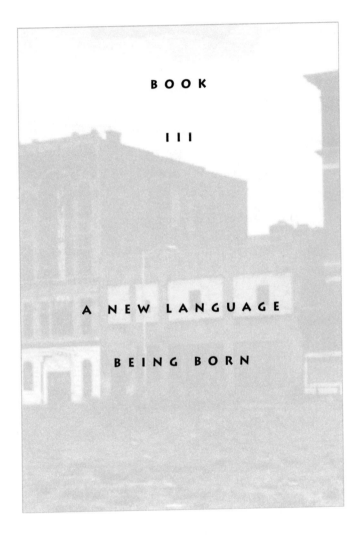

BOOK

III

A NEW LANGUAGE

BEING BORN

dreamt i was this poeta
words glitterin' brite & bold
in las bodegas
where our poets' words & songs
are sung

MIGUEL PIÑERO
— "La Bodega Sold Dreams"

Pa'lante, Siempre Pa'lante

HER mother didn't know for sure when or where Nazario and Vera first met, but Bodega never knew about it. Now everything fell into place: Nazario and Vera had been planning this for some time. I figured that Bodega remained in the dark right up until Nazario reached for his gun to shoot him. His eyes must have bulged in pain, his mind must have spun in disbelief. In those few seconds, his heart must have broken. Again. I wasn't there, but sometimes you just know.

Vera just wanted her husband dead. That's why the day they arrived at my door, all silly and drunk, she asked Bodega to teach her how to fire a gun. She had planned on killing her husband with Bodega's gun. She knew Bodega would do anything for her, even take the rap for killing her husband.

And Bodega would, too, confident that Nazario would get him acquitted or at least a light sentence. Bodega was more than ready to go to prison for Vera. Vera and Nazario knew Bodega could still run things from his cell. That's why he had to be killed.

That day when I first met Bodega he had said, "Should something happen to me, people will take to the streets." But it never happened. When he was killed, no cars were overturned. No fires were set. No cops were conked. Nothing. The people in Spanish Harlem had to go to work. They had families to feed, night schools to attend, businesses to run, and other things to do to improve their lives and themselves. No, no one took to the streets.

The day of Bodega's funeral, which came the day after Negra and Blanca visited me, I went looking for Sapo. He was easy to find. Not because of his big, shiny BMW but because of the sky. See, when something really bad happens, Sapo still likes to fly kites. So I woke up early that morning, left the house, and looked at the sky. I saw a kite flying nearby and tracked it. I took the dirty, pissed-up elevator to the four-teenth floor, then up the stairs to the roof, not worrying about the alarm because I knew it had been broken since we were kids. I stepped out onto the roof and circled around, looking for Sapo. Then I saw him looking at me, his kite string tied to a pole.

"I knew you'd come."

"Negra call you?" I asked.

"Yeah, that bitch called me."

"So you know, then."

"I know."

"So what should we do?"

"I can't do shit. Man, I got my car someplace in the Bronx. Cuz right now, I got to lay low. I got to walk through the streets as if I'm a second-class citizen. I got to go out and get groceries and come right home. Right now, I can't do shit."

"And later?"

"Later, Chino, when this shit all dies down, I still can't do shit. Cuz Bodega might be dead but his empire is out there for the takin'. And this time I plan on bein' the Man. Maybe, later, I'll go after that motha-fuckah."

Sapo untied the string and started to fly the kite again.

"Are you at least goin' to the funeral?"

"Crazy? I got to lay low."

"Good luck, bro." I was about to leave him.

"Hey, Chino! 'Pera, no corra."

"Wha' you want?"

"Why don'cha paint anymore, Chino? 'Membah back in school

when you painted a lot? Good pictures, too. You did a lot of cool R.I.P.s, and at school all the teachers would, like, ask you for somethin'."

"I don't know, it's just one of those things that ends."

"You evah gonna paint again?"

"Sure," I said, but I knew I didn't mean it.

"Thass good. You should do one last R.I.P.—for Bodega, you know?"

"Later, bro." I started to walk away, wondering why Sapo wanted to know why I didn't paint anymore.

"Whass your rush, bee? 'Membah when we would do Kid Comets up on this roof. 'Membah that?"

"Yeah. It was cruel, but fun."

Kid Comets was catching a pigeon, spilling gasoline over it, then lighting the bird with a match, just as you let it go. The bird would fly for a few seconds and then turn into a fireball and come crashing down. We would do this at night. On the roof. We would see the bird fry extra-crispy in midair and laugh.

"They're rats with wings, anyway. Plenty of them to go around," Sapo said.

"I gotta go, man." I knew he didn't want me to go and I wanted to stick around remembering things and laughing with Sapo, but I had things to take care of.

"Chino," he said when he saw me start to walk toward the roof's door again. "I just wanted to know if you remembah, cuz you my only friend." In his own way Sapo was telling me that his childhood memories were important to him. And a large part of them were made up of times with me.

"I remembah," I said. I left him up there on the roof and walked back downstairs and took the elevator to the lobby.

Like many others, Sapo didn't want to be seen at the funeral. Sapo was right, Bodega was gone and his dreams had dissolved like a wafer in water; his buildings would be reclaimed by the city, which would raise our rents. But his underground empire was still there for the taking. It was a game of chicken, and after the smoke cleared, all the cocks would fight for Bodega's spoils. My money was on Sapo. Because Sapo was different.

I went back home and fixed myself some breakfast and read a little. I wasn't going to go to work because I planned on attending Bodega's funeral later on that day. What I dreaded was making that phone call. I was never one to rat on people. But the neighborhood had been betrayed. Knowing Nazario fairly well, I knew it was only a matter of time before Nazario would erase me from the picture. I mean, I was the only one who had been there, I knew the truth. I wasn't afraid; I was angry. I just hated going to the cops. I wished it could be people from the neighborhood that would punish him and Vera. Hang them from a lamppost like old sneakers.

But I had no choice, so I called Ortiz and DeJesus, met them at the precinct, and afterward went to the funeral.

•

THE PEOPLE from the neighborhood might not have taken to the streets like Bodega thought they would, but that didn't mean they had forgotten him. At the funeral the entire barrio was there. It seemed as if everyone had set aside everything and had gone to pay Bodega their humble respects and show their appreciation. The service was held at the redbrick Methodist church on 111th Street and Lexington Avenue—the same church the Young Lords had stormed and taken over, and from which they had launched their great offensives: clothing drives, free breakfast, door-to-door clinics, free lunches; they even picked up the trash the Sanitation Department always neglected. The church was jam-packed and outside people crowded the streets as if for a parade.

After the service, Bodega's sister had asked the managers of a minimarket on the corner of 109th and Madison to let the public view Bodega's body there. The three Dominicans, a husband and wife and their business partner, agreed because Bodega had twice helped them make their rent. The place was cleared for the wake.

Everyone knew Bodega had loved that minimarket because it had once been the Gonzalez Funeral Home. It had been where the wake for the Young Lord Julio Roldan was held after the cops had arrested him, killed him, and then claimed he hanged himself in his cell. Bodega had attended that funeral, decades back, when he was a teenager and death was too far away to scare him. Back when his street name was still Izzy. In those days he was a small-time thief whose heart was stolen by Veronica Saldivia. He thought Veronica was as madly in love with him as he was with her, and as ardent as he to advance the status of Puerto Ricans. Bodega had attended Roldan's funeral with Veronica at his side, before Vera Vidal and Willie Bodega had been invented. The young Izzy had stood guard under the funeral home's clock, which freely gave the time to Madison Avenue, alongside his fellow Lords with their berets and empty rifles. They were watching the neighborhood's back. It was a time when hope for El Barrio seemed fertile, and love at last seemed attainable.

And so the wake was held at that spot. Puerto Ricans and Latinos from all five boroughs came to pay their respects. The line snaked across 109th to Fifth where it turned downtown, all the way past El Museo del Barrio, the International Center of Photography, the Jewish Museum, and the Cooper-Hewitt, and ended by the Guggenheim. For three days Fifth Avenue was colored like a parrot. The Rainbow Race, Latinos from the blackest of black to the bluest eyes and blondest hair, all splashing their multihued complexion at the edge of Central Park. The entire Latin continent was represented, including the thin waist of Central America and all the islands that decorated it like a string of pearls. Everyone was there like in some pageant for a dying monarch. And to pass the hours on line, Bodega tales began winding around the avenue. Almost everyone had one, and those that didn't added to the tales by retelling them.

"He once helped me with my rent."

"He helped put my daughter through school."

"He helped me and my sister get jobs."

"He once bought me a case of Miller beer."

∙

AFTER THE three-day wake, a hearse, long, black, shiny, and sleek like Ray-Ban Wayfarers, took Bodega's body to a Queens cemetery. Lines of cars, with their lights on, clogged Third Avenue. Clogged 125th Street. Clogged the FDR Drive. And all along the endless convoy as it made its way out of the neighborhood and onto the highway, you'd hear a passerby ask, "Who they burying?"

"Bodega," someone would answer.

"Who was this Bodega?"

"A Young Lord. William Carlos Irizarry. Man, where you've been? It was all over *El Diario.*" And as usual it was the only paper that covered the story.

The passerby would cross himself. *"Bendito, que Dios lo cuide."*

And those that didn't come out to the street would stare out of their windows. Young women would holler and scream. Older women would bring out pots and pans, and bang on them with wooden spoons. It was to let the world know this wasn't just any empty body inside that hearse. It once held the soul of Willie Bodega. So the people *had* taken to the streets, but in honor, not anger.

AT THE cemetery, the crowds gathered like moss around the plot, where a Jesuit from San Cecilia, with the sign of the cross, scattered earth over the coffin. There were a lot of young people, too many for me to count. I knew these were the students whose college tuition Bodega had been paying. His great society, as he had explained it to me that day I first met him. They held hands and began to sing a song I couldn't make out. I was too busy staring at Vera. Her elegant black dress and perfect posture, her matching black handkerchief to wipe her tears, her shoes with heels that punched holes in the grass. It was Veronica Saldivia–become-Vera at her best.

A few minutes later Nazario helped lower the coffin with Nene. Nene stood there, dignified, but cried and cried, inconsolable. The rest of Bodega's pallbearers were ex–Young Lords: Pablo Guzman, Juan Gonzalez, Felipe Luciano, Denise Oliver, Iris Morales. Standing near them were some artists from Taller Boricua: Fernando Salicrup, Marcos Dimas, Irma Ayala, Jorge Soto, Gilbert Hernandez, and Sandra Maria Esteves, along with some ex-cons and poets. Miguel Algarin, Reverend Pedro Pietri, Martin Espada, Lucky Cienfuegos, and even Miguel Piñero cried their eyes out next to Piri Thomas, Edward Rivera, and Jack Agueros. Nearly the entire East Harlem aristocracy.

Afterward everyone lowered their heads for an interminable moment of silence. When the silence was broken, the people scattered like crows. Everyone headed for the buses that would take them to the subway. Those who had cars gave lifts to those who hadn't, and a growl of motors drowned out the chirping birds.

As the cemetery was emptying, I waited until Nazario and Vera had embraced the Jesuit and whomever else they were continuing to fool. Then I made my way over to Nazario. Vera, along with Nene, was waiting for him in a car.

"I know everything," I said to Nazario. His eyes narrowed. He got closer to me, turning his back to the car where Vera was. "You killed Willie." He got even closer, his face almost next to mine.

"This works for all of us. For all the people. We all had to cleanse ourselves. Only by killing Willie and laying all the blame on him could that be accomplished. Everyone is clean, Julio. The neighborhood is better off." Always the practical one. To Nazario, what he and Vera had done was justified.

"No, the only one better off is you. You keep Vera, she keeps her husband's money, and you keep Willie's power."

"Just go home, Julio." Nazario was a reptile, his veins as cold as a razor in the morning.

"You betrayed all those beautiful things."

He looked at me as if he wanted to kill me. He didn't notice Ortiz and DeJesus behind him until they tapped his shoulder and arrested him. Nazario went peacefully. He smirked as if embarrassed that he'd been caught, and then smiled lightly at the detectives and brought up his hands for them to cuff. Vera and Nene had already been brought out of the car, handcuffed, and placed in separate squad cars. I saw Vera resisting, kicking the car door from inside, screaming and cursing like Negra.

Another squad car waited for Nazario. Ortiz and DeJesus guided him toward it. As Nazario walked, sandwiched by the detectives, he stopped for a second, turned around, and yelled, "Tell Sapo, when he gets it all, he's going to need me." I didn't answer. I only felt for Nene. He kept crying because his cousin was dead. I felt sad for him and knew he had no idea what had happened. Nene had just done what he had been told. All he wanted was his cousin back. I promised myself to visit him in jail and take him a ghetto blaster and oldies CDs. Like all of us, he had had no idea. Nazario had kept everyone in the dark.

At the cemetery, after the cops left with Vera, Nazario, and Nene, I sat down near Bodega's grave. I wished that I was a smoker; that way I'd have something else to do. I stopped thinking and just looked around. The cemetery really wasn't a bad place. It was spring and the sun was kind, the grass was green and freshly cut. There were weeping willows and rows of apple trees leading up a hill. There was a feeling of ozone in the air and a hawk soaring in the sky. There were little sounds of insects. A couple of crows flew by and landed on a tombstone not far away. There was a lot of life in that cemetery. I stayed right until the last bus was about to depart.

On my way back to Spanish Harlem, I figured that it wasn't Fischman that had set that fire in retaliation for Salazar's death. Nazario must have set that fire himself. That's why he was at the scene so quickly, presenting himself to the tenants as if he were Christ. I realized that those Italians in Queens weren't who he made them out to be. It was all a farce. I knew something was wrong when Bodega told me that Nazario had handpicked me to go with him. It was because Nazario knew he could fool me and thus fool Bodega as well. Nazario could report back to Bodega that he had met with that big Italian and been told it was okay to kill Fischman. Nazario had taken me along as evidence that the meeting had actually taken place.

So Vera killed her husband with Bodega's gun. Nazario killed Bodega. And since everyone thought there was trouble between Bodega and Fischman, the latter would have taken the rap for Bodega's death. It would have left Nazario and Vera with everything.

When I got back to Spanish Harlem, the sun had set. It had set for the first time on the remains of William Carlos Irizarry.

As I walked home the neighborhood was silent. Like the anthem in Bodega's new country. There was no salsa in the streets and the people looked as if they had just arrived home after a long day's work.

An old man and a young boy carrying suitcases approached me.

"Do you know where we can find Willie Bodega?" the old man asked in slow Spanish. "My grandson and I just arrived from Puerto Rico and my cousin told us that this man would find us a place to live and work. My cousin was a super for one of his buildings."

I stared at them. They had missed the party.

"Willie Bodega doesn't exist," I said to him. "I'm sorry."

"No, my cousin would never lie to me. He said a man named Willie Bodega would help me. I have to find him." The old man gripped his grandson's hand tighter, picked up his suitcase, and walked away. A few steps on, he asked someone else. Someone who would hopefully know where Willie Bodega was and wouldn't disappoint him. But the person just laughed at the old man and continued walking.

"*'Pera!*" I yelled at him to wait. He kept on walking, so I went after him.

"You can stay with me. I have an extra room. My wife left for a few weeks."

He was grateful. Told me his name was Geran and his grandson was Hipolito, and then he made me all sorts of promises that I knew to be true. He had come to work and start a new life and would get out of my hair as soon as possible. I told him there was no rush.

When we got home, I saw all those unopened boxes on the floor and I missed Blanca. I wanted to call her but I knew she was at school. Just then I remembered papers that were overdue; I had missed a lot of classes. There was no way I would catch up. My semester at Hunter was shot.

"Are you Willie Bodega?" Geran respectfully asked, looking at all the unopened boxes. "You must be rich," he said, thinking the boxes held valuable things. I looked at the boy. He was tired and silent.

"No. I'm not Bodega and I'm not rich," I said, and tousled the kid's hair. I didn't think the old man believed me. I showed them to their room, which Blanca and I had hoped would belong to the baby. He thanked me repeatedly. Both were exhausted. They didn't want anything to eat, just sleep. I moved the sofa bed into their room and said we would talk in the morning.

•

THAT NIGHT, I dreamed I heard a loud knock. In the dream I elbowed Blanca, who was there, next to me. I was happy.

"Mami, there's someone at the door."

"I didn't hear anything," she mumbled, moving slowly, catlike, and then settling back to sleep.

"Blanca, someone is knocking," I said, and this time she didn't even move. So I kissed her and got up from the bed, walked to the door, looked through the peephole, and instantly recognized who it was. I opened the door. He was dressed as a Young Lord and had on his beret and pin, a copy of *Pa'lante* under his arm.

He walked in and looked around and then asked me, "Do me a little solid, Chino, and open the fire escape for me. I have to show you something."

I opened the window and we climbed out onto the fire escape. East Harlem loomed below and ahead of us. He stretched out his arms and took a deep breath, like he had done when he showed Vera his renovated tenements.

"See, it's alive," he said, and right that minute, at a window next door to us, a woman yelled to her son down on the street. "*Mira*, Junito, go buy *un mapo, un contén de leche,* and tell *el bodeguero yo le pago* next Friday. And I don't want to see you in *el rufo!*"

We both laughed.

"You know what is happening here, don't you? Don't you? What we just heard was a poem, Chino. It's a beautiful new language. Don't you see what's happening? A new language means a new race. Spanglish is the future. It's a new language being born out of the ashes of two cultures clashing with each other. You will use a new language. Words they might not teach you in that college. Words that aren't English or Spanish but at the same time are both. Now that's where it's at. Our people are evolving into something completely new." He winked at me. "Just like what I was trying to do, this new language is not completely correct; but then, few things are." He started to walk up the fire escape. He walked up and up until there was no fire escape left and he was lost in the night sky.

In my dream I felt sad. But the new language Bodega had spoken about seemed promising.

Alone on the fire escape, I looked out to the neighborhood below. Bodega was right, it was alive. Its music and people had taken off their mourning clothes. The neighborhood had turned into a maraca, with the men and women transformed into seeds, shaking with love and desire for one another. Children had opened fire hydrants, and danced, laughing and splashing water on themselves. Old men were sitting on milk crates and playing dominoes. Young men left their car doors wide open, stereos playing at full blast. Young girls strutted their stuff, shaking it like Jell-O, proud to be voluptuous and not some bony Ford models. Old women gossiped and laughed as they sat on project benches or by tenement stoops, where they once played as children with no backyards—yes, they were happy too. Murals had been painted in memory of Bodega. The entire graffiti hall of fame was covered with tributes. Some had him as a Young Lord, beret, rifle, *Pa'lante*, and all. Others had painted him as Christ, with a halo and glowing with the Holy Spirit, sharing his divine power and good deeds all over the neighborhood. Others had painted him among the greats: Zapata, Albizu Campos, Sandino, Martí, and Malcolm, along with a million Adelitas. But they were all saying the same thing: "Here once walked Bodega; these were the things he left for us."

The way a picture that's been hanging on a wall for years leaves a shadow of light behind, Bodega had kicked the door down and left a green light of hope for everyone. He had represented the limitless possibilities in us all by living his life, striving for those dreams that seemed to elude the neighborhood year after year. But in that transitory moment when at last the pearl was about to be handed to him, like Orpheus or Lot's wife, he had to look back to find Vera.

No matter.

Tomorrow Spanish Harlem would run faster, fly higher, stretch out its arms farther, and one day those dreams would carry its people to new beginnings. The neighborhood sensed this, and in my dream the people were jumping, shaking, and jamming as if the rent weren't due for six months. Like Iris Chacón inside a washing machine during an earthquake, Richter scale 8.9. There was salsa and beer for all. The neighborhood might have been down, but it was far from out. Its people far from defeat. They had been bounced all over the place but they were still jamming.

It seemed like a good place to start.

Para Leonor y Silvio Quiñonez

ACKNOWLEDGMENTS

I would like to thank my agent, Gloria Loomis, and my editor, Robin "Max" Desser, for their endless labor and unwavering confidence. I am indebted to Frederic Tuten for his aesthetics and passion; Walter Mosley, whose work is always teaching me new tricks; and Professor Ed Rivera, another product of Spanish Harlem, for his insight and sound advice. I will always remember Juanita Lorenzo and Cesar Rosado's generosity and kindness, and their couch. I am grateful to Darnell Martin for "getting it" from the very beginning. Finally, Jeanne Flavin has been a good friend as well as a significant influence on how I view issues of crime and justice. I like to think this book would have happened even without all her help. But I'm glad I didn't have to find out.